BY LIV CONSTANTINE

The Senator's Wife

The Stranger in the Mirror

The Wife Stalker

The Last Time I Saw You

The Last Mrs. Parrish

THE SENATOR'S WIFE

THE
SENATOR'S
WIFE

[A NOVEL]

Liv Constantine

BANTAM BOOKS
NEW YORK

The Senator's Wife is a work of fiction. Names, characters, places, and incidents are either the products of the author's imagination or are used fictitiously. Any resemblance to actual persons, living or dead, events, or locales is entirely coincidental.

Published in the United States by Bantam Books, an imprint of Random House, a division of Penguin Random House LLC, New York.

BANTAM BOOKS is a registered trademark and the B colophon is a trademark of Penguin Random House LLC.

Hardback ISBN 978-0-593-59989-1
Ebook ISBN 978-0-593-59990-7

Printed in the United States of America on acid-free paper

randomhousebooks.com

2 4 6 8 9 7 5 3 1

First Edition

To three special men:

our brothers, Stanley and Michael,

whose love and support is unfaltering—

Mom would be proud that we're all best friends—

and to our cousin Leo Manta,

who with his wit and enthusiasm for our work

always makes us smile.

We promise it's safe to drink the tea.

False face must hide what the false heart doth know.

—*Macbeth*, act I, scene 7

THE
SENATOR'S
WIFE

SLOANE

The events leading up to the destruction of Sloane Chase's carefully ordered world had already been set in motion. She just didn't know it yet. She was tired and irritable, thanks to the Category 5 argument their houseguests had subjected them to late last night. She yawned as she walked into the kitchen and saw Robert, her husband, standing at the counter, pouring himself a cup of coffee.

"Good morning," Sloane said as she rose on tiptoe to kiss him.

"Good morning, gorgeous," he said, pulling her closer. "I made coffee." He poured her a cup and handed it to her.

"Thanks." She took a long sip. "What in the world is going on with Whit and Peg? I thought they'd never stop yelling."

Robert raised his eyebrows. "I know. Did you notice how hard Peg was hitting the wine? They were at each other's throats all evening. Something's not right between them."

Sloane nodded. "I'm glad we're heading back to DC today. This is not how I envisioned spending our last weekend at the beach."

A loud shriek made them both freeze. Peg's voice rang out. "You're a lying son of a bitch!"

Sloane and Robert exchanged a look. "What's going on now?" Sloane whispered.

They moved to the hallway just as Whit came running down the stairs, with Peg close behind him.

"I'm not going to talk to you while you're like this," he said as he swept past Sloane and Robert. The next thing they heard was the slamming of the screen door to the beach.

"Don't you dare ignore me!" Peg screamed after him, her face red and eyes wild.

Robert blocked her from going any farther. "Peg, hold on, you need to cool down. Let me go talk to Whit."

She collapsed into Robert's arms, sobbing. "I hate him!"

Robert gave Sloane a helpless look.

"Peg, why don't you and I go talk?" Sloane put her arm around the woman and, with a nod to Robert, indicated that he should go after Whit.

Sloane led her to the kitchen and poured a cup of coffee, letting the silence sit between them as Peg took a sip. Robert's first cousin Peg had not been herself lately. She was an attractive woman who'd always taken care with her appearance, but this past weekend she had shown no interest in how she looked and had been drinking heavily.

Finally, Peg spoke. "Everyone thinks he's so wonderful." She put the cup down and looked at Sloane. "You have no idea."

Sloane had sensed that things hadn't been great between them the last few months, but Peg's open hostility was something new.

Sloane put a hand on her arm. "What is it?"

Suddenly, Peg jumped up from her chair. "I need a drink." She grabbed the wine bottle on the counter and poured some into a glass.

Sloane watched in distress. "What are you doing? It's barely eight o'clock. That won't help anything."

Peg lifted the glass to her lips and took a large gulp, then poured more and drank again. She put the glass down on the counter and looked at Sloane with eyes full of fury.

"I hate him. He's a pig and a bastard."

"What's going on, Peg?" Sloane took her hand and led her back to the kitchen table, where they sat, Peg still clutching the wine bottle.

She raised it to pour another drink and wrenched her arm

away when Sloane tried to stop her. "I'll drink if I want to!" Peg slammed the glass down. "He's nothing but a liar and a cheat."

"What are you talking about?"

"He's screwing that bitch. Been screwing her for months."

Sloane raised her eyebrows. "Who?"

"You look surprised." She gave a bitter laugh. "He's discreet, I'll give him that. But all those late nights, the weekends at work. All bullshit."

"We're both married to senators, Peg. Those late nights and weekends come with the territory. You know that. Senate sessions run long, votes run over. Everyone in DC works those crazy hours. That doesn't mean someone's having an affair."

Peg's eyes were cold. "That's true for Robert. He would never look at another woman. He worships you, so how could you possibly understand? But Whit's different. I know he's been sleeping with Madelyn Sawyer for over a year now."

"What?" Sloane knew the woman, as did anyone who was anyone in DC. Madelyn Sawyer was a barracuda—smart, rich, and powerful, with a voracious appetite for equally powerful men. But surely Peg was wrong. She'd always been jealous, and having a husband who looked like Whit didn't help. He was fit and toned, with thick dark hair and a face that looked as though it had been sculpted by one of the masters. Robert, blond and blue-eyed, was good-looking, but Whit was startlingly handsome. Journalists seemed unable to resist mentioning his "movie star good looks," as trite as the expression was.

"Are you sure about this?"

Peg leaned forward, so close that Sloane could smell the wine on her breath. "He denies it, but I know he's lying, and I'm going to prove it. And when I do, Whit is going to be one sorry son of a bitch."

Sloane sighed, wondering if Peg, who seemed to revel in discord, could be mistaken. She'd been a witness to Peg's jealousy and possessiveness over the years and had often wondered how Whit was able to put up with her. On more than one occasion, Peg had caused a scene at parties when she'd had too much to drink and thought Whit was paying too much attention to another woman— even if he was just making polite small talk. "Maybe it's not what you think. Madelyn and Fred Sawyer have both been supportive of Whit's Senate campaigns. Maybe that's all it is. I've never seen them together, and I've never heard one word of gossip to that effect. Don't you think Robert would know if that were going on? The two of them are so close."

Peg huffed. "I know what I know. And besides, Whit wouldn't be foolish enough to tell Robert. I may have been wrong in the past, but this time I can feel it in my gut." She took another long swallow from her glass. "After my parents died, things got worse. I know now, he only married me for my money."

Sloane frowned. Everyone had been surprised when Peg's parents left their millions to charity through the Giving Pledge, but for Peg it was the final cruel act of parents who had been cold and disapproving, and for whom she could never measure up. Robert had always looked out for his ill-treated younger cousin and took on the role of Peg's protector. He was always there, and when she and Whit became engaged, Robert had been both pleased and relieved. But even after Peg was married and seemingly settled, her father never stopped referring to her as the drama queen of the family. And when she failed to produce a grandchild, her parents had essentially disinherited her.

"Sloane, are you listening to me?"

"Yes, sorry."

Peg scowled. "He was furious when I took the little money they left us to buy our house, so you know what he did? He took the insurance money we got for Dad's World Time watch that burned in the fire and bought himself that damn Porsche. Without even asking me."

"I'm sorry you're so upset. Why don't I ask Robert to talk to

Whit? In the meantime, try to put it aside for now. It won't do you any good to keep accusing Whit with no proof. Maybe you two should consider seeing a marriage counselor."

Peg closed her eyes and put her head in her hands. Then without saying another word, she stood up and walked out of the room, leaving Sloane shaken. Peg had always been overly fond of her wine, and on many of the weekends she and Whit had been guests at the beach house, Peg awakened with a hangover. Whit had confided to Robert that Peg's drinking was getting worse, that she was becoming increasingly argumentative and combative. Had her drinking reached the point where she'd become paranoid, convincing herself of things that weren't true? But what if it *was* true? Sloane would keep her eyes and ears open to any hint of gossip about Whit and Madelyn. As much as she liked and respected Whit, she wouldn't dismiss Peg's belief out of hand. How awful it must be, though, to live day to day in such a troubled marriage.

She walked to the sunroom and stood, looking out at the beach as Robert and Whit walked back toward the house, Whit's face animated and his hands gesturing. Robert was nodding as he listened. She couldn't hear what Whit was saying, but could tell from his body language that he was disturbed. Before they might notice her watching them, Sloane returned to the kitchen and began loading the dishwasher, when the sound of a ringtone got her attention—it was coming from Whit's phone sitting on the counter next to her. She glanced over and drew a breath when she saw the name on the screen: *Madelyn Sawyer.*

2

WHIT

Despite Whit's attempts to calmly talk things out with Peg, she'd been cold and belligerent since their blowup at the beach two weeks ago. He'd suggested they take some time apart, but Peg wouldn't hear of it. Now, as he pulled into the driveway, he frowned. What was Robert's car doing here? Leaving his golf clubs in the Porsche, he quickened his pace, anxious to see what was going on.

"Peg?" he called out as he entered the hallway, but she didn't answer. He heard voices coming from the living room. There he found Peg sitting on the sofa, a crumpled tissue in her hand, her face mottled, and her eyes wet with tears. Robert looked up as Whit entered the room, his expression somber.

"What's going on? What are you doing here, Robert?" Whit asked.

"Peg called me this morning and asked me to come over. As you can see, she's quite upset," Robert said.

Whit sighed and, walking over to the bar cart, poured himself a bourbon. He sat in one of the chairs across from the sofa and leaned forward, his gaze fixed on his wife. "What's wrong now, Peg?"

Her eyes were blazing with pure hatred, her lips pressed together in suppressed fury. Whit closed his eyes and rubbed his fingers across his forehead, wearied by the expression on her face and the unending loathing that greeted him every night.

"You really are a complete shit," she said. "But why should it surprise me given that you're such a damn liar?" She got up and left the room, coming back in a minute with a folder, which she thrust at him. "I've been having you followed for a month now. It's all there. Photos of you and Madelyn. Records of conversations between the two of you. I knew you were lying! All this time trying to make me believe I'm imagining things." She ground out the words through clenched teeth.

"You hired a detective to follow me? How dare you!" Whit grabbed the file from her and scanned the contents. The photos showed him and Madelyn at various public places looking very cozy, but they proved nothing. He threw down the folder. "Look, you know I've had to spend time with her, flatter her a little to get her support, but that's all it is."

Robert shook his head. "I thought you were better than this."

Peg snatched the glass of wine from the table, downed it in one gulp, and hurled the empty glass across the room, where it crashed against the exposed brick wall and shattered. "The report," she said. "It shows you going into a suite at the Salamander hotel and staying for hours. You're not talking your way out of this!"

Whit sank into a chair and put his head in his hands. He was so tired of fighting with her. "Yes, I went to the Salamander, but it was to meet with Madelyn *and* Fred. I've told you that before. He doesn't typically like to meet at his house. You shouldn't have involved Robert in your paranoid fantasies. Do you want me to air all your dirty laundry in front of your cousin? How you're always drunk, and half the time I don't know where you are? You're the one who's been cheating on *me* for years."

"What the hell are you talking about, you liar! *You're* the cheater, not me."

He turned to Robert. "Do you have any idea what I've had to put up with all these years? Her drunken rages? The constant accusations. I've had it with your crazy cousin."

Robert's face hardened. "Now just a minute . . ."

"He's lying, Robert." Peg was sobbing now. "The only reason I drink so much is because he treats me like shit! He's never home. He tries to make me think I'm crazy." She wiped the tears from her cheeks and looked daggers at Whit. "I hate you!" she shrieked.

"If you hate me so much, why are you still here?"

"Where am I gonna go? You took my best years!"

But there had been no best years, he thought. The woman he'd married turned out to be very different from the one he'd romanced. He couldn't take it any longer. "My best years too." Whit's voice was flat. "I can't waste any more of them. I want a divorce," he said without looking at her.

"You're crazy if you think I'm going to let her have you." Peg's hand dug under the couch cushion, and suddenly she was moving toward him. Whit's eyes widened when he saw what she was holding: the Colt double-action revolver that had belonged to her grandfather.

"Peg, what the hell?" Whit shouted, springing up from his seat. "Put that gun down!"

"You used me to get close to Robert and help your career. Now that you're a big senator and you don't need me anymore, you're going to throw me away like a piece of trash?"

Robert's face turned white. "Peg, don't do this! Give me the gun."

Peg's eyes were bulging, and she was screaming obscenities at Whit, frantically waving the gun at him. "Say goodbye, Whit. I hope she was worth it."

"No!" Robert yelled, jumping in front of her. Whit watched as if in slow motion while Robert grabbed her.

"Get out of the way!" she yelled, struggling with him.

"Peg, stop!" Robert reached for her hand, and the gun went off. Peg stood, frozen, her mouth wide in horror as a scarlet stain spread across Robert's shirt. He staggered back, falling to the floor, and she began to scream, a loud wail that pierced the silence.

"Oh my God, what have you done?" Whit knelt on the floor next to his friend, helpless as he watched the pool of blood spread under his body. Peg was sobbing hysterically, and as Whit looked up, he saw that she was still gripping the gun. "Peg, give me the gun." He jumped up, grabbing her arm in an attempt to get his hands on the weapon. He struggled to wrest it away, but her grip tightened, the gun dangerously close to her face. The second shot was deafening, and he recoiled in horror. Peg slid from his arms and fell to the floor next to Robert, whose body was still. Whit heaved, unable to hold back the vomit rising from his belly as he picked up the phone and called 911.

"Hurry, please. There's been an accident. My wife. Oh, God, my wife. She shot her cousin, Senator Chase!" His voice broke with a sob. "Then she turned the gun on herself. Please hurry!"

3

SLOANE

Two years later

Newlywed Sloane Montgomery slipped the vintage Balmain evening dress over her head and gently ran a hand through her thick chestnut hair, fluffing it back into the salon blowout she'd gotten that afternoon. She was looking forward to the evening at the White House, but the anticipation was tinged with sadness. The last state dinner she'd attended had been with Robert, and she felt once again the sharp pang of loss as an image of her late husband filled her mind. Even after twenty-four years together, he had still been able to make her heart beat a little faster when he gave her that smile reserved only for her. They'd never lost the passion and desire of their early love.

Leaning closer to the mirror, she applied a light dash of clear lip gloss and stepped back to appraise herself. She'd been told that she looked younger than forty-eight, her face still smooth and fresh-looking, and the small laugh lines around her blue eyes only accentuating the warmth of her generous smile. The simple but elegant black dress fit perfectly her tall, slender frame, but her fingers fumbled nervously as she fastened the clasp of her great-grandmother Emerson's pearl choker.

She glanced down at the emerald cut diamond on her ring finger. It still felt strange not to see the sapphire-and-diamond engagement ring that Robert had given her. After she and Whit had gotten engaged, Sloane had given the ring to her daughter, Emmy, who'd accepted it with a mixture of gratitude and melancholy. Even though Emmy said she was happy for her mother, it was still hard for her to see Sloane wearing another man's ring.

Yet Whit had been a source of comfort and strength for them both during those dark days following Peg's and Robert's deaths, and no one had been more surprised than Sloane to find her feelings for him blossom over time. Their friendship and shared loss had grown into love; a love that was different from what she'd had with Robert, but something exceptional, nonetheless. Whit had been particularly considerate of Emmy, talking at length to Sloane about the best way to let her know of their plans to marry, and Sloane had been greatly relieved to have Emmy's blessing.

She sometimes wondered if her illness made both Emmy and her more mindful of the fragility of life and therefore kinder to each other. Sloane had been diagnosed with lupus in her late twenties and had taken steroids and other toxic medications through the years, but had always refused to succumb to the severe ups and downs of her condition. Sometimes she remained in remission for years, until the disease attacked like an invading army. After Robert's death, she'd had a bad flare, but fortunately it had been alleviated. However, the steroids Sloane had taken ultimately took their toll on her bones, and her left hip was now causing her pain. She'd put off the hip-replacement surgery for as long as she could, but the pain had reached a point where she could no longer ignore it, so she'd finally scheduled the surgery and was going in in two weeks. She and Whit would be interviewing home healthcare workers next week so she had someone to drive her to her charitable foundation, as well as help with home therapy.

Enough dwelling on the past, she thought. This was a new start, and it was time to look ahead. As she grabbed the light cashmere wrap and her evening bag from the bed, Whit entered the room and walked over to her.

"You look gorgeous as always," he said, flashing his megawatt smile and letting his fingers glide down her bare arm.

"Thank you. You look rather gorgeous yourself, Senator," Sloane said, giving him an admiring glance. With his strong jawline and deep hazel eyes, Whit was one of those men who became even more handsome as they aged.

"Shall we go?" Whit held his arm out for Sloane to take, and together they walked from the bedroom and down the curved staircase of the three-story Georgetown home she'd lived in with Robert for sixteen years.

It was a sublime evening in September, one of the few months that lent Washington the treasured days of pleasantly warm weather and low humidity. Whit and Sloane settled into the waiting limousine, and their driver pulled onto M Street for the short drive to Pennsylvania Avenue.

Sloane had been to her fair share of White House state dinners, but this would be the first time she attended not as Robert's wife, but as Whit's. When they arrived, she was struck all over again by a feeling of reverence for this iconic building. She and Whit entered from the East Colonnade and walked past the phalanx of cameras and press. They mingled with the other guests in the large East Room with its magnificent cut-glass and gilded brass chandeliers, amid circulating trays of wine and hors d'oeuvres, as they waited to be summoned to the Blue Room and the receiving line of the president, first lady, and their visiting dignitaries, the prime minister of Greece and his wife.

Most of the faces were familiar, some extremely good friends after Sloane's many years in the nation's capital. Outgoing and friendly, she enjoyed the social side of political life, and her philanthropic work and service on the boards of Washington institutions like the Kennedy Center for the Performing Arts and the National Archives had brought her admiration and respect.

"How are you feeling, darling?" Whit leaned into her, his hand cupping her elbow as they moved from the group they'd been chatting with. He looked so elegant, she thought, dressed formally in black tie.

"Not too bad." She smiled at him, although the earlier pain in her hip was now shooting down her leg. "But maybe we should skip out before the dancing and leave after dinner."

"Of course. You say the word when you're ready."

They continued around the room together, greeting and chatting. Sloane took in the beautiful designer gowns the women wore. Bethesda, Georgetown Park, and The Shops at Wisconsin Place might be fine for everyday wear, but formal events were a different animal, calling for designer gowns that were one of a kind. No one wanted to see the dress she was wearing on another guest, which meant buying couture or a call to your own stylist who knew exactly what became you, and who took care of finding the perfect dress. Every designer was represented tonight. The Balmain Sloane wore was over five years old. Her foundation work made her even more aware of what other women lacked, and she reckoned that the combined money spent on the evening wear and jewels in this room could easily pay for several shelters that would help families get back on their feet.

"Sloane!" An older woman, Congresswoman Faye Chambers, a good friend of Rosemary, Sloane's former mother-in-law, gushed in a deep southern accent, and brushed her cheek against Sloane's.

"Faye, how nice to see you," Sloane said.

"If you ladies will excuse me, I need to have a quick word with Justice Meyers," Whit said.

Once he'd walked away, Faye moved in closer to Sloane and said in a quiet voice, "So, how's married life? I have to admit I was a tad surprised when I heard. Rosemary wasn't too pleased about it. But then again, she's not been herself since Robert died. I certainly hope it hasn't put a strain on your relationship with her." She raised her eyebrows and gave Sloane an exaggerated smile. "But of course, I hope you'll both be very happy."

Sloane had no intention of discussing her relationship with Rosemary. "Thank you," Sloane said. "I hope you enjoy your evening." As Faye walked away, another woman approached and held out a hand.

"Mrs. Montgomery, I wanted to introduce myself. I'm Grace Minnows. I worked with your husband, and I just wanted to say what a wonderful man Robert was. We were all so sad when he passed."

Sloane recognized her name. She was a senator that Robert had mentioned favorably. They had worked together on several initiatives. Her eyes filled, and she reached out to grasp the woman's hands. "Thank you so much. He spoke highly of you as well."

"That's so nice to hear. Well, I think we'll be lining up soon to greet the president, so I won't hold you up. It was very nice meeting you."

Sloane spotted Whit across the room and began to walk toward him, but her progress was blocked by Madelyn Sawyer, the woman Peg had accused Whit of being involved with during their marriage. Whit had assured Sloane that there was no truth to Peg's accusations and that Peg was the one who had been cheating on him for years, picking up strangers at bars in a drunken haze. Madelyn, in a magnificent black velvet gown with a plunging neck, stood in front of her, the spicy scent of her Roja perfume filling the air. In the hollow of her throat, a necklace with a huge round diamond sparkled against her pale skin. In fact, she was covered in diamonds, Sloane realized, with diamonds dangling from her ears, a bracelet of thick baguettes on her wrist, and her famous diamond engagement ring sparkling on her finger. The woman was beautiful, no question about that, and had made plain her interest in Whit at other gatherings they'd attended. Sloane could understand why Peg had felt threatened by her.

"Ah, Sloane, just the woman I wanted to see." When Sloane merely looked at her, saying nothing, Madelyn continued, reaching into her evening bag as she spoke. "Assuming you'd be here tonight, I brought something I've been meaning to give you." She held out a check. "It's a contribution to your foundation."

Sloane and Robert had started the Emerson-Chase charitable foundation twenty years ago, to build and maintain domestic violence shelters all over the country. Sloane took the check from Madelyn and, without looking at the amount, folded it and slipped it into her clutch. "Thank you," she said.

"It's for two hundred thousand, in case you didn't notice." Madelyn turned to leave, then swiveled back to face Sloane. "You're looking pretty good. I've always admired how you've soldiered on despite your illness. How are you feeling?"

"Just fine," Sloane replied.

Madelyn raised her chin, staring down her nose at Sloane. "I think it's just wonderful of Whit to take on a woman with a serious disease. But I've always thought Whit was quite gallant."

A rush of feelings swept over Sloane, the primary one distaste. She wouldn't allow herself to be baited. But Madelyn moved in closer, her lips curled in a snarl. "By the way, congratulations on the nuptials. Whit's so lucky to have made such a good match." She tilted her head and continued before Sloane could respond. "Although some people were surprised by how fast you were both able to bounce back from such a tragedy."

It took every ounce of restraint for Sloane not to turn on her heel and walk away from this contemptible woman.

"I wouldn't exactly say we've bounced back. But life does go on, Madelyn. Even when you lose someone you love very deeply. But then again, that's probably something you know little about."

Madelyn's eyes narrowed. "What are you—"

Sloane patted her shoulder and smiled. "Oh, that didn't come out right. I meant, fortunately you haven't lost someone you love. I can only imagine how devastated you'd be if something happened to Fred."

Before Madelyn could reply, the announcement came that the presidential receiving line was in place and ready to greet their dinner guests.

"Well, that's our cue," Sloane said, turning just as Whit came walking up. "Hi, darling," she said, taking his hand. "See you inside, Madelyn."

"What was that all about?" Whit asked as they walked away.

Madelyn was brazen and audacious, and regardless of Whit's disinterest, continued to seek him out at events to which they were all inevitably invited. Fred and Madelyn were a Washington power couple, and Sloane didn't kid herself that Madelyn was merely arm candy. Sloane had never warmed to her, even before Peg's accusations. She found her cold and self-centered, but to her credit Madelyn had brains, was politically savvy, and could more than hold her own. That, along with her stunning looks, was a formidable combination. She'd certainly intimidated Peg, but Sloane was not Peg. She wasn't about to allow this woman to make her insecure, and she wasn't going to let Whit think that she didn't have faith in him. "She gave me a donation for the foundation," was all she said.

They moved arm in arm up the line until finally their names were announced: "*Senator Whitaker Montgomery and Sloane Montgomery.*" President Marshall Beckermann and the first lady had become good friends of Sloane and Robert's when both men had been in the Senate together. A good-looking couple in their midfifties, they were both popular and generally well liked by the media. Sloane and Anne Beckermann had been new Senate wives together in those early years, forming a fast friendship that continued to this day, and their daughters, who'd grown up together, were close as well. The night after Robert's funeral, Anne had spent the night with Sloane, and on many nights after his death, Sloane had dinner with the first family in their private quarters at the White House. She was forever grateful to Anne for her thoughtfulness in those first months after Robert's death, when the house felt so cold and empty with him gone and Emmy living in California.

"Oh, Sloane. So darn good to see you," the first lady said, hugging her close. "It's wonderful to see you looking so happy; you deserve it. Your table is right next to ours," she whispered in her ear, her smile wide as she released her.

Sloane had called Anne when things had started to get serious with Whit. She'd wanted her advice and, if not her approval, then at least the opinion of her good friend who had known and loved Robert. Anne's voice had warmed when Sloane told her she was thinking of remarrying. Sloane could still remember her words: *You might be one of the few women lucky enough to have found two truly good men to love.*

Sloane gave Anne a broad smile. "We'll have to get together soon. I adore the dress, and I want to hear more about your trip to France." Anne's red one-shoulder Givenchy gown complemented her dark complexion and brought out the rich brown of her eyes. She had become so glamorous during her first two years in the White House.

Greetings finished, Whit and Sloane entered the elegant State Dining Room. In the centers of ten round tables covered in sky-blue cloths sat lush mounds of white roses in crystal bowls, since blue and white were the official colors of the visiting country. They were perfectly paired with the splendid Kailua Blue Obama china. The overall effect was stunning. Soon Anne would be unveiling her own china pattern, a tradition for all first ladies. She had confided to Sloane that the only complete sets of china were those dating from the Reagan administration to the present, because cups and dishes had broken over the years, rendering sets incomplete.

Whit held out Sloane's chair, and once seated, she gazed directly across the room at Healy's 1869 portrait of Abraham Lincoln, who bore an inward-looking smile. Anne knew the portrait was one of Sloane's favorites and had deliberately seated her across from it. The diffused lighting and candlelight made the room seem to glow with a romantic old-world feel. Sloane picked up the embossed dinner menu with the gold presidential seal and read:

First Course

STUFFED GRAPE LEAVES

SPINACH AND GOAT CHEESE WRAPPED IN PHYLLO

Second Course

GREEK VILLAGE SALAD

Main Course

RACK OF SPRING LAMB
ROASTED COURGETTES WITH LEMON
DIJON GLAZED CARROTS

Dessert

GREEK HONEY BALLS (LOUKOUMADES)
VANILLA ICE CREAM WITH TANGERINES

But by the time all the guests were seated, and the president stood to give the toast, Sloane's hip was aching so badly she wondered if she could last through the other toasts, much less dinner. However, she gamely raised her glass of sparkling wine and took a small sip. Champagne wasn't served at the White House—only American wines.

The evening dragged on, with Sloane feeling worse every minute. Seated next to Greece's representative to the United Nations, she tried her best to keep up her end of the conversation, but with great difficulty, longing instead to get out of these clothes and into her comfortable bed. Inhaling a deep breath, she turned to him.

"Greece is such a beautiful country. My first husband and I honeymooned there on the island of Corfu."

"Did you swim in the Channel of Love?" he asked, a mischievous gleam in his eye.

Sloane laughed. "Of course! How could we resist, when we heard that all couples who swim there remain in love forever?" She glanced at Whit across the table and was relieved to see him deep in conversation. "Anyhow," she said, quickly changing the topic. "Of all the places I've traveled, I find Greece one of the most spectacular."

He smiled at her. "Oh, it's so nice to hear that you appreciate the beauty of my country. My family is from Samos. I moved to Athens after university, and now, of course, my wife and I live most of the year in New York, but we make sure to get back to the island every summer."

Delighted by her dinner companion, Sloane felt her mood lift. She was momentarily thrown back into the past, when Robert was still alive. Images of their time together in that magical land flooded her mind. She and the diplomat spent the next half hour discussing Greek literature, and for a while Sloane was able to push her pain to the back of her mind.

But then her thoughts were interrupted by Madelyn Sawyer's laughter. She and her husband, Fred Sawyer, paunchy and balding, were seated several tables away. Eighty-year-old Fred, a real estate developer and billionaire many times over, was one of Whit's key backers. It was clear to everyone in town that Madelyn's marriage was born of something other than love, but she'd turned herself into a political force to be reckoned with. Sloane understood that Whit needed to maintain a professional relationship with both of them so they would continue to lend their valuable support and finance to his campaigns. Sloane watched as Madelyn threw back her head, her thick black hair swaying, as she entertained everyone at her table, all of whom seemed entranced by whatever she'd said. Sloane grudgingly admitted that Madelyn was witty and fun, a welcome and sought-after addition to any gathering. Her eyes met Madelyn's from across the room, and Madelyn narrowed hers. She licked her lips, and then turned back to her dinner companion.

Sloane's hip began to throb again. When finally the plate of Greek desserts was placed in front of her, she closed her eyes to center herself, saying a silent thanks that the evening was soon coming to an end. When the dishes were cleared away, Whit rose. She stood up to follow him, but the first lady walked over to her.

"Are you all right?" Anne rested her hand on Sloane's forearm.

"I'm not feeling very well. I'm not up to staying for the dancing."

"Can I get you something? Would you like to go upstairs and rest for a bit?"

"No, no. We'll just go home. Thank you, though."

"I worry about you." Anne's face was filled with concern. "Is everything okay?"

Sloane sighed. "Everything's fine. I just need to get this hip surgery behind me."

"If you say——" Anne's words were interrupted by the invitation for everyone to adjourn to the East Room for after-dinner dancing.

Sloane picked up her handbag from the table. "Well, my dear. Another beautiful and successful state dinner. It was a wonderful evening."

The two women talked a few more minutes while some of the other stragglers stood by the empty dining tables, still conversing.

"I'm away all of next week, but I'll call you when I get back. Let's have lunch together," the first lady said.

"I'd love that. You be safe on your travels." Sloane scanned the room for Whit, but he was nowhere in sight. "Hmm. Whit seems to have disappeared."

"Must be waiting for you out front. I'll walk with you."

Together they walked along the Cross Hall, but there was no sign of Whit.

"Perhaps he's waiting for you in the East Room," Anne said, leading the way to the music and dancing.

They stood at the entrance, searching the room, and simultaneously spotted him.

Anne cleared her throat. "There he is. Talking to Madelyn Sawyer."

Sloane could feel the veins in her neck throbbing as she watched them deep in conversation, their heads tilted toward each other. An image of Robert, unbidden, filled her mind, and she found herself comparing him to Whit. She'd never once doubted Robert or felt unsettled while seeing him talk to another woman across the room. Had she, as she knew some believed, moved on too soon? After a few minutes, Whit looked up and his eyes locked with Sloane's. He made haste coming toward her.

"Good night, dear," Anne whispered as she walked away.

Sloane stood waiting while Whit hurried over. Before she could utter a word, Madelyn appeared beside them.

"Leaving so soon, Sloane? My goodness, such bad form to leave early. But I suppose when one is sickly, you can't really blame them."

"Madelyn . . ." Whit began

Sloane put a hand up to silence him. "Thank you for your concern about my health, but the reason Whit and I are leaving is because we're still on our honeymoon. You remember what it was like when you first got married, don't you? How much in love you were? Whit and I want to be alone to enjoy each other. Good night, Madelyn. Enjoy the rest of your evening."

Sloane took Whit's arm and left her standing there. For once, Madelyn seemed to have nothing to say. The woman couldn't be trusted; that much was sure. Sloane's faith in her husband was rock solid, and that was all that mattered. Madelyn, however, was a different story.

ATHENA

Athena was ready for a new job. She drank from her coffee cup as she read over the information Clint had sent her earlier that morning, circling a few lines here and there. Taking a final sip, she stood and put the cup in the dishwasher, then grabbed a sponge and wiped the counter again. She surveyed the kitchen and adjoining living room, satisfied that everything was in its place. She'd always taken great pride in keeping her surroundings immaculate. Athena's Adams Morgan loft in a modern DC midrise with rooftop garden, fitness center, and parking garage had been a real find in an area where two-bedroom condos were selling for a lot more than she could afford. The only time her 765 square feet of space seemed small was when Clint—all six foot four of him—was there. He always joked about her miniature rooms and furnishings, his dark brown eyes crinkling in mirth. She never suggested they meet at his place, because, of course, that was out of the question.

At precisely ten o'clock, there was a knock at the door. Clint. Always on time.

She opened it, and he entered without a greeting. He didn't bother taking off his leather jacket and sat at the island, then raised his eyebrows. "Did they call?"

She nodded. "First thing this morning. I have an interview with the senator next week."

"You've gone over everything, all the job requirements? They're looking for admin help with the wife's charity as well as the home healthcare bit."

"I know. I'm prepared."

"Good. Make sure you impress upon him that you can handle the other aspects of the job."

"I plan to spend the rest of the day on donor management software tutorials. They'll never know I haven't worked for a charity before."

WHIT

The Russell Senate Office Building was exactly 4.2 miles from Whit and Sloane's Georgetown home, and yet it was a twenty-four-minute drive in the best of conditions. But he didn't mind the commute and wouldn't trade living in the Chase mansion, even if he had to crawl on all fours to the office. He'd always admired the graceful dwelling, imagining what it must be like to live there. Now that he was married to Robert's widow, he no longer needed to imagine.

Whit always got in early so he could have a short period of quiet before the demands of the day bombarded him. He'd been in meetings since 8 A.M. and was finally back in his office. He tapped the keyboard on his desk and brought up his schedule for the next two days, glancing at his watch. He had just enough time to go over material for this afternoon's meetings before heading out for his lunch date with Sloane. Whit buzzed for his assistant.

"Linda, can you bring me the notes for the committee meeting on Friday? And a cup of coffee as well."

"Of course, Senator. Right away," she replied, and closed the door behind her.

He didn't look up as he heard the door open. "Just put it on the table over there."

"Should I lock the door first?"

His head shot up. Madelyn was standing in his office. "What are you doing here?" he asked.

"Now, is that any way to greet me?" She sauntered over to the desk. Perching on the edge, she crossed her legs, showing them off to their best advantage in a black Akris pencil skirt and mile-high Gianvito Rossi Plexi pumps. In the past, she'd modeled her designer purchases for Whit in the privacy of the suite she kept at the Salamander hotel for her rendezvous. He realized now what a colossal mistake it had been to ever get involved with her. His marriage to Peg had long been over in all but name—their relationship was a disaster. But he'd made it clear to Madelyn when he'd married Sloane that he had every intention of making his new marriage work. He'd never admitted the affair to Sloane—she wouldn't have married him. How could he make her understand the special hell that his marriage to Peg had been? Madelyn's attentions had been a welcome balm to his ego, a pleasant diversion from Peg's constant criticism. He thought Madelyn viewed their relationship the same way that he did—something temporary, as they both had too much to lose if it ever became public. But the one thing he hadn't counted on was her falling in love with him. When he'd married Sloane, she went off the deep end, threatening to tell Fred. But in the end, she'd have suffered as much as he if Fred found out. Her prenup would have left her with a fraction of the wealth she now enjoyed. So she kept quiet. But that didn't stop her from continuing to throw herself at him at every opportunity, claiming he was the love of her life. He had to treat her with the same delicacy one would in handling dynamite. One word to either Fred or Sloane about their past could ruin him.

He sighed. She was nothing if not determined. "Madelyn, you can't be here. I'm meeting Sloane for lunch in half an hour."

"Change of plans, darling. Text her and cancel. You and I have important business to discuss about your next campaign strategy. Your opponent is gaining popularity. We need to put our heads together and figure out our next move."

Whit groaned inwardly. Why did she have to show up on the day he was meeting Sloane? But Madelyn was right, they needed to figure out their next steps. He pulled out his phone and texted Sloane, telling her he had a meeting.

"Where do you want to go?" he asked.

"I've already made reservations at the Woodmont Grill. My driver will take us."

Wisely, she'd chosen a restaurant in semidiscreet Bethesda instead of a place in DC. One of the things he admired about Madelyn was her impeccable political acumen. She knew what to expose, and what to hide. He picked up the phone and buzzed his assistant again. "Please reschedule my two o'clock with Congressman Belle."

"Shall we?" He looked at Madelyn.

She licked her lips and gave him a seductive smile. "We definitely should. But first . . . ?" Madelyn pushed him backward onto the leather chair, pulled up her skirt, and straddled him. She ground her hips into him, her cherry-red lips parted suggestively. Her mouth came down on his as she guided his hand past the low vee of her blouse until he was cupping her naked breast. He pulled his hand away.

"What the hell, Madelyn? We can't do this."

"Sure we can, lover. I locked the door, like always."

"Stop," he said as he pushed her off him and stood, straightening his tie. "I told you. I need to make this marriage work. Sloane understands that you and Fred are major supporters of my campaign and that we have legitimate reasons to interact. I don't want to give her any reason to distrust me."

In a flash she dropped to her knees in front of him. Before he could object, she'd nimbly undone his belt and pants. His zipper was halfway down when she looked up at him, her eyes filled with lust.

"Why did you marry her? I bet she doesn't do this for you."

It took every ounce of restraint for him to push her away and zip his pants. Sex with Sloane was nothing like with Madelyn, who was the consummate lover—wild, inventive, and decadent. With Sloane it was urgent but tender, not this insatiable hunger. "Enough, Madelyn. Get up." He extended his hand to her.

She slapped his hand away and stood, her eyes slits. "You'll regret this."

He had to say something to appease her. "Don't be angry. You know how much I want you, but I can't jeopardize my position."

She didn't answer, but he could tell he was off the hook. For now, anyway.

As they walked outside, Whit spotted the familiar black Rolls idling at the curb on Constitution Avenue. How many times had the two of them had sex in the back seat of that car?

The driver gave a brief nod and touched two fingers to his cap. "Hello, Senator," he said, opening the door for them.

"Hello, Derek," Whit replied.

Madelyn slid in first, but only as far as the middle of the seat, leaving no room between them. As she ran her slender hand along his thigh, the enormous diamond she loved showing off sparkled in the sun.

Whit felt like he was balancing on the edge of a knife. It had always been easy for him to excel and rise to the top in any and all pursuits: outstanding student, star athlete, Ivy League academic scholarships, successful senator. But he knew his one weakness— women—and with Whit's good looks and charm, they'd thrown themselves at him all his life. He was summoning all the strength he could muster to fight that weakness. What made it difficult was that he needed Fred Sawyer's money for his next reelection campaign, and if he didn't stroke Madelyn's ego, she'd get her husband to pull his support. But he also couldn't risk losing Sloane. He patted Madelyn's hand. "Sloane is on high alert where you're concerned. We can't give her any reason to doubt me. It was different with Peg. Please try to understand; we've talked about this before."

Madelyn sniffed, pouting. "Your wife is a snotty bitch. I can't stand her."

"She's not exactly your greatest fan either," he joked.

Madelyn burst out laughing. That was one thing he appreciated about her—her ability to laugh at herself. It was an important quality in this town. She was one of the power players now, but Whit knew it hadn't always been that way. Raised in a small backwater in Arkansas by her auto mechanic father and stay-at-home mother, Madelyn had excelled in high school, easily winning acceptance to several top universities. She chose Columbia, but left at the end of her sophomore year after a modeling agent approached her on West Fifty-second Street. She signed with the agency and never looked back. Madelyn pursued a modeling career with her usual single-mindedness, and although she never reached the top ranks, she moved in the kind of circles where rich men were looking for beautiful women. She fell madly in love with one of those men and believed him when he said he'd marry her, but in the end, he moved on to the next long-legged wonder, leaving Madelyn brokenhearted. She was thirty-seven, still hurting, and no longer an innocent young hopeful, when Fred Sawyer came into her life.

Whit recalled the misty-eyed candor with which she'd recounted her first meeting with Fred. They were seated next to each other at a pretheater dinner party. She'd found him interesting and non-threatening, and when he asked to see her again, she said yes. Fred fell hard for Madelyn. This gruff and powerful man who evoked fear and dread in others had a tenderness and care for Madelyn that made her feel safe and cherished. They married a month later. That was twelve years ago, and now Madelyn was at the top of her game, even if she wasn't enamored with Fred anymore. She complained to Whit that Fred was no longer the knight in shining armor who showered her with gifts and attention and love the way he did in those first years of marriage. Now she was another of his possessions, a footnote in Fred's workaholic world. And so she'd not only accepted her changed position, but had transformed herself into a major power broker.

As Madelyn snuggled closer, Whit felt the vibration of his cellphone between them. She thrust her hand into his jacket pocket and took the phone, holding it up. Sloane's name appeared on the screen. As Whit reached out to take it, Madelyn pressed decline.

"She'll have to wait her turn." She laughed and tossed the phone onto the seat.

6

SLOANE

It was so good to get away from Washington for the weekend, Sloane thought. The sky over the ocean was suffused with swaths of bright yellow and orange as the sun rose, sending ripples of tangerine strokes through the wave crests. The cool air was refreshing as Sloane and Whit walked hand in hand along the water's edge. She was grateful that her hip wasn't aching at all today and she could enjoy the stroll. The sand was still warm after the sweltering months of July and August, and at seventy-two degrees, the ocean water was the perfect temperature.

"This is wonderful. I'm so glad you suggested we get away, especially with my surgery next week. I'm really dreading it," Sloane said.

Whit released her hand and put his arm around Sloane, his fingers gently rubbing her shoulder. "Everything is going to be fine. You won't be in pain anymore."

"I know. But the idea of being out of commission for weeks is not appealing."

"That's why we're bringing in someone to help. She can drive you to the foundation, help you with everything until you're back on your feet."

Sloane sighed. "I guess. It's just that I don't love the idea of a stranger living with us. Selfishly, I wish Emmy wasn't so far away and could be here instead."

Emmy had been offered her dream job as a junior associate at an entertainment law firm in Los Angeles a few months before Robert had been killed. She'd been willing to come back to DC, but Sloane wouldn't hear of it. As much as she missed her daughter,

Sloane was more concerned with Emmy's happiness. But at times like this it was hard for Sloane not to wish that she'd found her dream closer to home. Sloane leaned her head on Whit's shoulder as they walked.

"I'm sure Emmy wishes she could be here too," he said.

"Don't get me wrong. I'm glad that Emmy is happy, but I miss her so much. I've always tried to be the best mother I could, but I didn't have a model to go by. I have so few memories of my mother. I can't even remember what her voice sounded like. When you're six years old, you don't really understand what it means when someone dies, that it will be forever, that you'll never see them again." Sloane pictured her father's broken face, tear-stained, as he told her in a halting voice that her mother was now in heaven.

Whit lightly squeezed her shoulder. "It's a terrible thing for a young child to lose her mother."

"My father never remarried. I don't know if that was a good or bad thing. He might have had more children. Maybe I'd have had brothers or sisters. Who knows? He was a good man and a wonderful father. We were extremely close. He died the day of my college graduation. It was the worst day of my life. Until Robert died." She shrugged and kicked up a splash of foamy surf as they continued to walk. The sun had fully risen, a huge orb of yellow above the blue-black water.

More people appeared on the beach, joggers running along the shoreline, couples ambling along, solitary walkers wearing baseball caps and earbuds, nodding a silent greeting as they passed.

"How about we sit over there and finish our coffees?" Whit said, steering them to dry sand.

Sloane put down the covered mug and took off her light windbreaker, then plopped onto the warm sand, burying her toes in it. Whit sat next to her, his knees drawn up.

"This is perfect," he said, taking a sip of coffee.

"It's a great relief valve from Washington. Buying this house was one of the best things we ever did. Robert was always working so hard, stretched and consumed by it all. I had to get him away from it, even if just for a few days now and then. And I see you working the same way. You need a place to get away, a refuge, and this is it."

"It *is* pretty wonderful. I always loved spending time here with you both. I can almost imagine them back at the house." He got a faraway look in his eyes. "When I was a kid, we spent two weeks in Virginia Beach every summer." He shook his head as if to dispel an uncomfortable thought. "My friends . . . most of their families had their own places at the shore, so I'd get invited to go down a week or two here and there with them as well."

Sloane detected a note of sadness in Whit's voice. He didn't talk about his family much, but when he did, she always sensed something missing. At times she felt almost embarrassed by the wealth she'd grown up with—the large homes in Virginia and Washington, the clapboard beach house here in Rehoboth, and the pastel-colored Conch home with the wraparound veranda in Key West. But her father had instilled in her from a young age that wealth should be used to better the world. How many times had he said, *Sloane, my girl, always remember to love people and use things. Never the other way around.*

Robert had come from the same world of privilege, and the two of them had resolved that they would use their good fortune to help others. The foundation they established had been as much a labor of love for Robert as it was for her. And now that he was gone, she felt even more passionate about continuing the work they had started together.

They sat a while longer, chatting and enjoying the warmth of the sun. Suddenly, Sloane got up, pulling the T-shirt over her head and stepping out of her shorts. Now in only her bathing suit, she reached down to grab Whit's hand. "Come on," she said, pulling on him. "Last one in's a rotten egg."

Taking her off-guard, Whit scooped her up in his arms and ran into the ocean, Sloane squealing in feigned distress as the waves splashed over her. The water was rough, with a powerful undertow. Even though they were strong swimmers, it didn't take long for them to tire and retreat, dripping wet, to flop onto the sand.

"How's your hip feeling, darling? Any pain?" Whit asked after a bit.

"Amazingly none. I can't believe it," Sloane said.

"Good. Shall we walk back then? I'm getting hungry."

"Okay," she said, rising. "I'll make us breakfast."

"That's not what I'm hungry for." He stood, pulling her into his arms and kissing her.

Sloane felt desire build as they hurried back to the house. They showered together, lathering each other and afterward massaging lotion onto each other's bodies before making love. Whit's body was lean and strong against hers, his hands and mouth so expert at bringing her to a boil. The first time they'd made love, Sloane had been astounded, and also a little ashamed, that her body responded to Whit with such passion. It had felt disloyal to Robert, almost as if she were betraying him. In time, though, she'd come to believe that it was what Robert would have wanted, and she realized that to deny herself a life would not bring Robert back. Whit made her feel like a woman again, quickening the excitement and desire that she thought had died with Robert. Sloane had loved Robert, her best friend Camille's big brother, from the time she was a young girl, mooning over the older boy all through her school years. He would always be her first and purest love, but Robert was gone.

"Thank you again for suggesting we come. It's been a wonderful weekend." He showed that smile she loved so much. "This is a great house. A good place to leave the world and all its worries behind."

"What kind of worries?"

He pressed his lips together. "Work, of course. And us. I worry about Rosemary. It's pretty obvious that she's not too happy about our union."

Sloane thought back to a couple of weeks ago when she'd invited Robert's mother and sister to have lunch at the Georgetown house. She had been looking forward to the gathering. The afternoon, however, had been a disaster, cold and formal. Rosemary, usually so warm and lovely, had actually been insulting to Whit when she'd said, "It doesn't seem to have taken you long to make yourself quite at home in my son's house."

Whit had remained silent, but Sloane's ire made it impossible for her not to say something. "This happens to be *my* house." She looked at her husband. "And Whit's."

Rosemary remained rigid in her chair. "You're right, Sloane. It *is* your house. You can let whomever you choose live here." She'd turned to Camille, who appeared dumbfounded at her mother's rudeness. "I think it's time we leave," she said to her daughter as she rose from the seat. And even though Rosemary had called to apologize the very next day, Sloane was still hurt at the way she'd treated Whit. Now she tried to temper any distress he felt.

"You have to understand that Rosemary lost a son two years ago. She's still having a hard time seeing me with someone else," she said. "And as you know, she and Peg were quite close. She saw the struggles Peg was dealing with, and I think it's difficult for her to see us together. It's only natural, but time will take care of that. She'll come around; you'll see."

He shrugged. "Maybe. I still miss Robert so much, and it's hard having his mother be mistrustful of me."

Sloane didn't know what else she could say to allay his concerns. "Listen, I've been thinking. There's something I want to do to put our marriage on a more equal footing."

"What do you mean?" Whit asked.

She worried that Whit might in time come to resent the inequities in their finances. The more she thought about it, the surer she was of what to do about it.

"Our prenuptial agreement doesn't include the houses, which

are all in trusts with me as trustee. I want to make you a trustee as well, so that we share in the ownership. I think it's only right that you feel you're an owner of the houses you're living in."

Whit raised his eyebrows. "You don't have to do that, Sloane. I know you're just doing it to make me feel better about what Rosemary said."

"Of course I don't *have* to do it. I *want* to do it," she insisted. "End of discussion. I'm going to take care of it as soon as we get back to Washington." She reached out to take his hand. "Equal partners." Not *completely* equal, she thought, since there were certain things she wasn't ready to share yet.

7

ROSEMARY

Rosemary Chase put down the book she'd been reading for the past hour and winced at the stiffness in her legs. Getting old was for the birds, she thought, feeling all of her eighty-two years, despite the fact that her hair, still thick and shiny, was now a beautiful silver, and her bearing continued to embody the elegance of her earlier years. An avid tennis player, gardener, and sailor, she was in good shape, but when she pushed herself too far, her body was quick to remind her that she was no longer a young woman.

She rang for Matilda as she walked to the window to enjoy the view of the pond from the living room window. This was her favorite room in the immense house she and her late husband, Chapman, had bought in McLean, Virginia, over fifty years ago, when Robert was only nine and Camille a baby. They'd celebrated countless happy events and marked so many milestones here. She pictured the glittering parties she and Chapman had hosted over the years, the men so handsome in their dinner jackets, the women so glamorous. The house had been noisy then, full of life, and many times she'd yearned for a quiet moment to herself.

Now it was too quiet with just her and the staff rambling around the halls. But she loved this house—it contained a lifetime of memories both sweet and bittersweet. She was fortunate to have the means to stay here until she passed from this life to the next, regardless of the ravages of age. But she fervently hoped that when the end did come, it would be swift and take her while she was still in full control of her faculties. She sighed. Her thoughts lately were bordering on the morose. Straightening her shoulders, she admonished herself. *Enough feeling sorry for yourself. Life is good.*

She had plenty to fill her days—her charity work, her friends, and, of course, her family.

Despite grieving over the loss of her only son, Robert, Rosemary was able to find joy in the company of her daughter, Camille, to whom she'd always been close. And Sloane, her daughter-in-law—she would never think of her as anything else—kept in close contact with her as well. And then there was her beloved granddaughter, Emmy, the apple of her eye, on whom Rosemary had always doted. She did her best to count her blessings, but there would always be a hole in her heart that only Robert could fill.

Matilda, her longtime housekeeper, came into the room. "What can I do for you, Mrs. Chase?"

"Camille should be here soon for an early dinner. Would you please set everything up on the screened-in porch? It's such a lovely evening, it would be a shame to waste it."

"Of course."

She'd had a full and remarkable life, and a good marriage to a wonderful man. Despite her sorrow at losing him five years ago, she was grateful that he hadn't been alive to bury his son. Truth be told, at times she wished she hadn't still been alive either. Even though two years had passed since the shooting, she often caught herself expecting to see Robert walk through the door, calling out her name. She couldn't count the number of times she'd picked up the phone, ready to dial his number, only to remember that he was no longer here. And to lose both of them, Robert *and* Peg, who was like a daughter to her, had been almost unendurable. She sighed and, glancing at her watch, saw that she still had a few minutes before Camille was due to arrive.

What the hell, she thought as she opened a drawer of the chinoiserie desk, lifted the top off the glass case, and pulled out a cigarette. She slipped out the French doors and stood on the patio, feeling a small thrill of rebellion as she lit it and took a deep pull. Camille would have her head if she knew. Rosemary had quit years ago, before the children were even born, but since her husband's passing, she had kept a pack in the house and, every once in a while, indulged. It made her feel—young wasn't the right word, but youthful and in control. And really, at eighty-two, was an occasional cigarette going to kill her?

After a lovely meal spent catching up, Camille and Rosemary took their coffee and went to sit by the pool while it was still light.

"What time is your flight to Lisbon tomorrow?" Rosemary asked.

Camille gave her a quizzical look. "My trip was canceled. I told you that yesterday, remember?"

Rosemary nodded. "Oh, that's right. You said the conference was postponed till next month." She took a sip of her coffee and sighed. "Not too many more nights by the pool. It'll be time to close it soon."

"I love it out here. Remember all the cookouts we used to have in the summer? Sloane and I used to spend all day working on our tans, trying to look cool for the friends Bobby would bring over. Not that they ever looked at us." Camille laughed.

Rosemary felt a pinch in her heart at Camille's use of her old nickname for her brother. There'd been an eight-year difference in age between Camille and Robert, and during his prime teenage years, he'd viewed her and Sloane as little kids. Of course, that all changed when Sloane grew up. "I could always tell that Sloane had a crush on him. I was so happy when they finally started dating," Rosemary said. "They were perfect together." She cleared her throat. "Camille, what do you think about her being with Whit?"

Camille put her coffee cup down. "It doesn't really matter what I think, although you certainly made it clear what *you* think when we had lunch at Sloane's. What matters is that Sloane is happy. After what she's been through, she deserves it. Losing Robert that way was horrible for all of us, of course. And then Sloane was thrown into the terrible lupus flare that knocked her off her feet for weeks. I'm glad to see her happy, and I hope that Whit will take good care of her."

Rosemary sighed. "I know we've talked about this before, but I just can't stop wondering . . . how did things escalate so quickly? I know accidents happen with guns, but it doesn't ring true to me that Peg would react so violently. It doesn't make any sense."

"The police investigated the shooting. So did the FBI. They didn't find anything suspicious," Camille answered.

"That's true, but I ran into Michelle Sommers on Sunday. You remember her; she was a good friend of Peg's."

Camille shook her head. "I don't know the name."

"She's an artist and was in town to see the Whistler watercolor exhibition at the Freer. Anyway, she said something that I can't stop thinking about."

"What did she say?"

"That Peg had called her husband for legal advice because she was afraid that Whit was leaving her for another woman. She also said Peg believed that he was putting money away in a secret account."

Camille was staring at her. "Mom, what are you saying? That Whit orchestrated this whole thing to keep Peg from finding some hidden stash? Maybe he was secretly putting money aside so she wouldn't spend it all. And besides, Peg is the one who called Robert and insisted he come over, remember? Whit didn't even know he was going to be there that day."

Rosemary contemplated this last comment. That was true, but something still rang false. Rosemary had always believed that Whit was an opportunist. In her estimation he'd latched on to Robert and Peg, using them both to further his own agenda. Rosemary had observed him over the years and seen the occasional flicker of resentment in his eyes when he looked at Robert, or the way he would admire a costly piece of art in her home, lingering over it a tad too long. Her son's one failing was that he had always looked for the best in others, but Rosemary looked for the truth, and despite the fact that Camille accused her of having an unreasonable bias where Whit was concerned, Rosemary wasn't convinced. And now Whit was living in Robert's house, married to his wife, and living the life Robert should be living. Whit was hiding something; of that, she was sure. Rosemary had some investigating to do. And she knew exactly who to call.

8

SLOANE

The weekend away was just what they'd both needed, and this Monday morning Sloane felt rested and refreshed. She walked briskly from the elevator and into the seventh-floor offices of the Emerson-Chase Foundation in Alexandria, Virginia, stopping briefly at the receptionist's desk. "Good morning, Rebecca."

"Good morning, Mrs. Montgomery." The young intern smiled up at her.

"I have a ten o'clock." Sloane glanced at her watch. "You can send them right to my office, but would you buzz me when they arrive?"

"Of course."

"Thank you." Sloane headed down the hall to her office, the budding ache in her hip cautioning her to slow her gait. The space was light and airy, the pale green walls covered in framed photographs except for the wall opposite her desk, where a large de Kooning painting, one that had been in her family since 1948, hung. She faltered when she saw the large vase of sunflowers on her desk. She'd mentioned once to Whit how much she loved them, and ever since he'd put in a standing order at the florist to have them delivered to her office—each week with a different message. She picked up the card: *I'm still on cloud nine from our weekend. Can't wait to wrap you in my arms tonight.*

She felt a buzz of delight, smiling to herself as she remembered their lovemaking. They'd stayed up late afterward, talking about their plans for the future and the traveling they would do once she'd recovered from hip surgery. But now, as she looked at the flowers, she couldn't help remembering the trip to Tuscany with

Robert and being surrounded by the happy flowers when they'd driven past fields and fields of them, a sea of gold facing the sun. It had made her want Robert to stop the car so she could run into the field to stand in their midst.

Her feelings were so conflicted that she wondered if everyone who remarried after the death of a spouse felt guilty for finding love again. Robert was gone and she had forged a new life, but sometimes it felt like she was replacing him. That first year after Robert died, she thought she would never smile again. Whit had been such a good friend to her, had never tried to cross the line into anything romantic. The change happened slowly, and she and Whit seemed to realize simultaneously and with surprise that they were in love. Perhaps it was partly the realization that life can change so quickly and without warning that made them decide to grab this new chance at love regardless of the timing or what people might think.

She sat at her desk and picked up a silver-framed photograph of Robert and her taken in front of a Washington shelter they'd built for battered women. That had been one of their first undertakings when they established the foundation. They both looked so young, Sloane thought as she examined the picture more closely, tracing his face with her finger. She sighed and put it back in its place among the other photos, remembering those early days.

The foundation's name—Emerson-Chase—was the combination of Sloane's maiden name, Emerson, and Robert's surname, Chase. It was divided into two entities: the Emerson-Chase Foundation and the Emerson-Chase Foundation Trust. The foundation focused on philanthropic works, while the foundation trust managed the assets and transfer proceeds. From the beginning, Sloane had been chair of the foundation, and she and Robert the joint trustees of the trust. An advisory board of eight members included Camille. With an endowment in the millions of dollars and valuable real estate in Washington and Virginia, it wielded enormous power in addition to its good works. Sloane wasn't naïve. It had opened doors all over the city and would now be a great asset to Whit. She bit the inside of her lip as she contemplated her next move, then buzzed her executive assistant.

"Miles, can you come in?"

"Be right there." In a moment, he was through the door and seated in front of her desk.

"Will you take a look at my calendar and set up an appointment with our lawyers? The meeting can be here or at the law firm, whichever they think best. You can let them know that I need to discuss some changes to one of the trusts."

"Will do. Is there anything else?"

"No, that's all. Please leave the door open on your way out."

Brianna had asked for a meeting this morning, and now Sloane pressed her extension. "Brianna. Good morning. Are you free to meet now?"

Within minutes the older woman rolled into Sloane's office in her wheelchair, a stack of paperwork in her lap.

Brianna Rifkin had been at the foundation for the last ten years. Sloane had come to know her and her story during the three months Brianna had stayed in one of the foundation's domestic violence shelters all those years ago. She'd seemed to be gaining so much strength and confidence that Sloane was beside herself when Brianna announced she was going back to her abusive husband, who had apologized for the beatings—crying and promising that it would never happen again. Sloane had tried to talk her out of it, but when she saw that it was useless, she'd given Brianna her direct phone line and told her to call anytime, day or night, if she was in trouble.

Just two days later, a frantic phone call came while she was at the office. The beating had been especially vicious, and Brianna was hysterical, sobbing into the phone and trying to speak, cowering in the bathroom behind a locked door with her husband raging on the other side. Sloane ran to her car, dialing 911 as she left. By the time the police and Sloane got to the house, Brianna's husband had broken down the bathroom door and shot her as she tried to get away from him. The bullet lodged in her spine, paralyzing her from the waist down. When Robert found out what had happened, he was furious with Sloane for putting herself in such a dangerous situation, but she'd told him he had to accept the fact that she'd never refuse any woman's call for help. That was behind them now, and Brianna had become a valued member of the team, going back to school and eventually earning her degree in accounting.

"Why don't you bring me up to date?" Sloane said, eyeing the stack of folders Brianna held.

"The groundbreaking for the women's shelter in Philadelphia is in two weeks. They're estimating it should be operational within six months." She placed a paper in front of Sloane. "If you can sign this, I'll release the first portion of funding this morning."

"Wonderful. I'm happy to hear everything is on track."

"I've gone through the most recent grant applications and have made my notes. I'll leave them for you to review, and you can let me know which you want to be sent to the committee for voting."

For the next thirty minutes, the two women went over every-thing item by item until they were finished.

"We're looking good, Sloane," Brianna said, closing the last folder. "Even better than last year."

The rest of the morning seemed to fly by. Sloane was reading a grant request when Miles popped his head into her office and said, "It's twelve fifteen. You remember you have a one o'clock lunch date with Camille, right?"

"Oh my gosh, I completely lost track of time. Thanks, Miles." She gathered up the file and put it away, then sat for a moment, picking up the old photograph once again, her eyes resting on the image of her late husband. She swallowed the lump in her throat, put the photo down, and, straightening her shoulders, left the building.

*   *   *

Twenty minutes later, Sloane pulled into the parking garage on F Street, still lost in thought as she maneuvered into the spot she'd reserved ahead. Despite the short walk from the garage to the Old Ebbitt Grill, where she was meeting Camille for lunch, the sleeveless linen sheath she wore was inadequate on this unusually chilly September day. She picked up her step, wincing at a sudden sharp pain in her hip, but looking forward to spending time with her dear friend, hoping Camille might intervene on Sloane's behalf with Rosemary. She understood how hard it must be for her former mother-in-law to see her with someone other than her son, but as Whit often reminded her, Robert wouldn't have wanted Sloane to be alone for the rest of her life. Surely Camille could help Rosemary understand that.

Sloane deliberately arrived a little before their reservation time, hoping for once to get there before Camille, who was always early. As the hostess led her to the table, Sloane shook her head when she saw that Camille was already seated, her blond hair loose and wavy. Her stunning Thai silk skirt and jacket of bright turquoise looked great, Sloane thought as the slim woman rose to embrace her.

"So happy we've finally found time for lunch," Camille said, smiling at her.

"Me too. Between the two of us, our schedules are so hectic."

Camille's job at USAID took her to countries around the world on assignment, and she'd been gone off and on the better part of the past year. Her travels were the genesis of her exotic wardrobe, and she often brought back something unique for Sloane and Emmy. When Robert was alive, Sloane and Camille carved out a week each year for what they called their girls' trip. They took turns choosing the location, with the only rule being it had to be somewhere neither of them had been before. "We need to start our trips again," Sloane said as she took a seat.

"I think it's my turn to choose," Camille said, a sparkle in her eye.

"Maybe we can finally do the hiking trip we keep talking about, now that I've got my hip replacement scheduled."

"I'm so glad you're finally taking care of that. Is Emmy going to come stay and help you afterward?"

Sloane shook her head. "No, I've already put a call in to a care agency your mother recommended. I won't be able to drive for six weeks and will need physical therapy. Emmy can't take that much time off from work, and I don't want her to. This way someone can ferry me around and help with some of my admin duties at the foundation. Help me cut my workday down a bit."

The server appeared at their table, and Sloane ordered a glass of iced tea. When it arrived, she clinked her glass against Camille's.

"Cheers." She took a long sip, feeling herself relax.

"How's Emmy doing in her new position?" Camille asked.

"She loves it and is really enjoying California. I was hoping one day she'd take over the foundation, but obviously I want her to follow her passion."

Camille arched an eyebrow. "You're too young to be thinking about who's going to take over. You mentioned that you met with a new donor last week. How did it go?"

This was Sloane's opening, and she took it. "Great. It was Whit's doing. Congressman Horner made a significant contribution. Whit has drummed up quite a bit of support. He's really gone above and beyond. So . . ." She took a sip of her wine. "What do you think about asking him to join the board?"

Camille nodded. "I think it's a great idea. Whit could be a real asset."

"I was hoping you'd feel that way. I am concerned, though, about your mother. I know it's been very hard for her seeing us together, and I would hate to upset her further."

Camille's eyes filled, and she reached out to take Sloane's hand. "Mom will come around. You just need to give her time. It was incredibly hard for her, losing both Robert and Peg. I know she feels guilty for not realizing how unwell Peg really was. And, frankly, I think she blames Whit, although you and I both know how Peg could be. I didn't have a blind spot where she was concerned, the way Robert and Mom did."

Sloane hesitated to speak ill of the dead, and so she refrained from commenting further on Peg's destructive self-absorption and Robert's devotion to her, despite the fact that she agreed with Camille.

"Your mother couldn't have known. None of us did. And I'll admit, I never would have imagined Whit and me together, but it isn't as if we planned it. There's something about shared grief, I suppose. He and Robert were so close that it feels like I still have a part of Robert with me."

"You don't have to justify anything to me. I'm glad you've found happiness again, and I've always liked Whit. I'm sure he put up with a lot behind closed doors; things that we have no idea about."

"Thank you. I hope one day Rosemary will feel the same way."

Camille cocked her head to the side. "I wasn't going to say anything, but I don't want you to be blindsided."

"What is it?"

"Mom believes there could be something to Peg's assertion that Whit was cheating on her."

Sloane remained quiet.

Camille put up a hand. "I don't agree, mind you. But she may call you and tell you this, so I'd rather you be prepared. Last night Mom had dinner with Liz Dvorak, who works in Senator Mackai's office in the Russell Building. She happened to see Whit get into Madelyn's car last Wednesday. I'm sure it was just a business meeting, but Mom's determined to make something of it."

Sloane felt her stomach drop. She was supposed to have met Whit for lunch after a meeting at the foundation that day, but he'd texted at the last minute to say he'd been called in to a meeting. She held her breath, hoping Camille wouldn't see how rattled she was, and then said the first thing that came into her mind. "Madelyn picked him up for a meeting. Whit told me about it. Of course, there's nothing going on, just as you said," Sloane said, improvising. She didn't want Camille to know that the revelation had taken her by surprise. Or that she was royally pissed that Whit hadn't mentioned it to her.

"Why don't we order lunch and change the subject? Tell me about your time in Brussels," Sloane said, her voice a little too bright.

9

ATHENA

Athena placed a mug of black coffee on the table next to Clint, where he sat reading the four pages of notes she'd given him. His lanky frame sprawled from the chair, one long leg crossed over the knee of the other, and he rubbed two fingers against his temple as he scanned the text. Athena sat opposite him in her kitchen nook, watching his face for any reaction, but as always, he betrayed no hint of what he might be thinking. It was something she'd learned from him and tried to emulate, not always successfully.

When he flipped two pages back to reread something, Athena began impatiently tapping her finger on the arm of the chair. Clint stopped reading and stared at her.

"Do you mind?" he said.

Athena crossed her arms and raised her chin. "Not at all. Take all the time you want."

He put down the papers and picked up the coffee, taking a long swallow before speaking. "Look, we're on the same side, remember? We'll have all the bases covered before your interview with the senator, so let's relax and address the things you've outlined here. I know you're a little nervous, but everything will be fine."

Athena closed her eyes and let out a big breath. "You're right," she admitted. "I think I'm more impatient than nervous. I just want to get this interview over with and stop playing out scenarios in my head."

"I get that. Too much thinking can drive you crazy," he said, picking up her notes and turning to the first page. "Don't let the vaunted Senate office and all the trappings of power intimidate you. You know the saying—he puts his pants on the same way everybody else does."

"I know, I know."

"If you get a tough question, buy yourself time. Don't rush. Take a deep breath and ask him to repeat the question. You've got this."

Athena gave him a probing look. "There's a lot at stake. A lot to play for." Clint had no idea exactly how much was at stake for her personally, and she had no intention of telling him.

"There is. And that's why we're overpreparing."

"Do you want a refill before we go on?" she asked.

"I'm good."

"I've done extensive research into the foundation, poring over the annual reports to see what kind of money is flowing in and out of there. Of course, the real story will come once I have access to the foundation's actual financial records. I've also read up on the senator's voting record and acquainted myself with his priorities so I know what his hot buttons are."

"Good." Clint nodded, his dark gaze becoming hard. "Anything come up on the first husband, Robert Chase, that we might have missed?"

"No. I've even looked into his family background: his mother, Rosemary Chase, and the cousin, Peg Montgomery. And a deep dive into Sloane, the senator's widow," she said.

"No longer a widow. Now a wife again." Clint cocked his head.

"Righto. I'm curious to meet the eminent Sloane Emerson Chase Montgomery. Quite the cushy life—born with a silver spoon and living in her Georgetown mansion without a worry in the world."

Clint smirked and looked at his watch. "It's later than I realized. I need to get going."

Athena tried not to let her disappointment show as they walked to the door.

"See you tomorrow," he said.

"Okay." She watched him walk down the hall and into the elevator. Closing the door, she felt the familiar loneliness descend upon her. Nights were the worst: dinner by herself and an evening alone stretching ahead of her. Too much time to think about how empty her life was. It hadn't always been that way, of course. But it was even more painful to remember what had been.

She clenched her jaw, berating herself for being so self-absorbed. Crossing the room, she grabbed her keys. A walk would do her good, get her mind off herself, she thought as she left the condo and headed to the lobby.

The evening was warm, and the streets of Adams Morgan crowded. She walked along Eighteenth Street, past the colorful shops and eclectic restaurants, until she came to Lost City Books, one of her favorite haunts. Athena loved the comforting smell of old books, the fine feel of rare volumes. She pulled a book from the shelf—*A Room with a View*, by E. M. Forster—and, opening to a random page, read. *We cast a shadow on something wherever we stand, and it is no good moving from place to place to save things; because the shadow always follows.*

She closed the book and, with tears in her eyes, wondered for the millionth time what her life would be like if she'd made a different choice that day. And if the shadow would follow her forever.

10

SLOANE

Sloane was shocked when she opened her eyes and read the time on the bedside clock. Three thirty in the afternoon? She couldn't believe she'd slept the day away. She'd finally given in and taken a sleeping pill last night to try and dull the pain. The room was dark, the blackout shades still tightly drawn, and Whit's side of the bed was empty. She'd had trouble sleeping the past few nights, her body aching and her mind racing. She calmed herself with the knowledge that after next week, she'd have a new hip, and the pain would be gone. It was bad enough that over the years, at times, the lupus had rendered her weak enough to be bedridden, but she hadn't anticipated that the treatment would come with its own host of problems. The steroids reduced the inflammation and pain that came with her swollen joints, but now her bone density was compromised as well.

When she'd first been diagnosed with the chronic disease that caused the immune system to attack the body, Robert had been by her side in every way. She thought back to that dark day twenty-one years ago. She could picture it as if it were yesterday. Robert sat next to her across from the doctor's desk, clutching her hand in his.

"I wish I had better news, Sloane." The doctor's eyes were filled with compassion.

As he went on to explain the disease and her options, the room seemed to fade, and she felt as though she couldn't breathe. She tried to focus on the doctor's words, but all she could think about was a future cut short by illness and suffering. She sat, numb, as Robert took notes, asking all the questions she couldn't. Her body was attacking itself. The possibilities . . . were daunting. They rode home in silence, with her staring out the window and Robert giving her the space she needed. She worried that if her disease took too heavy a toll, Robert wouldn't be able to take care of her. And Emmy—what would happen to Emmy if she lost her mother just as Sloane herself had? It was all too awful to think about. She felt herself sinking, drowning in fear, and then her thoughts went back to that night, the summer before her junior year in college. She'd just turned twenty-one, and she and Camille sat at the bar sipping beer at O'Leary's Sports Pub, feeling so grown up. Sloane swiveled around on the barstool and to her surprise saw Robert at one of the pool tables across the room. "Look. Your brother's here. C'mon." She slid off the stool, her heart beating faster, and walked over to him, putting her money down under the bumper.

"Well, if it isn't Sloane Emerson, all grown up with a beer in her hand and ready for a game of pool." He chuckled. "It's my table, but you can break."

"No, you're the winner. You break," she said.

"Nah, I'll give you a fair shot. You're up."

"Okay." She shrugged and took a cue from the rack, chalked the tip. Placing the cue ball slightly off center, she hit it, scattering the balls across the table, but sinking none.

She thought she saw a slight smirk and heard something like a *tsk-tsk* from Robert as he bent over to line up his shot, but first he looked back at her and said, "Six ball, corner pocket." He sank the ball, then two more, but on the fourth shot he missed.

"My turn?" she asked.

"All yours."

Sloane smiled inwardly as she proceeded to run the table, sinking every ball, then turned to him and said, "Eight ball, corner pocket, just in case you're wondering where I'm going." And sank it.

Robert was a good sport and laughed with her. "Do you always win in two shots?"

"No, I usually win on the break, but I didn't have my personal cue." She told him how her father had taught her the game when she was still in grade school, and they'd played almost every night at home.

The two of them closed the pub and spent the dwindling days of summer together every chance they got. He told her later that he'd fallen in love with her that night—with her steely confidence and grit, with her sense of playfulness and love of life.

She breathed in deeply as they pulled into the driveway, repeating those words over and over in her mind. Confidence. Grit. Love of life. This was a time to bring to bear every ounce of her inner strength, not fall apart and feel sorry for herself. She would find out everything she could about lupus and its treatment, learn all that she needed to do to keep her body strong. She wasn't going to let this illness beat her. She would face it head-on and fight like hell. For her daughter, for her husband, for her life. When they walked into the house, Robert stopped her in the hallway and embraced her.

"We're going to get through this. It's going to be okay," he whispered in her ear.

"I know," she said. "I know."

They rode out the flares together; the days she had only enough energy to walk to the bathroom because of the joint pain and fever and spent endless hours sleeping. He'd been kind and supportive, encouraging her and never impatient. Even though she was not in a flare right now, that could change at any moment.

Now Sloane finished dressing and walked down the stairs in navy slacks and a white pullover. First she went to the kitchen to speak with Yvette, the cook, about dinner, then poured herself a glass of pomegranate juice. She sat in the living room to wait for Whit to come home.

Alone with her thoughts, Sloane twisted the wedding ring on her finger, becoming more and more impatient for him to arrive. She'd been incensed at Madelyn's catty remarks the night of the White House dinner but had never said anything to Whit. When she'd reached the point where she thought her nerves might snap, she heard the front door open and his footsteps on the marble floor of the entrance hall.

Rising from her chair, she walked toward the foyer and called, "I'm in the living room."

He came in and kissed her lightly on the lips. "How are you, darling?"

"I'm fine. You didn't wake me before you left this morning."

"I tried. Even gave you a kiss. You were really out of it, so I figured you needed the sleep."

She cocked her head and regarded him, wondering if he'd been relieved that she hadn't been awake. "Dinner isn't for another hour or so. I want to talk to you about something. Do you want a drink?"

He chuckled. "Am I going to need one?"

"Maybe," she said, her face serious.

Sloane sat down as Whit went to the bar cart and poured himself a whiskey. "So." He sat in a chair near hers, putting his drink on the small table between them. "What is it you want to talk about?"

"Madelyn."

"Right."

She frowned. "I don't want to belabor the point. You've said that your relationship with her is strictly business, and I believe you." She sighed. "But when you lie to me, it's hard not to be suspicious."

"What are you talking about?"

"I had lunch with Camille yesterday. She told me someone saw you getting into Madelyn's car, the day you canceled lunch with me because a sudden meeting came up. Why didn't you tell me you'd canceled our lunch to see her?"

He took a long swig, finishing the whiskey in the tumbler. "I should have told you, but I didn't want to upset you. That's the only reason I didn't mention it. I wasn't trying to hide anything. You have to believe that. The thing is that I still have ties to both of them—political and financial. Fred's been a huge backer, and I just can't discount his influence and deep pockets. You know how it works. Besides, I don't want Fred as an enemy, and Madelyn can be vindictive. If they decide to back someone else, it could be very difficult for me."

"I get that. I'm not asking you to make an enemy of either of them. But I do expect transparency. You should have told me that you were canceling to have lunch with her. It was so embarrassing when Camille told me about it. I don't like being made a fool of."

Whit rose from the chair and knelt at her side. "You're right. I'm sorry. It won't happen again. I promise to be one hundred percent up front." He stood, taking her hand and drawing her up and into his arms. "You are everything to me. And I will show you every day of your life that you will never, ever have to doubt that. I love you."

Sloane lifted her face to his. "I love you too," she said. Sloane wanted to believe that Madelyn Sawyer was a nonissue, but it was clear that Whit was very much in her sights. Peg had obviously seen this too, and Sloane felt remorse as she remembered that last beach weekend when she'd accused Peg of overreacting. Peg had never possessed the strength or self-assurance to go up against a woman like Madelyn, but Sloane was different. Still, the last thing she wanted was to remind Whit of Peg with accusations and insecurity. She would never have married him if she didn't trust him. But that didn't mean she wouldn't keep her eyes wide open. She knew all too well that even in the closest marriages, people kept secrets.

WHIT

Whit leaned forward over the desk in his office and reviewed the file. Total Care Agency had sent the name of their recommendation—Athena Karras—after calling to let him know the applicant they had originally intended to send was now unavailable. He'd been disappointed, since it had been difficult to find someone with both the healthcare background and computer skills Sloane wanted—not to mention that he'd already vetted one applicant and was now forced to expedite a new background check on another.

He closed the folder containing the report from the private investigator. There were no red flags, as far as he could tell. Whit turned on his computer and opened a browser. Even though Sloane had told him the agency had stringent vetting procedures in place, he still wished to conduct his own investigation before allowing anyone into their home. He was interviewing the woman today, and he wanted to make sure there was nothing in her background that would make her an unsuitable hire. So far, she had checked out fine.

According to the report, she'd been with the agency for three years and had a spotless record. They had hired her when she'd returned from Greece, where she'd lived with her late husband for twelve years prior. Even though she was of Greek descent, she'd been born in America to parents who'd immigrated to the States before her birth. Her husband had been a lawyer in Athens, and they'd met when he'd come to New York on business. After a whirlwind romance and marriage, she'd moved with him to Greece. She had been a communications major in college, but had dropped out in her junior year, moved away, and begun working as a healthcare aide soon after her marriage. The photos in the file showed her looking at her husband adoringly. He had died of a brain injury sustained in a motorcycle accident while they were vacationing on the island of Rhodes four years ago.

Whit typed her name in the search bar on Facebook, and her profile came right up. Leaning in to get a closer look at the last post, he noticed she hadn't added anything in over four years. All her previous comments were from her time in Greece, mostly pictures of landscapes and beaches. A few showed her and Yiannis, her late husband—one with him on a red motorcycle and Athena seated behind him, her arms wrapped around his waist. He checked Twitter and Instagram next, but nothing. Clearly, social media was not a priority for her, which was good. Even when she had been active, her posts rarely shared information that disclosed anything too personal.

He clicked on a picture of her at the beach and enlarged it. Slender women had always appealed to Whit, but he couldn't deny that Athena's curves were attractive. She had smooth olive skin, sultry brown eyes fringed with thick black lashes, and lush rosy lips. Her long black hair fell in abundant waves.

He would do the initial interview, but ultimately Sloane would have to approve hiring her. Between Athena's communications background and her experience with helping patients who had chronic illnesses, she seemed to be the perfect candidate. But until he spoke with her in person, he wouldn't be able to tell if she was truly up to the task.

Whit heard a quick tap before his office door opened. His assistant, Linda Rodriguez, led a woman into his office.

"This is Athena Karras, Senator," she said, and left the room.

"Hello, Ms. Karras. Thank you for coming in today." Whit rose from his seat behind the ornate wooden desk and, extending his arm, indicated a chair. "Please, won't you have a seat?"

"Thank you," Athena said. "I've never been in this building before. It's just beautiful."

"Yes, it is. The Russell is the oldest of all the Senate office buildings."

"Oh, I didn't know that. So much history here. I saw a tour group downstairs when I came in."

He tilted his head as if struck by a thought. "Would you like to take a tour with one of my staff when we're finished here?"

"Oh my gosh, I would love that!" Athena exclaimed.

"Make sure you ask to see the Caucus Room if you're interested in history. The investigation of the sinking of the *Titanic* took place in that room. Also, the investigations into Teapot Dome and Watergate."

"How interesting. That's so kind of you. Thank you."

"You're welcome." He smiled and looked down at the pages in front of him for a few seconds. "Before we begin," he said, "I want you to know that my wife is very independent and doesn't like asking others for help."

Athena said nothing, waiting for him to go on.

"She's having hip replacement surgery next week. She's been living with lupus for over twenty years, and her meds have kept it mostly under control, but when she has a bad flare, it can render her very ill. Hopefully the surgery won't stress her body and put her into a flare, but that is a possibility."

"I've worked with lupus patients before. I'm familiar with its ups and downs."

"You know that this is a live-in position, and not your typical healthcare job, in that it involves more than just care. We're looking for someone who will also act as an assistant to Mrs. Montgomery. Help her with administrative duties and drive her where she needs to go. According to your résumé, your computer skills are up to date, and I infer from your study of communications that your writing skills are up to par?"

She met his steady gaze. "Absolutely. I was planning on combining my love of patient care with writing, after a marketing internship with a national assisted-living company." She paused. "My personal circumstances changed, and I ended up moving to Greece. At that point I found work in home healthcare, and I've never looked back."

"What made you return to the United States?" he asked.

"Well . . . my husband died, and it was time to start over."

"I'm sorry for your loss." Whit cleared his throat. "All right, I'd love for you to meet my wife tomorrow."

"That would be great. And in terms of assisting with her schedule and appointments, the agency made that clear, and I'm more than happy to help with that."

"Normally I wouldn't be too worried, but given that Mrs. Montgomery has lupus, I want to take extra precautions. Make sure she doesn't push herself too hard after the surgery. She hasn't had a flare in almost two years now, but since lupus can involve the central nervous system, her condition can turn urgent very quickly, and her organs can be affected. She's always been worried about it attacking her brain, so you must let me know if you see any decline in her mental condition so we can stay on top of things. Right now she's not experiencing any symptoms, but I'm hoping you will be able to see that she doesn't overdo it, that she gets rest and follows doctor's orders."

Athena nodded. "I think I can manage that without making her feel she's no longer in control of her life. And I've also worked with many patients in chronic pain. Several integrative therapies might be helpful as an addition to regular treatment—but certainly not as a replacement."

"Like what exactly?" he asked.

"There are several Eastern modalities that might be helpful. Touch is important."

Whit frowned. "As long as she's not in a flare, I suppose that would be okay. She experiences joint pain sometimes, which massage could exacerbate."

"Absolutely. Massage would be contraindicated during a lupus flare. But extremely gentle and light touch is so important for the patient."

Whit glanced briefly again at the paper in front of him and said, "I see that you've been with the agency for three years. You say you're familiar with the illness."

"Yes. I've cared for two patients with lupus, and also patients with other autoimmune conditions. I believe that's why they recommended me for this position."

"Good," he said, and then went on. "Mrs. Montgomery takes her work at her foundation very seriously and won't be kept away. You'll need to drive her back and forth to Alexandria on the days she works. Of course, we wouldn't expect you to use your own vehicle. One of our family cars would be at your disposal."

The interview continued for another half hour, and finally he said, "You'll need to sign a nondisclosure agreement pertaining to our personal matters as well as foundation business. Do you have any problem with that?"

"None whatsoever," Athena replied.

"Great. If you're able, I'd like you to start as soon as possible, and get up to speed on what she'll need you to do as far as the foundation work goes. Her surgery is a week from today. Assuming of course that Mrs. Montgomery agrees, after she's conducted the final interview."

"Thank you, Senator. I'll do my very best to help Mrs. Montgomery."

"Wonderful. I'll call the agency to let them know we're close to a decision," he said, rising. "Could you come by the house to meet Mrs. Montgomery in the morning? Say, eight o'clock?"

"Yes. Eight is fine," Athena said, getting up from the chair. "I look forward to meeting her."

Whit spoke into the intercom. "Linda, we're finished, but I promised Ms. Karras a tour of the building. Would you ask Roland to show her around?" Without waiting for a reply, he came around the desk to where she stood and handed her a card. "Here's my mobile number and our address. Enjoy your tour, and we'll see you tomorrow," he said, leading her to the door. Athena was perfect, he thought.

12

ATHENA

After the tour, Athena descended the grand marble staircase to the Rotunda level and exited the building. The interview had gone well, she thought, and her nervousness had evaporated quickly. The senator was charming, and oozed charisma from every pore. He was even better-looking in person than the handsome and vibrant image he projected in photographs. Thick dark hair, warm brown eyes, a straight nose, perfect white teeth, and dimples combined in classic good looks. He could easily be a model or an actor—which, she supposed, being a politician, in a way he was.

She pulled her phone out, tapped Clint's name, and raised it to her ear as she walked to the Union Station Metro.

"Hey." His deep voice came over the line. "How'd it go?"

"It went well. We're one step closer. The senator is smooth. And he's whip smart. I can see why he is where he is."

"Well, we knew that, didn't we? Where are you headed now?"

"Back to my place," Athena said, stepping onto the down escalator.

"Okay. I'll be over later."

"All right. Gotta go. I'm at the station."

Three minutes later, she took a seat on the Red Line to her Woodley Park stop, going over in her mind what the senator had told her about the job. Athena would be with Sloane pretty much 24/7, and she'd have access to the foundation offices as well. There would also be that slice of time during Sloane's surgery, when Athena would be in the house alone. This was all good. Now the only thing standing between Athena and the position was the interview with Sloane, but the more she'd learned about the woman, the more confident she felt. They had a lot in common, actually, despite the fact that Sloane came from ridiculous money, and Athena's background was humble.

For a start, they'd both experienced the death of a husband. And in an old magazine interview that Athena had read, Sloane talked about her honeymoon in Greece with her first husband, and how much she loved the country where their daughter, Emmy, was conceived. Athena's Greek heritage would definitely be a plus in her favor. She planned to build on that and establish a connection that would make Sloane trust and confide in her.

She rose as the train approached her stop and headed to the doors. As she walked from the platform to the escalators, she heard the senator's words in her head: *She hasn't had a flare in almost two years now, but since lupus can involve the central nervous system, her condition can turn urgent very quickly, and her organs can be affected. She's always been worried about it attacking her brain.*

As well she should, Athena thought.

13

SLOANE

Sloane reviewed Athena's résumé over breakfast and was impressed with her background. She jotted a few notes, put down her pen, and looked at her watch when she heard approaching footsteps. She was right on time. Good.

"Miss Karras is here to see you, Mrs. Montgomery," Doris, the housekeeper, said.

"Thank you, Doris." Sloane rose as Athena entered and tried her best to keep her expression impassive as she took in the woman's stunning looks. Sloane felt a moment of anxiety at the thought of this gorgeous young woman living under the same roof with her husband. She immediately regretted the thought. What kind of person was she to judge someone on her looks? Athena's beauty was irrelevant.

She reached out to shake her hand, noticing Athena's short nails with approval. Sloane disliked overly long fingernails, an image of Madelyn's blood-red claws forming in her head. "So nice to meet you. Please come sit down." Sloane took the file and led Athena to the two club chairs in front of the window. As they sat across from each other, Sloane sensed the woman's nervousness and decided to start by trying to put her at ease.

"I love the name Athena. The goddess of wisdom." Sloane paused before continuing. "And war. I see that your parents were born in Greece."

"Yes. My father was born in Athens, and my mother is from the island of Crete."

"Crete, yes. I've been to Greece but haven't visited Crete."

Athena nodded. "My family is from Chania on the northwest

coast of the island—it's a paradise. The harbor with its waterfront cafés has touches of Venice and Egypt. The old lighthouse dates back to the fourteenth century. It's an intoxicating place."

"You make it sound enticing enough to plan a trip." Sloane shifted in the chair, feeling the discomfort in her hip grow stronger. "I'll be glad to get this surgery over with. I think my husband told you that I'm looking for help not only postsurgery, but also with administrative duties."

"He did, Mrs. Montgomery."

"Please, call me Sloane."

Athena smiled. "The senator said you wanted someone who could drive you places and assist you at the foundation. I have to say that it's what made the position sound so interesting to me. I'm familiar with the work your foundation does to help women, and any way in which I could help would be a privilege."

Sloane studied her with interest. "Have you done work in this area?"

"I have. When I lived in Greece, I volunteered weekends at a homeless hostel in Athens. Over time, I even learned how to help them with some of their accounting and donation tracking using donor-management software."

Sloane raised an eyebrow. "How nice to hear. Well, Athena, I think you'd be of great assistance with the work you've done and your administrative skills. We have an accounting department, so I won't need your help there, but emails and correspondence build up quickly, and I don't want to fall behind. I see that you were a communications major, which will also be an asset." Sloane looked up from the résumé to Athena. "I've been told I'll have a physical therapist come to the house three or four times a week, so your PT experience will be very helpful as well." Sloane closed the folder in her lap and rested her hands on it.

"Now, as my husband told you, the surgery is next Thursday. If you could start tomorrow, that would give us time to do some preparatory work before the operation. You can come with me to the office and get familiar with some of the work. Also, get to know the staff and the lay of the land here at the house. I should only be in the hospital overnight, so I'll be home and moving around with the help of a walker the day after surgery. They've stressed to me that it's important to take it easy. And to be careful not to fall. The last thing I want is to hurt myself and end up back at the hospital."

"I can start tomorrow. It's tempting to try to do more than you're ready for in those first few weeks, but my job will be to see that you don't."

Sloane laughed. "You'll have to forgive me if I get impatient with you. Taking it easy and going slowly are not my strong suits. And I really can't imagine not being able to drive for six weeks."

"Six weeks will be up before you know it, and everything will be back to normal. You'll see," Athena assured her.

Sloane rose from her seat. "Thank you, Athena. I look forward to seeing you first thing tomorrow. Sound good?"

"Sounds perfect." She smiled.

14

ATHENA

The meeting with Sloane Montgomery yesterday had gone exactly as Athena had hoped. She could tell she'd made a good impression, and that Sloane felt at ease with her. Athena was used to making others feel comfortable. Her mother had always told her she had a gift for getting people to open up.

It was a fifteen-minute drive to the Georgetown home of Senator and Mrs. Montgomery. On this beautiful fall day, Athena put her window down as she steered her six-year-old Toyota Prius up Wisconsin Avenue, passing high-end boutiques and distinctive restaurants. The streets pulsated with life, throngs of people strolling the sidewalks and filling the tables of outdoor cafés. It must be great to live here, she thought, peering down tree-lined avenues of distinguished homes before she reached the Montgomery residence. Quite a far cry from the small condo Athena worked so hard to afford.

The three-story red brick house was set back from the street and surrounded by a low brick wall. Tall trees and lush shrubbery gave the impression of permanence and longevity. After her interview with Sloane, Athena had searched the address online and found that in addition to its seven bedrooms and ten bathrooms, the back terrace overlooked a heated swimming pool. She texted the link to the listing and floor plan to Clint. It wasn't difficult to find that the last time the house had sold was sixteen years ago, to Senator Robert and Mrs. Sloane Chase, for $6.2 million. And that was just the DC house; never mind the Rehoboth Beach house or the place in Key West.

Athena pulled her car into the driveway as she'd been instructed.

She turned off the engine just as Senator Montgomery came walking out.

"Good morning," he said, giving her a warm smile as she got out of the Toyota. "Can I help with your things?"

"Thank you, Senator. I can manage. I'm a famous overpacker."

"So is my wife." He laughed and Athena followed him to the house.

Sloane appeared in the foyer as they entered, and Doris, the tall older woman she'd met yesterday, her dark hair pulled into a bun, stood next to her.

"Good morning, Athena," Sloane said. "Doris will show you to your room. After you get settled, come downstairs and we'll go to the office and get you familiar with things."

"I'm heading out," the senator said, and leaned forward to kiss his wife.

Athena climbed the stairs, keeping up with Doris while taking in the art lining the walls. The paintings looked important with their ornate gold frames and old-world themes, but none of them were familiar to her. She'd promised herself that she would take an art history class one day, but other things had taken priority.

As they reached the second-floor landing, Athena stopped in front of a large window with a stunning view of the Potomac River.

"Oh my. How beautiful," she couldn't resist saying.

"Yes. This house sits on one of the highest points in Georgetown. You can see the Capitol and the Washington Monument from here too," Doris said with pride, leading Athena down the hall and past three bedrooms before finally stopping. "This will be your room, miss. Mrs. Montgomery is the next bedroom down, right next to yours. If you need anything, just use the intercom phone beside the bed to call me."

"I will. Mrs. Montgomery mentioned that you're the one who keeps things running smoothly around here. She's very lucky to have you." Athena hoped she wasn't laying it on too thick.

Doris said nothing for a moment, then leveled a look at Athena.

"I've been with her for over twenty years now. I'm the lucky one. Mrs. Montgomery is one of a kind."

Athena turned to open the bedroom door. "Thank you, Doris," she said, noting the tone of protectiveness in the woman's voice.

"You're welcome, miss. I hope you'll be comfortable." And with that, she excused herself.

Athena liked what she saw when she walked into the room. Light blue walls that looked as if they'd been washed with sun and saltwater, and polished hardwood floors covered in thick white area rugs. She sat on the king-sized bed, running a hand over the white duvet cover, marveling at the deep plushness of the feather mattress. Walking to the French doors leading to a small balcony, she let her gaze linger on the river in the far distance. She stepped out onto the balcony, closed her eyes, and breathed in the fragrant smell of honeysuckle.

She went back inside and began to unpack, grateful to see that the bureau was empty and the closet had ample hangers. Her iPad held all her books, and she'd brought only a few personal items. The lone photograph she'd packed was a reminder of the life that no longer existed. When she hung the last dress, she took one more look around the enchanting room before closing the door behind her and heading downstairs. She was tempted as she passed it to open Sloane's bedroom door and take a quick peek in, but she resisted. There was time enough for that.

15

WHIT

Sloane had been taken into surgery almost two hours ago, and Whit was getting antsy. The doctor said the operation would be about an hour and a half, so what was taking so long? He paced up and down the small waiting room until finally Rosemary sighed in exasperation.

"You're going to wear a hole in that carpet," she said, raising an imperious brow.

Sitting in this room with her and Camille for the past two hours had been agony. Between the polite conversation and the pregnant pauses, he was ready to jump out of his skin. He didn't need the added stress of Rosemary's hostility while he waited to see how Sloane's surgery had gone. But he knew she was worried too, and so he gave Rosemary a benign smile.

"I'm getting a little worried. Seems to be taking longer than expected."

Just then the surgeon came through the door. They all stood and rushed toward him.

"Everything went great. She's in recovery now, and we'll watch her for a couple of hours before moving her to her room. She's still pretty out of it." He looked at Whit. "Someone will be out to take you back to see her in a little while."

"That's a relief," Camille said as the doctor walked away. "Would you like us to wait with you? I imagine Sloane won't be up to us all converging on her tonight."

"Thanks so much, but it's not necessary. I'll give Emmy a call to update her, and then they'll probably take me to see Sloane."

"All right, then. Please give her our love and tell her we'll both be back to see her tomorrow," Rosemary said.

"Will do. Thank you both for being here."

"Of course. She's our family," Rosemary said with an edge to her voice.

Whit didn't bother responding. The woman was never going to approve of him, so what was the point?

Camille put a hand on Whit's arm. "Please let me know if there's anything you need."

Once they'd gone, he called Emmy.

"All good. Your mom's in recovery, and the surgery went great."

He heard a sigh of relief over the line. "Thank God! I've been on pins and needles all day. When can you see her?"

"Soon. I promise when she's fully awake, we'll FaceTime you."

"I hate not being there."

"I know. But, sweetheart, your mother told you that she didn't want you to jeopardize your new job. She knows you've got a lot on your plate learning the ropes. I'll take good care of her. There's nothing for you to worry about."

They chatted for a few more minutes and he ended the call. He had always wondered what it would have been like to have a child of his own. Peg had made it clear early in their marriage that she wasn't up to a pregnancy. Neither of them had been interested in adoption. In retrospect he realized it was probably for the best. He couldn't imagine what kind of mother she would have been. But he wished he could understand the kind of unconditional love that seemed to exist when the parent/child bond was strong. Sloane's love for Emmy was unselfish and generous, so different from the give-and-take in most relationships. As much as she would have loved for Emmy to live close to her, Emmy's happiness trumped her own desires.

He glanced at his watch, impatient now, and eager to see Sloane. He was relieved that Athena had started and would be at the house to help. With his crammed schedule he wouldn't be able to give Sloane the care she required. Neither of them had expected her to need a new hip this soon, but her pain had gotten much worse soon after they'd become engaged, and the surgery she had hoped could be put off for another year could no longer wait.

His phone buzzed and he looked down at the incoming call. Madelyn. He groaned.

"Hey."

"Hi, lover, where are you?"

He bristled at her words. She was relentless. "Sloane had surgery today, remember? I'm at the hospital."

"Oh, that's right. I forgot that was today. You're not staying there all night, are you? Won't she be out of it?"

"Of course I'm staying. Is there something in particular you need?" he asked.

"I'm not sure you want me to answer that."

He shook his head. "I can't talk now."

"Oh, boo. Fine. I'll catch up with you tomorrow. Give my regards to Sloane." She laughed. "On second thought, don't."

Whit put the phone into his pocket and sighed. Madelyn was becoming more and more of a problem. She couldn't get it through her head that he was committed to Sloane. Was he going to have to spend the rest of his life paying for the mistake of sleeping with Madelyn?

16

ATHENA

Athena walked down the curving stairs, letting the tips of her fingers glide lightly along the smooth wooden banister. The house was quiet, and she realized that no sounds from the outside world were discernible. It was like being in a fortress. She supposed that was an apt term for this imposing structure that kept the outsiders out and those who lived within its walls sequestered and secure.

The senator and Sloane had left for the hospital hours ago. The staff had been given the day off, with the exception of Doris, who had finally left to run some errands, saying she'd be back in a few hours. As Athena reached the landing, she paused, considering where to start. She had at least two hours alone, and Sloane wouldn't be home until tomorrow at the very soonest. The senator would most certainly be at her side when she came out of surgery and would continue to stay with her through the night. She decided to take a quick stroll through all the rooms before she began to look in earnest.

During the past week of her stay here, Athena had seen most of the house, but now she was able to take more time to drink it all in. The thick rugs under her feet, the deep cushioned chairs and sofas in muted creams and whites, the gracious chests and cabinets. Nothing was overdone; all of it in exquisite taste born of generations of wealth and privilege. Yes, she knew interior decorators could approximate this look, but they could never completely replicate that elusive element of old-money confidence and nonchalance. It was mind-blowing the way some people got to live while most of the world struggled to just get by. What would it be like, she wondered, to grow up in a home like this?

Before Athena left the living room, she stopped at the grand piano, on which a dozen gold-framed photographs sat. Her eyes locked onto one of Sloane and her daughter, Emmy, at the beach, both of them sitting on the sand. Emmy must have been six or seven in the picture, her long blond hair grazing Sloane's shoulder as she leaned her head against her mother. They were both grinning, their faces filled with joy. Athena wondered if it had been Robert behind the camera. She picked up the photo next to it, one of Robert and Sloane. It looked like it might have been taken on their honeymoon, the two of them standing arm in arm in front of the Parthenon. They made a stunning couple, Robert tall and good-looking, his blond hair the color of Emmy's, and Sloane with a beauty that was girlish and elegant at the same time. Sighing, Athena replaced the picture. We take so much for granted, she thought, never realizing how life can change in an instant.

Enough, she said to herself, turning away from the piano. It was time to get down to business. She strode with purpose to Whit's office, but when she tried to turn the handle, nothing happened. Locked. She bent down to take a closer look and read the name on the lock. Bowley. Snapping a photo, she texted it to Clint. She'd never seen that kind before and would have to talk to him before attempting to pick it. Her tool could get stuck in the lock if she didn't know what she was dealing with, and that would mark the end of her employment here. Whit's office would have to wait for another time. She sighed in frustration and moved instead to Sloane's office, where the door opened easily. Sloane's perfume lingered in the room, fresh and pleasing. Athena sat in the chair behind the desk and opened the top drawer, finding the usual supply of paper clips and pens. She continued until she'd opened every drawer, but there was nothing out of the ordinary in any of them—a to-do list of things to take care of prior to her hip surgery, a list of instructions for the caretaker at the house in Key West, a notebook with names and numbers of repairmen and important phone numbers in Florida, Rehoboth Beach, and Georgetown. And more of the same. She pulled out her phone and snapped pictures of the pages and texted them to Clint. You never knew what information could be useful.

She sat back, exhaling a disappointed breath, and looked around the room. The only other furniture were two chairs and a small table between them. The bookshelves, however, held a few carved boxes, and Athena rose to take a look. One held a glass set of turquoise worry beads; one was empty; in the third sat two ceramic birds' eggs. Oh well, it would have been too much to ask, she supposed, to strike gold on the first try.

Closing the door behind her, Athena went to the kitchen. She made a cup of coffee in the gleaming cappuccino machine and sat drinking. She finished her coffee and rinsed out the cup. Now for the bedrooms.

She'd been in Sloane and Whit's bedroom only once, although after tomorrow, when Sloane returned from the hospital, this room would become more and more familiar. It was large but inviting nevertheless, with an air of intimacy and luxury. Athena went first to the nightstand, a small Chinese chest with beautiful painted designs on its doors. She pulled the hanging gold rings and swung open both doors. Books, and some papers. She looked through them one by one. A few book reviews cut from the newspaper, an unused notepad, and a journal. She flipped through it, but all it contained was a list of books with comments about each one.

This was getting her nowhere. Perhaps Sloane's office at the foundation would yield something more useful. As she walked to the door and turned to survey the room once more, her gaze came to rest on the low three-drawer bureau. Most likely only clothing, but it didn't hurt to check. Sliding each drawer open without expectation, she found what she thought she would—lingerie, sleepwear, workout clothing. Nothing else. On impulse she went to Sloane's closet, curious to see what magnificent things were hiding behind its doors. As she stepped inside, she thought how ludicrous it was to call this room a mere closet. Custom-built shelving for shoes and handbags, slide-out drawers for sweaters and other folded items, and in the middle of the room a center island with drawers that looked like they might hold jewelry and other accessories. A large floor-to-ceiling mirror with an elegant ornamental frame stood at one end of the room. Athena had only seen rooms like this in photographs.

She moved to the wall where Sloane's dresses hung, grouped by color from white to turquoise to black and everything in between. She moved the hangers one by one, feeling the expensive fabric between her fingers and admiring the beautiful designs. Pulling out an especially exquisite black cocktail dress, Athena went to the mirror and held it up against her body, turning slightly and tilting her head from side to side as she studied her reflection. She'd never owned anything this magnificent. Sighing ruefully, she put the dress back and turned to leave.

"What are you doing?" An indignant Doris stood in the doorway.

Athena jumped. She hadn't heard her come up the stairs. Doris was staring at her with open hostility, and Athena gave the woman what she hoped was an unperturbed look. "I was just making sure everything is ready for Mrs. Montgomery's return. She left me a note with a list of items she wanted me to pick up and put in the closet for her."

Doris held out a hand. "May I see that? She didn't mention needing anything extra to me."

"Since I've been here, I've seen how invaluable you are to Mrs. Montgomery and how much she depends upon you. I'm sure you know how much pride she has. These items she asked me to pick up are . . . um . . . of a personal medical nature. She probably felt more comfortable asking me, as her home healthcare worker, to pick them up. I'm thinking perhaps she would prefer I kept them private."

"Oh . . . of course. I didn't mean to pry."

"I know you're only looking out for her. I hope you'll advise me on how best to support her, since you've been with her for so long."

She saw with relief that her words seemed to mollify the older woman, whose expression relaxed a bit.

"I'd be glad to give you any advice you need. In the meantime, I came up to tell you there's red lentil soup the cook left. If you'd like some for dinner, you can just heat it up."

"Thank you." Athena smiled again. "I'll take care of a few things and have it a little later."

She headed to her room and from the corner of her eye saw Doris descend the stairs. She'd have to tread lightly with Doris. Having someone in the house who didn't trust her was something she couldn't afford.

When Athena got the call from the senator, saying the surgery had gone well and Sloane would likely be released in the morning, she went to Whole Foods and picked up a large bunch of white calla lilies. When she returned to the house, she asked Doris for a vase.

"Lilies?" Doris wrinkled her nose. "They always remind me of funerals. Such a strong smell. They're not really a favorite of Mrs. Montgomery's. Did you see the beautiful bouquet of pink roses the first lady sent? Much more cheerful to my mind."

Athena hid her annoyance and instead gave Doris a sweet smile. She'd seen the roses that morning, along with the handwritten note from the first lady. How nice for Sloane that she was so important that the wife of the president remembered to send her flowers. That must have taken the first lady all of five minutes to ask some staffer to handle. Athena had actually taken the time to go out and get the flowers herself, but to these people she was just an unimportant underling.

"Well, I'm sure Mrs. Montgomery will enjoy both arrangements."

Doris shrugged, then brought her a crystal vase. Athena placed the large bouquet on the dresser in Sloane's bedroom. She hoped the flowers would make an impression not only on Sloane, but on the senator as well. She moved the roses the first lady had sent downstairs into the entrance foyer.

Athena was waiting in the entrance hall when they arrived, Sloane looking tired and leaning on her walker as she took a few careful steps.

"Welcome home. I'm so glad everything went well," Athena said.

"Thank you. I'm happy to be home. Looking forward to sleeping in my own bed."

"Well," Whit said. "Shall we head that way now? Or would you rather stay downstairs for a while?"

"No, let's go up. I think I'd like to rest." Sloane stopped a minute to admire the roses and read the card. "How nice of Anne! She leaves tomorrow for Oregon to meet their new grandson. I'm sure she'll decide to stay awhile, and I don't blame her. Such a happy occasion." She looked from the flowers to the staircase and inhaled. "Okay, I'm ready. Maybe one of you can stay behind me, and one next to me. They told me I should be able to go up by myself, as long as I take it slowly. I may as well begin getting everything back in working order. Good leg going up, and bad leg going down: That's what the physical therapist told me."

The walk upstairs was painfully slow. Athena continued to utter encouraging words to Sloane. By the time they reached the bedroom, the woman was exhausted.

"Let me help you undress and get into bed." Athena pulled the covers back and patted the mattress, where she'd already laid out a loose-fitting pair of pajamas for Sloane.

"We can handle this, Whit. I'm just going to sleep the day away, so why don't you go ahead to the office. You've taken enough time off, and I know things must be piling up," Sloane said.

"Are you sure?" Whit asked.

"Of course. Go."

Athena backed away from the bed as he kissed Sloane. "Okay, ladies. I'll see you tonight." And with that, he was gone.

"Oh my," Sloane said as Athena helped her change. "You've thought of everything. The flowers are just beautiful. Thank you."

"You're welcome. Flowers always cheer me up."

"Me too." Sloane got into bed and adjusted the pillow under her head. "Mmm. This feels great. I hate hospital beds."

"Yes." Athena smiled. "Did they give you instructions? Like how often to change the dressing? Medications?"

"Yes, look in the small case over there. It's there, along with all the meds they prescribed, my phone, and the other things I took to the hospital. Can you bring my phone over, please? You can just set it on the nightstand. Thanks."

Athena took a sheaf of papers from the case, reading quickly through them. "Okay, here we go. All the medication amounts and times are listed, so I'll make up a chart for myself. We don't want to miss any doses."

"That's not necessary, Athena. I can take care of my medication."

Athena thought before answering and then said, "I'm not sure that's such a good idea. After surgery, when a patient is taking pain medication, they can lose track of time, or get confused as to when they took the last one. We really don't want that to happen. It's better if I keep track of everything. That's what the agency recommends too."

Sloane sighed. "Maybe you're right. I *have* been rather groggy on and off. I certainly don't want to make a mistake, so if you think it's better for you to handle it for now, that's fine. All the meds for the surgery are over there, and my lupus meds are still downstairs. Whit can show you."

"Good. Is there anything I can get you? Some food? Something to drink?"

"No, thanks. I just need some sleep. Would you draw the curtains before you leave?"

Athena pulled the door closed on the darkened room and took the instructions and medications with her. The protocol was rather simple: just pain medication and an antibiotic. Athena knew that sulfa drugs like Bactrim or Septra were typically prescribed to hip replacement patients to prevent infection, but Sloane had been prescribed Augmentin. Sulfa drugs were contraindicated in lupus patients because they could cause flares. She was glad that Sloane had so easily acquiesced to her suggestion to let her handle the meds. It would make her job that much easier.

17

ROSEMARY

Rosemary paced as the phone rang.

"Mac Slade."

"How are you, my old friend?" she asked with no preamble.

"Rose! Damn, it's good to hear your voice, woman."

Then his tone became somber. "I was awfully sorry to hear about Robert. I would've come, but I was out of the country. Anyway, I've been meaning to call, but didn't quite know what to say. You must think I'm terrible."

She shook her head, even though he couldn't see her. "Nonsense. There's no need for apologies between us. Besides, you sent a lovely note and flowers." She sighed. "But I could use your help now."

"Name it."

"I want you to look into Whit Montgomery. As you know, he was married to my niece, Peg."

Mac cleared his throat. "The senator who was there when Robert was . . ." His voice trailed off. "I hear he married Robert's widow."

Rosemary exhaled. "Yes. I still have suspicions about his role in the shooting, but I can't prove it. Before she died, Peg told me that Whit was cheating on her with a woman named Madelyn Sawyer. Can you see if there's anything going on between them? I also need you to come down here. Talk to some of Peg's friends in Arlington. I'll send you the details in an email."

"You got it. How quickly do you need it?"

"The sooner the better." She hesitated a moment, then went on. "One more thing. Whit hired a new home healthcare worker.

Athena Karras. Check her out. Can't be too safe with who we have around us. I'll send you a link to her Facebook page. Camille showed it to me. Then you'll have her picture."

"Sure thing. And as for Peg's friends, I'll head down in the morning. Give me a couple weeks to see what Whit's got going on. I'll have him tailed. Once I have something, I'll come see you in person. It'll be good to catch up."

She smiled. "I'd love that."

She ended the call, feeling a modicum of relief, and emailed him Michelle Sommers's name and address, so he could find out if Peg ever met with Michelle's lawyer husband about her concerns about Whit, and what Michelle knew about the money Peg thought Whit was hiding. Maybe Michelle could also shed some light on the reason that Peg had called Robert in a panic, the day they were both killed.

Once she hit send, Rosemary sat at her desk, absently drumming her fingers on the wooden surface. If she was going to go down this rabbit hole, she had to open her mind to all the possibilities. If Whit had married Peg only for her money, could he have been frustrated to find out she'd inherited just a small portion of her parents' estate? Maybe he killed her for her life insurance money. No one was there to see what had happened. Whit was the only witness. But she thought again of Camille's point about Peg having been the one to call Robert there that day. Surely even Whit was not Machiavellian enough to have manipulated her into doing so and then staging a shooting. And the investigation had supported Whit's explanation of events.

As much as Rosemary disliked him, murder was quite a stretch, yet the news was full of stories of seemingly model citizens committing horrific acts. Men killed their pregnant wives, their children, their parents. And didn't witnesses consistently claim the guilty party had seemed like a perfectly nice person? If Whit was capable of such an atrocity—shooting his wife and his supposed best friend—the question was why.

Suddenly, the answer seemed so obvious that Rosemary felt like a fool for not seeing it before. Sloane! In one fell swoop, Whit had dispensed with both of their spouses, freeing him up to marry Sloane and obtain access to all her millions. What did they always say about the motive for murder? Love or money. Occasionally both.

Whoa, slow down, she admonished herself. Before she continued with this noir thriller idea, she needed to see what Mac found. Besides, Sloane was no fool. Rosemary knew she'd had Whit sign a prenuptial agreement—Camille had assured her of that. But there was also the foundation. She hoped that Sloane hadn't given Whit any control over it.

She stopped in the kitchen to let Matilda know she'd be ready for dinner in half an hour. Filled with new resolve, she headed upstairs to change. Even though she ate alone most nights, she continued her custom of dressing for dinner. She could do what many of her widowed friends did and eat her dinner in front of the television, but she liked to maintain a routine. On the nights she did not have guests for dinner, she still had the cook prepare a proper meal. Her mother had taught her a long time ago not to discount one's own company, and Rosemary was fortunate in that she very much enjoyed her own.

When she returned downstairs, she walked into the living room and poured herself a healthy glass of scotch. After she took a long swallow, her nerves began to settle. She had to think clearly, and not allow herself to go off half-cocked. She thought back to her last conversation with Peg. At the time, she had thought her niece was exaggerating; that her assertions about Whit were over the top. Now she wished she had paid more attention.

18

ATHENA

The first week had gone well. Athena could see that Sloane was progressing, and although the PT sessions were painful for her, she never complained. Athena had to admit the woman was driven and determined. She didn't need to be coaxed to do the PT "homework," and pushed herself, proving diligent about doing the exercises. The physical therapist had come to the house for all three sessions last week, but today Athena would be taking Sloane to the therapy office. Sloane had complained about having cabin fever and wanted to get out of the house.

Athena rose very early, as she had each day since arriving, and was dressed, breakfast behind her, before Sloane awoke. Now she went to Sloane's door and knocked.

"Come in," Sloane said.

Athena entered the room and saw that Sloane was in her robe and sitting on a straight-backed chair near the bed. "Good morning. How did you sleep?" Athena asked.

"Really well. I'm looking forward to going out today."

"I bet." Athena opened dresser drawers and took out underwear, socks, sweatpants, and a loose top, carrying them over to Sloane. "I'll help you with these, and—"

"Oh no." Sloane shook her head. "I can't go out in sweatpants. Before the surgery, I put some loose outfits together and moved them to the front of the closet. There's a pair of gray slacks with a white pullover on a hanger. Would you bring them over, please? I'm going to try using my reacher-grabber to help me dress."

Athena watched as Sloane dressed, helping when needed. Overall, Sloane did well. "Okay, how about shoes? Which ones?" Athena asked.

"I bought a pair of slip-on sneakers. They told me they're good flats for after surgery. The box is on the floor next to the dresser."

Athena picked them up, noticing they were Prada.

Sloane slipped on the shoes with the help of a long shoehorn and stood, smiling. "Okay. A little out of breath, but ready to go."

She'd only seen Sloane in sweatpants or pajamas since the surgery, but the woman who stood before her now was the same effortlessly chic woman she'd met that first day. Even wearing casual sneakers, she managed to look elegant.

After they arrived, Sloane was quickly called back. As she stood to follow the nurse in, she turned to Athena.

"Would you hold on to this?" Sloane handed her a small light-blue purse and left.

Athena flipped distractedly through a month-old *People* magazine. She put it down, looked at her watch, and then at Sloane's handbag, which she'd sat on the chair next to her. It was fine leather, Athena could tell by the feel of it, but very plain, with some metal studs across the front and a small leather loop stamped with a capital D hanging from the handle. Looking around the room first, Athena picked up the bag and opened it. Imprinted on the inside flap was a small crown and the name Delvaux under it—a brand she'd never heard of. Inside was a small leather credit card holder, a mini Montblanc pen and pad, and an Hermès lip balm. She closed the bag and returned it to the chair, guessing it was probably expensive, just like its contents. Understated, not obvious.

Athena scanned the pile of magazines on the table and glanced at her watch again, figuring Sloane should be finished in another ten minutes or so, but when she looked up, Sloane was walking toward her.

Athena got up. "How did it go?"

"A little painful, but my range of motion is increasing, so that's good. Let's go have a nice lunch, and afterward we can drop by the foundation."

Half an hour later, they sat across from each other at The Warehouse in Alexandria. The restaurant wasn't far from the foundation offices, and Athena could tell by the warm greetings Sloane received that she came here often. They placed their order, both deciding on the seafood gumbo. Athena watched as Sloane squeezed some lemon into her water glass and took a sip.

"It's wonderful to be out and about. The four walls of my bedroom were beginning to close in on me." She laughed.

"It's hard to be confined, I know, and you're making great progress. But you do have to be careful not to overdo it."

"You sound like my husband. So . . . enough about my recuperation. Let's talk about something else," Sloane said.

Athena thought about the best way to get Sloane to open up and to build a good rapport with her so her guard was down. Their love of Greece was common ground, so she decided that would be a good tactic. "You mentioned that you and your first husband honeymooned in Greece. I miss it. I'd love to hear about your time there."

Sloane stared past Athena. "It was spectacular. I can still see us on the beach, Robert so tall and athletic, standing in the sand, pulling me up from the beach towel. The two of us running, splashing into the water together." She looked back at Athena. "Those three weeks of sun and surf, those lazy afternoons, were absolutely magical. We had dinner late—nine or ten. We feasted on Greek delicacies, that delicious flaming saganaki cheese, tender lamb with rice cooked to perfection. I still remember the taste of the kumquat liqueur we'd end every meal with." Sloane's mouth curved into a small smile. "Some nights we missed dinner altogether."

"They sound like happy times," Athena said, wondering if Sloane was as happy with her current husband.

"Yes. The happiest. Robert's sister, Camille, was my best friend from the time we were little. We went to the same boarding school.

He was the cute older brother who teased us and called us little pests. Of course, he never saw me as anything but his sister's friend, but he was always kind. I'll never forget the night of his parents' annual Christmas party. Robert brought Amanda, his steady girlfriend. I was so jealous of her." Sloane's rueful laugh filled the room. "Anyway, soon after that, he went off to college and then law school, so I hardly saw him. We reconnected the summer before my junior year at Amherst. He was studying for the bar, and, well, the rest is history. We fell in love and got married a year after I graduated."

"That's so romantic," Athena said. "How long were you and Robert married?"

Sloane sighed heavily. "Almost twenty-five years. He turned thirty the day we got married. Robert always joked that he planned it that way, so that he'd never forget the date of our anniversary. We had a rule . . . no purchased presents for birthdays or anniversaries. We each had to make something for the other. Our anniversary was a fun celebration every year, even if it was just a candlelit dinner at home and dancing the tango like we were in a scene from *Scent of a Woman*. We had so much fun together." She looked down for a few seconds, and when she looked up her eyes shone with tears. "I miss him."

"He sounds wonderful. Do you have a picture of him on your phone?" Athena asked.

"I do." As Sloane took the phone from her purse and set it on the table, then tapped in her password, Athena watched carefully and committed it to memory. "Here," Sloane said, swiping to a photo and handing the phone to Athena.

The photograph was obviously taken when Robert was in his thirties and showed an all-American-looking guy with sun-bleached hair and penetrating blue eyes. "He was very handsome," Athena said.

"Sloane," a voice rang out. A tall young woman came rushing over to their table.

"Abby, how good to see you," Sloane said, but remained seated.

"I heard about your surgery. How did everything go? You look wonderful."

"It went well, thank you for asking. Abby, this is Athena Karras. Athena, Abby Thompson," Sloane said.

Athena smiled, uttering a brief hello, and then listened to the exchange between the two women. It was apparent that the younger woman was a little in awe of Sloane, and Athena watched with interest as Sloane put her completely at ease by the time they'd finished. And it didn't escape her notice that Sloane introduced Athena as if she were a friend, never referring to the fact that Athena worked for her.

"So, Athena," Sloane said brightly after Abby left. "Tell me what you do when you're not working."

Taking a deep breath, Athena thought for a moment, recalling Sloane's full bookshelves. "Well, one of my favorite things to do is poke around old bookstores. I could spend hours looking through the shelves."

"Mmm. I love that too. What do you like to read?"

"I'm all over the place. I love biographies, especially ones about strong women. I've always been drawn to Greek tragedy." She smiled. "I guess it's in the genes. And I read a lot of nonfiction."

"I love biographies too. And I've gone back and reread many of the classics I studied in college. Such a different take, almost thirty years later. But I have to say that I'm a sucker for a good love story," Sloane said.

Athena did her best to keep her expression impassive. Love stories always ended badly. Didn't Sloane know that?

SLOANE

Fifteen days postsurgery, and Sloane was doing well—at least as far as her hip was concerned. But a feeling of alarm filled her, as if her very breath were being squeezed from her body. What her rheumatologist had feared was coming to pass: her joints were achy, her feet swollen. A lupus flare. Athena had driven her to the doctor's two days ago for blood tests, and Dr. Porter, her rheumatologist, had confirmed it when he called her yesterday with the lab results. Her sedimentation rate was elevated, which meant that she was experiencing inflammation. Sloane had a follow-up appointment in an hour, and he would give her an injection of triamcinolone to see if that would mitigate the flare instead of upping her prednisone, which came with a host of side effects. She hoped the steroid shot would work. No wonder the physical therapy had become more arduous instead of less so.

Sloane put down her toothbrush and leaned against the vanity, drawing in a breath to steady herself. Just the effort of washing up this morning had already drained her.

She heard the sound of an incoming FaceTime call and picked up the phone from the vanity top, smiling when she saw Emmy's name.

"Hello, sweetie! How are you?"

Emmy's smile faded and her eyes clouded with concern. "Mom? Are you okay? You don't look good."

Sloane forced a cheerful note into her voice, trying to sound better than she felt. "Just a little under the weather. Nothing to fret about." She didn't want to tell Emmy about the doctor's appointment. It would only worry her. Although when she looked at the image projected on the screen, she could see why Emmy had asked. She had dark circles under her eyes, and her color was gray.

"Mom. You have to take it easy. That's the whole point of Athena being there; you're supposed to rest. Maybe I should take some time off and fly home."

"No. I'm fine. You haven't been there long enough to take time off. I have Whit and Athena here." Sloane took a deep breath and tightened her free hand on the cane for support.

Emmy didn't look convinced. "I don't know."

"You'll be home for the donor party in a few weeks. And by then I'll be as good as new. Now stop worrying!"

"Okay. Love you, Mom."

"Love you more."

Sloane ended the call and inched slowly to a chair. She felt bad lying to Emmy. She still hadn't told Whit about the flare either—she was hopeful the shot would do its magic and she'd be back to normal. She'd tell him about it after her appointment today. She thought again of Madelyn's cheap shot about her illness and was filled with anger. She could just imagine the elation Madelyn would feel if Sloane became sick again.

The truth was that people lived a lifetime with lupus and kept it well under control with their medications. Sloane had been lucky so far, but the fact that she had central nervous involvement put her at a higher risk of serious illness. Central nervous system vasculitis could cause inflammation of the brain and spinal cord vessels. If that happened, the complications ranged from fever and headaches to terrifying seizures, psychosis, depression, and coma. It was something she tried not to think about, but in these quiet moments, the fear tormented her. She pictured herself unable to move or speak, a prisoner of her own body. She had a living will and had specified that she didn't want to be kept alive by any artificial means. But she also knew from her support group that she could be sick enough to lose control of her faculties, but still able to live unassisted for years. That was the nightmare she lived with.

*　　*　　*

Sloane heard the door chime and looked up from the book she was reading: it was only five thirty, early for Whit to be home. He walked into the living room and sat next to her on the sofa, leaning toward her for a kiss.

"This is a nice surprise. What brings you home early?" she asked.

"I have a meeting with my staff later to go over a new bill. I wanted to stop home and check on you, since it could be a long night."

Sloane saw her opening and took it. "I need to tell you something. I had Athena take me for some bloodwork. Dr. Porter ran more tests. It, uh . . . it seems I'm in a flare."

Concern filled Whit's face. "Why didn't you tell me?"

"I *am* telling you."

He leaned forward for emphasis. "I meant right away. How bad is it?"

"It'll be okay. He gave me a steroid shot today, and that should reduce the inflammation. I need to take it easy for a few days; not that I'll be doing any calisthenics with this hip thing going on, but I'm sure everything will be fine."

"Sloane, you can't keep things like this from me. I'm your husband, and I love you. If you're not well, I'm the first one you should tell. As a matter of fact, I want to go with you when you see the doctor. I want to be with you through this."

"But you're so busy . . ."

He shook his head. "Not too busy for you. Your health is the most important thing."

She felt relief flood through her. "I didn't want to burden you. Especially so soon."

"That's nonsense. I *want* to be here for you. In sickness and in health, remember?"

She nodded.

"How about I make you a cup of your favorite tea. I have time before I need to go back. We can sit together for a while."

"I'd love that. Thanks."

"Okay. Be right back. And promise me, no more secrets."

She nodded, but it was a promise she was unwilling to make.

20

ATHENA

Emmy surprised Sloane by flying home for the weekend. She and Sloane had been out all morning, and Athena had taken the opportunity to call Clint and bring him up to date. They'd agreed from the beginning that it was safer for her to communicate with him from the mobile phone she kept locked in the glove compartment of her car.

She'd taken a long walk after they spoke, savoring the fresh air and sun on her face, and the freedom just to be herself. She got back to the house a little after Emmy and Sloane returned and went up to check on Sloane. The bedroom door was slightly ajar, and she poked her head in. Sloane was sitting on the love seat, scribbling away on a yellow legal pad. She stopped writing and looked up when she saw Athena.

"Come in," she called.

Her color seemed better, her face more relaxed, Athena noticed. "You look like you're feeling better," she said.

"I *do* feel better." Sloane smiled brightly. "And I'm thrilled to have my daughter here."

"I can see that."

"I've missed her so much."

"It's hard to be apart from the people you love." Athena felt a pang of loneliness.

"Yes. But it helps to know she's happy in California."

"Do I hear myself being talked about?" Emmy said as she swept into the room with a flourish.

"Hi, sweetheart, only good things."

Athena moved toward the door. "Why don't I leave you two alone? I'll go down and see what's happening with dinner."

Emmy pivoted to her. "Oh, wait. I'll come with you. Help you."

"Go ahead. Off with both of you," Sloane said, waving them away and returning her attention to whatever she'd been writing.

"We didn't really have much of a chance to talk last night when I got in," Emmy said as they walked side by side down the stairs. "It's still early. How about a cup of tea and a chat?"

This was precisely what Athena had been hoping for, and she'd been about to make the same suggestion. With Emmy living in California, this might be the only chance she'd have to probe. "Sure," she said.

Yvette was busy at work in the kitchen when they entered. "Hey, Yvette. We're going to make some tea," Emmy said.

"I'll do that for you," Yvette said.

"No, no. We'll take care of it and get out of your way," she told Yvette, and turned to Athena. "I'll put on the kettle, and you get the mugs," Emmy said, already opening the cabinet door for her.

They took the steaming mugs into the yellow sunroom, where the pale afternoon light sifted gently through the window.

"Your mom seems better now that you're here. I think your visit has done her a world of good. She's always talking about how proud you're making her by following your dreams. I know you wish you could be here longer, but your mother wouldn't want you to jeopardize your career."

A shadow crossed Emmy's face. "I do wish I could stay longer. I'm worried about her. She can be so hardheaded at times. It's obvious she's not well, but she insists on doing things she shouldn't be doing right now." She clasped her hands together, her fingers threaded through each other. "I *am* relieved, though, that you're here to help."

Athena drew her hands together in her lap, mirroring Emmy's. "I know how hard this is for you. To be so far away while your mother's ill." She locked her gaze onto Emmy's. "I want you to know that I will take care of your mother as if she were my own. She can, as you say, be hardheaded, but I will *not* let her overwork or harm herself. I'll be with her all the time." Athena saw the relief in Emmy's eyes as the young woman unclenched her hands and relaxed her shoulders.

"Hearing you say that makes me feel so much better." Emmy looked pensive, as if considering what she was about to say. She pressed her lips together for a second and then spoke. "I've felt so conflicted about taking the job in LA. I mean, not when I first went, when my father was still alive, and Mom wasn't alone. But after he died, I really struggled about whether I should just come home and find work here."

Athena concentrated, listening carefully to every word Emmy uttered. "Yes, I can see how conflicted you must have been."

"I told her I was going to leave the job, but she insisted that I stay; said I shouldn't give up on something I love. I knew she had Gram and Aunt Camille. She has good friends too. And she had her work, of course."

Athena nodded, but said nothing, encouraging Emmy to continue.

"And then all of a sudden she was with Whit." Emmy stopped. "He was my dad's best friend. I guess it was a little strange to me when Mom first married him."

"You often read about people marrying a good friend after a spouse dies. I imagine your mother was always fond of him as a friend. And maybe it's easier to be with someone who knew and liked your spouse."

"I guess that's true."

"You've known him a long time, haven't you?"

"Since I was a kid, yes. He was always so much fun. Peg was my blood relative, but I always liked Whit better. And then, after what happened—" Emmy stopped, her face hardening. "I'll always hate her. My father would still be alive if it weren't for her."

"It was a terrible tragedy. So awful." Athena thought about how to word her next question. "I might have it completely wrong, but I remember reading about it at the time and wondering if Peg was a jealous person."

"Totally! Always accusing Whit of flirting if he even spoke to another woman. She was even jealous of my mother. There was this time at the beach, Mom and Whit went for a morning walk together. Dad was still in Washington and Peg was asleep. She never got up early, always slept till ten or later. Anyway, when she finally got up and they weren't back, she went batshit crazy. Like a raving lunatic. When they walked in, she started in on both of them, accusing them of cheating. I mean, my mother, really? She's the last person in the world to do that. She has more integrity than anyone I know."

Interesting, Athena thought. Had Peg been onto something?

"I'm sorry if I was ranting. It always gets me when I think about that night."

"I understand," Athena said, recognizing that Emmy was finished pouring her heart out.

"I did want to talk to you about next week," Emmy said.

"Next week?"

"The donor party. Mom puts so much into it, and I had planned on being here to help, but I'm not going to be able to take the time off now. Will you make sure she takes it easy and doesn't overdo it?"

"Of course. I told you, I am going to watch her like a hawk."

"Thanks. I feel so much better knowing you're here." Emmy stood and picked up her empty mug. "I'll go check on Mom. See if she's ready for dinner."

"Okay. Here," Athena said, extending her hand. "I'll take everything inside; you go ahead upstairs."

Athena watched Emmy leave the room, grateful that she'd be going back to California tomorrow. Having a doting daughter around who watched Athena's every move was the last thing she needed.

21

ROSEMARY

Mac had called that morning to say he had the information she needed. He was due to arrive any moment, and Rosemary was so anxious to hear what he'd found out that she hadn't been able to concentrate on anything. After rereading the same sentence four times, she threw down her book and looked at her watch just as the doorbell rang. She heard Matilda open the door, and then footsteps in the hallway. Standing as her old friend entered the living room, she smiled at the sight of his jaunty trademark fedora. Removing the hat from his head, he put it down on a chair and opened his arms to her. Rosemary embraced him and was surprised to feel tears spring to her eyes. She hadn't realized until now just how much she'd missed him.

"You look wonderful, Roe," he said as he leaned back to take her in.

"So do you. Still have a full head of that gorgeous silver hair," she teased. He did look good. Much healthier and fitter than the last time she'd seen him. He'd been sober for over ten years now, and it showed. Mac was one of her oldest friends from her childhood; they'd grown up together. And while there had always been a spark between them, the timing had never been right. Mac became a top defense attorney in a large firm in Philadelphia, and eventually partner. Over time, though, he couldn't stomach getting the guilty off, and when his last client went on to murder two children after Mac got him acquitted, he stopped practicing law. That was more than twenty years ago. Afterward, he became an investigator for those in difficult situations. A rich husband took off with the kids before the divorce and custody agreement? Mac would find them. He had connections everywhere, and a brilliant mind on top of that.

"Come, sit. What can I get you?"

He took a seat and handed her a manila folder. "I'm good. Your guy, Whit, hasn't had any rendezvous with the Sawyer woman in the past few weeks." He shrugged. "Not that that means nothing's going on, but I couldn't find anything. He's quite cozy with her husband, Fred. However, it does look like something's not on the up-and-up."

Rosemary leaned in, rapt.

"It appears he's having some secret meetings with another congressman as well as the head of a lobbying firm, Dominic Peterson. I wrote it all up for you."

She opened the folder and scanned the report.

SUBJECT: SURVEILLANCE OF WHITAKER MONTGOMERY

At approximately 6:00pm on Tuesday, the 23rd, the target, Whitaker Montgomery, entered the bar at the St. Regis Hotel, where he met with two unknown males.

(Note: Investigation later identified the unknown males to be Congressman Frank Horner and Dominic Peterson, President of Redstone Consulting, the largest lobbying firm representing private real estate developers in the United States as well as the Home Builders Association.)

Montgomery, Horner, and Peterson had several drinks at the bar.

At approximately 6:35pm, Horner departed the bar area and took an elevator to the 7th floor before the elevator returned to the lobby empty. The elevator did not appear to stop on any other floor on the way up or on the way down.

At approximately 6:45pm, Peterson departed the bar area and, also, took an elevator to the 7th floor before the elevator returned to the lobby empty. The elevator did not appear to stop on any other floor on the way up or on the way down.

At approximately 6:55pm, Montgomery departed the bar area and, also, took an elevator to the 7th floor before the elevator returned to the lobby empty. The elevator did not appear to stop on any other floor on the way up or on the way down.

A subsequent sweep of the 7th floor revealed no individuals in the hallways or stairwells.

The Vice President of the United States and his Secret Service security detail were observed in the hotel's restaurant, adjacent to the bar area. No attempt was made to follow the Vice President.

Rosemary stopped reading to digest the contents.

"I'm not sure this is really anything," she said.

Mac tilted his head. "I'm not done. I accessed the public visitor logs for the Eisenhower Executive Office Building. Sure enough, Peterson, Montgomery, and Horner, along with Madelyn's husband, Fred Sawyer, went on three separate occasions to meet with the vice president. On one of those occasions, Congresswoman Faye Chambers was also in attendance."

Rosemary sat back in the chair. "That *is* odd. I don't see why Peterson would be meeting with Whit and the VP." She wondered if Faye would be able to shed more light on this. She was a good friend of Rosemary's.

Mac leaned forward. "But this is where it gets really strange. I checked the flight manifests for Air Force Two over the past nine months. On three occasions, both Horner and Peterson were on it. One of the trips Whit was there too."

"Where did they go?" Rosemary asked.

"Once to Nebraska, once to Michigan, and once to Oklahoma. I did some asking around. The dates all coincided with the opening of a new HUD housing community. They were all there for the ribbon cutting. I get why the VP and senator and congressman were there; these are government initiatives to increase public housing. But what does Peterson, a lobbyist, have to do with them? He mostly represents commercial builders of privately owned housing projects. Something doesn't smell right." Mac shook his head. "I'm gonna keep digging." He exhaled. "On the other matter . . . I did go to Arlington, but Michelle Sommers wasn't there. Their housekeeper said they were out of the country, and she'll have Michelle call me when she returns. Athena Karras seems to check out. If the facial recognition program turns up anything strange, I'll let you know right away."

"I appreciate it. Now, I insist that you let me feed you. Come on, let's go into the dining room. I'll have Matilda bring us some lunch, and we can catch up. It's your favorite."

Mac's eyes lit up. "Corned beef and cabbage?"

Rosemary nodded. "Only for you."

After Mac left, Rosemary did some research on Peterson. When she was finished, she dialed Faye's direct line. She and Faye had been friends for over fifty years, and although she saw Faye less than she'd like these days, whenever they did get together it was as if no time had elapsed at all. After Rosemary's husband died, it was Faye who'd dropped everything and stayed with her day and night that first horrible week.

"Hello?"

"Faye, Rosemary here."

"Darling! Good to hear your voice. How've you been?"

Rosemary got right to the point. "Better. Do you have a minute?"

"For you, always."

Rosemary summarized what Mac had told her. "I need to know if Whit is involved in anything suspicious with this Peterson fellow."

"I seriously doubt it. Whit has a stellar reputation. Peterson's a powerful lobbyist and not a man to make an enemy of. I'm sure Whit's just playing the DC game like everyone else, and I'd be shocked to find that he was doing anything underhanded. But I'll make some discreet inquiries. See what I can find."

"Thanks. Why don't you come for dinner next week? Mac said he might have more information for me by then. We can compare notes. Wednesday?"

"You're on."

Next, she dialed Camille. "I'm not catching you at a bad time, am I?" she asked her daughter.

"No. Going over some files at my desk. Everything okay?"

"Yes, I was just wondering if you know anything about a man named Dominic Peterson."

"Why?"

Rosemary hesitated. "Um . . . Whit has been meeting with him."

She heard an exasperated sigh on the other end of the line. "Mom, you have to stop this!"

"Please, do you know him?"

"Yeah. His company represents the Home Builders Association. Head honcho now at Redstone Consulting. He doesn't have to hit the pavement anymore; he has a massive team of lobbyists who do that for him. All he has to do is sit behind a desk in his posh office and make a phone call."

"I've heard he's got a sketchy reputation."

"Well, there are rumors he's associated with some unsavory people. Nothing ever proven, but let's just say, nothing is out of the realm of possibility where Peterson is concerned."

"Why would Whit be involved with him?"

"I wouldn't jump to any conclusions. You know how this town is; you have to at least appear to be friends with everyone. All political friendships are expedient and conditional. Mom, you've got to stop trying to discredit Whit. It's only going to alienate you from Sloane."

Rosemary's frustration rose. Was she the only one who wasn't deceived by Whit's charm and magnetism? She decided not to tell Camille that she'd asked Mac to look into Whit. She'd wait until she talked to Faye and had more information.

"Okay, I hear you. Forget I mentioned it. I'll talk to you later."

Rosemary leaned back in the chair and closed her eyes. She was filled with a profound sense of dread. She felt like Pandora, her hand hovering over that damned box, about to unleash untold calamity.

22

ATHENA

Athena could see a difference in Sloane's frame of mind since Emmy's departure last week. She was sleeping later and had lost some of her usual cheeriness. This morning, Athena rose even earlier than usual, dressed, and walked down the hallway to Sloane's bedroom, opening the door just a crack. When she saw that the room was still dark, she quietly pulled the door shut and went downstairs to a house bustling with activity in preparation for the foundation's donor appreciation celebration. She'd learned from Sloane that it was a party held every year to thank everyone who had made a large donation to the foundation. The unfortunate thing was that the need for Sloane's hip replacement had come after the date for the event was set and preparations begun. Besides, it had been a month since the surgery, and if she weren't in an active flare, the party wouldn't have been too much for her. Tonight they were expecting two hundred guests, which would include the board members, employees, and volunteers of the foundation, as well as principals of the many charities they supported.

From her bedroom, Athena had seen the crew from Luxury Rentals unloading stacks of tables and chairs. Now, as she walked into the kitchen, cases of wine, silver chafing dishes, and serving platters along with tableware, crystal stemware, and sterling silver flatware were being unpacked by Blackwell Caterers. Athena shook her head. Only the best for this pampered crowd, she thought, her gaze resting on the fine white, gold-bordered plates. No plain dishes or stainless utensil rentals, but real china and silverware.

Athena poured a cup of coffee just as Doris came in from the back patio.

"Good morning," Athena said to her. "Thanks for making the coffee in the midst of all this hustle and bustle." She took a sip of the hot brew.

"I make coffee every morning. Why should today be any different? Is Mrs. Ch— uh . . . Montgomery up and maybe ready for some breakfast?"

"She was still sleeping when I came down about ten minutes ago. She was up so late last night, worrying about tonight and wanting to make sure nothing was being overlooked."

"She's doing too much. It's just plain ridiculous to have this big do when poor Mrs. Montgomery is so under the weather. It should have been postponed," Doris said, her lips pursed and shaking her head. "I wish she'd take better care of herself."

"Well, that's what I'm here for," Athena said. "I made her turn the light out last night, and I intend to let her sleep as long as possible this morning."

"Hmph. Still shouldn't have been up so late."

Athena topped up her coffee and turned back to the woman, trying to quell her own irritation. "I'm going to stroll around and check on things. I'll head upstairs in a little bit to see if she's awake, and let you know."

Before going upstairs to look in on Sloane, Athena walked outside to the backyard, where a luxurious arched-ceiling tent was being set up. As soon as they were finished, the small tables and chairs would be brought in, and the dance floor put together. Sloane had hired a band for live dance music. It was a shame, she thought, that the pool had been closed and covered at the end of September, because it would have been lovely to see it all lit up from the tent. But October weather was unpredictable in Washington and could go from pleasant to snow in the blink of an eye.

Satisfied that all was going as planned, Athena checked her watch and headed inside to see if Sloane had awakened, padding down the long hallway to Sloane's room and listening at the door. It was slightly open, and Athena could hear Sloane talking on the phone. She strained to hear what she was saying. She caught Brianna's name and leaned in closer.

"No, no. I don't want the funds held up. Send me the report. I'll go over it and sign off on the disbursement."

There was silence and Athena realized Sloane had finished her call.

"Ah, you're up," she said, opening the door all the way and entering.

Sloane sat on a chair, using the reaching tool with a pincher to put on a pair of pants.

"Can I help you with that?" Athena asked.

"No. I have to do this for myself." Sloane grabbed the cane and stood, tucking a white long-sleeved blouse into loose tweed pants. Taking a breath after her effort, she turned to Athena. "I took one last look at the guest list and didn't see Senator Marconi's name. Did we get an RSVP from her?"

"Remember? I phoned last week and was told she's out of town."

Sloane's glance flickered. "I must have forgotten."

Athena kept her expression neutral with difficulty. This was the third time Sloane had asked about her. Maybe it was the pain medication, but she'd been repeating herself a lot over the past week.

"Oh, another thing. There was a call from Fred Sawyer's office saying he was called out of town, and that his wife, Madelyn, would be attending alone."

"Oh, wonderful." Sloane's tone of contempt didn't escape Athena's notice.

"How's everything downstairs?"

"Great so far. They've probably finished setting up the tent and should be laying down the dance floor soon. Dancing under the stars—how romantic."

Sloane smiled but said nothing.

"What are you wearing tonight?" Athena asked.

"Come, I'll show you."

Athena followed Sloane into the large closet and dressing room, where a pale pink gown hung. "Oh my. It's gorgeous. I loved the gown you wore to the White House dinner a while ago too."

Sloane's brow wrinkled. "The White House dinner?"

Athena didn't miss the questioning look on Sloane's face. She and Clint had studied the video carefully. She shouldn't have mentioned it now. "Uh . . . yes. I watched you and the senator and all the other guests arriving on the C-Span telecast. I was excited that the Greek prime minister was in town."

"I see."

Athena cleared her throat. "Shall I let Doris and Yvette know you're ready for breakfast?"

"No, no. I'll go down now. Have something small, and then we can get to work."

Athena noticed that Sloane's eyes still looked tired, and her face pinched with pain every time she took a step.

When they reached the stairs, Sloane gripped the banister so tightly that her knuckles turned white, and her steps were slow and halting. How she'd get through the evening was a mystery to Athena.

Athena would talk to the senator tomorrow about Sloane's medications. She could suggest that stronger pain meds were called for. She hadn't really had any time alone with him since the interview, but now that his wife was going to bed so early, there would be time to catch him by himself. And time alone with Whit was crucial to her plan.

23

SLOANE

Sloane soaked in a hot bath, which helped ease the stiffness and muscle spasms, and afterward napped for a few hours. The time it had taken to check the preparations downstairs and go over everything with Athena had exhausted her. She needed to be rested for tonight, when she would be the hostess, and not able to duck out early if she was feeling tired or sick.

In an hour and a half, their guests would be arriving, so she threw back the covers and reached for her robe. As she tied the sash, there was a light rap on the door.

"Yes?"

The door opened and Whit stuck his head in. "How are you doing? Athena said you were taking a nap. Are you feeling better?" He walked in and closed the door behind him.

"I am. How's it going downstairs?"

"Everything's all set up. Looks great. Athena's got it all under control. Here," he said, handing her a cold bottle of water. "Thought you might be thirsty."

"Thanks." Sloane unscrewed the cap and took a long swallow. "How was your golf game?"

He grimaced. "Never got there. I got stuck at the office working on the figures for the appropriations meeting on Monday." He tucked a lock of hair behind her ear and kissed her lightly. "Anything I can do for tonight?" he asked, pulling away.

Sloane put her arms around his neck, kissing him back. "I miss you. I miss making love to you."

Whit held her closer, kissing her neck. "I miss you too. But it won't be long, sweetheart."

She pulled away, sighing. "I know. It's just . . ."

"C'mon. No brooding. You have a party to host. And lots of donors to thank." Whit took her hands and gave them a reassuring squeeze. "When you're well, we'll go away for a long romantic weekend. Okay?"

"Yes, okay." It angered her that her nightly tossing and turning was so disruptive that it had forced Whit into a guest room. He hadn't complained or even mentioned it, but they'd had a vigorous sex life before she'd gotten so sick.

"Okay," he repeated, and kissed her again lightly. "I'll go now and let you get ready."

By the time Sloane finished her makeup and hair, she'd pumped herself up for the evening. It was her favorite event of the year, and she reminded herself that tonight was about the work of the foundation and recognition to all those whose generosity in time and money had contributed to that work. She zipped up her dress and was surprised at how loose it was. She hadn't realized she'd lost that much weight. Cocking her head as she looked in the mirror, she frowned. The dress definitely looked baggy at the waist. She began to pull belts from the drawers, trying and discarding them until she buckled the metallic Brunello Cucinelli. With that finishing touch, Sloane walked slowly downstairs just fifteen minutes before the first guest was due to arrive.

Athena had followed the plans to the letter, Sloane saw as she walked through the house. The soft lighting and flickering candles gave the rooms a warm, inviting feel. Sloane hated harsh, too-bright lighting at parties.

Athena rushed over. "Oh, Sloane, you look wonderful. I'm glad you got some sleep."

"Thank you." She was relying more and more heavily upon Athena, and she didn't like it. Sloane wasn't used to delegating things in her personal life. She knew Athena was only doing her job, but she was finding it difficult not to be resentful. She had to remind herself that it was temporary and forced herself to give

Athena a warm smile. "And thank you for managing all of this so beautifully. I really appreciate it."

"I've enjoyed every minute. Come outside and see the tent. It's dazzling."

"People will be here any minute, and I need to greet them. I won't stay at the front door long, just until the first few arrive, and then I'll go take a look."

As she reached the foyer, Whit came zipping down the stairs to join her, and the first guests began to arrive. For the next hour, wine and liquor flowed, and the house was filled with the sound of loud talk and laughter. The vice president and his wife arrived late and with great fanfare just as guests were being seated for dinner, but there was still no sign of Madelyn. Could this be her lucky day? Sloane wondered happily. She was about to take a seat at one of the tables when Whit came up to her and took her hand.

"Come with me, darling. The vice president and his wife are sitting in the dining room. We should both be with them."

Sloane went along. Vice President Chester Bishop was a relative newcomer to Washington. When President Beckermann's vice president died in office a year ago, Beckermann had nominated Bishop, the former governor of Illinois, to take his place. Bishop was a seasoned politician, however, who had served as inspector general of the Chicago Housing Authority, three terms in Congress, and finally as a two-term governor of the state. Sloane had met him only a few times at social gatherings and didn't know him well, but Whit had formed a fast friendship with the new vice president. This was a good opportunity for her to get to know the man better, and she tried her best to keep her attention trained on the conversation around the table. It was informative and timely, but she couldn't help her attention occasionally wandering to the front door as she kept an eye out for Madelyn's arrival. To Sloane's delight, however, when the meal ended and the guests moved to the tent for dessert and dancing, she still hadn't arrived.

Before the band played, Sloane stepped gingerly onto the stage and took the microphone, leaning the other hand on the cane for support. "I want to thank every one of you here tonight for your generosity and great spirit of giving. You care about changing lives, and I love you for that." She spoke briefly about the work that had been accomplished, and about her dreams for bigger things to come. "So, thank you from the bottom of my heart on behalf of all those you've helped. And now, let's have a little music and dancing."

The applause was boisterous, but soon drowned out by the band's raucous rendition of "Celebration." Sloane looked across the room at Whit, who winked at her and walked across the crowded dance floor to stand with her as they watched the dancers. And then Madelyn was walking through the crowd toward them.

"Mind if I borrow your husband for a dance? Seeing as you're sidelined tonight?" Madelyn stood there, her scarlet lips spread in a wide grin, her breasts spilling out of a sequined bodice.

Before Sloane could speak, Whit said, "Excuse us, Madelyn." Putting his arm at the small of Sloane's back, he led her away.

"Ugh. That woman," Sloane said between gritted teeth. "I need to sit."

Whit pulled out a chair from the table and helped Sloane get situated, then sat down beside her. "Ignore her." He leaned in closer. "Look, the vice president is leaving soon, and he and I want to have a private chat. We're going to sequester ourselves in the library for a little bit. Okay with you?"

"Sure, it's fine."

"I love you. Don't forget that." His lips brushed her cheek.

Sloane sat alone at the table after he'd gone, still fuming, when Madelyn sauntered over. "Well, he seems to have abandoned you," she said. "But who can blame him? I mean, what man as young and virile as Whit wants to be saddled with a wife who needs a cane to get around?"

It took everything in Sloane's power not to whack her with it. She took a deep breath, reminding herself not to let Madelyn see how much she was getting to her. "He's not interested in you, Madelyn. Everything he wants is right here. When are you going to get that message?" Sloane was fighting to stay calm.

"Oh, really? Is that what he's told you?" Her smile was mocking.

"You're starting to sound desperate, Madelyn."

"You think so? I met that luscious piece of ass you hired. Athena? That's her name, right? She's enough to keep any man happy."

Sloane rose from her seat. "You really are despicable, you know that?"

She started to walk away, but Madelyn placed her hand on the cane, stopping Sloane. "You don't know him at all, do you? He wants it all, honey—lots of power, lots of money, lots of sex—and his appetites are huge. More than you could ever give him." Madelyn removed her hand, smiling cruelly.

"Get out of my house, Madelyn."

"Don't worry. I was just leaving. Whit's the only one I wanted to see here anyway," she said, then turned and walked away.

Sloane felt as if she were being attacked and torn apart on all sides—with a predatory bitch after her husband, and worst of all, the lupus that wanted to kill her. Fists clenched, she inhaled deeply and held her head up high. She'd survived worse things before, and she wasn't about to give up now. This flare would be behind her in no time, and once it was, she'd whisk Whit away for a long weekend so they could reconnect romantically. And when they returned, she'd have a nice chat with Madelyn and let her know in no uncertain terms that Whit was off-limits.

24

SLOANE

I t all went downhill for Sloane after the donor party. Over the following weeks, the familiar and all-consuming fatigue began to
creep in—not the "I need some rest" sort of tired, but the "I can't
even open my eyes or lift my arm" kind of exhaustion. Everything
hurt—the clothing against her skin, her swollen wrists and fingers, even her eyelashes. The headaches were constant, and nausea
swept over her in waves. She could barely uncurl her hands. Some
days were better than others, and on those days, Sloane was hopeful that she might be coming out of it. But for the last four days,
there'd been no letup. After the shot hadn't done the trick, Dr. Porter had increased her other medicines and ordered bed rest until
the flare was under control.

No healthy person could really understand what it was like to
live with a chronic illness, Sloane thought, particularly one like
hers that had no cure. When she was feeling good, she was always
aware in the back of her mind that this silent monster lying in wait
could strike her down at any moment. The most isolating feeling in
the world was knowing that others were going on with their lives,
taking walks, shopping, going to concerts, while she was stuck in
her room yet another day.

"Stop feeling sorry for yourself," she chastised herself out loud.
Pushing her body to the edge of the bed, she put her feet on the
floor and reached for her cane. Lying around in pajamas all day
wasn't helping. She made her way to the bathroom, doing her best
to ignore the pain shooting up her legs and the burning on the bot-
toms of her feet. She spent the next hour showering and doing her

hair and makeup. When she returned to the bedroom, she chose a pair of navy slacks and a gray sweater and sat on the bed while she changed. "That's better." She forced a smile to her lips and moved over to the chaise longue, where an anthology of poetry awaited her. She'd only read a few pages when Whit walked in.

"Don't you look nice! Having a good day?" he asked as he came over and gave her a peck on the lips.

"Yes, much better," she said, even though it wasn't true. "What do you have there?" She inclined her head toward the shopping bag he held in one hand. In his other hand was her Ember smart mug.

He sat on the edge of the chaise longue and handed her the mug. "Green tea to help with inflammation. No caffeine, of course."

"Thank you," she said, taking a sip.

"And now just a few things to show you how much I love you." He pulled out the first box and handed it to her.

She put the mug down and took the box. Bottega Veneta. She couldn't imagine what it was. Lifting the lid, she pulled out a gorgeous black-and-white halter dress.

Whit smiled at her. "As soon as I saw it, I thought of you. Once you're better, I'm taking you away to the islands and can't wait to see you in it."

For a moment, she allowed herself to imagine them on vacation, her healthy and wearing this beautiful dress. She reached out and squeezed his hand. "So thoughtful! Thank you."

"There's more." He grinned as he pulled out a smaller box.

"Gucci. What could this be?" Removing the top, she saw it was the Flora bracelet she'd admired a few months ago when they were shopping at City Center. She pulled the delicate gold and diamond piece from the box. "It's so lovely. But you shouldn't have."

Whit took it from her and fastened it on her wrist. "Of course I should. Anything to cheer up my beautiful wife. But there's more."

"Whit, this is too much. Really . . ."

"You know how I like to spoil you. Last one. Go ahead."

She dug her hand into the bag and pulled out a heavy package wrapped in gold foil.

"Careful opening that one," Whit said.

She peeled the paper back to reveal a book: *The Poems of W. B. Yeats*. He knew Yeats was one of her favorites.

"It's a first edition," he said proudly.

She clutched the book to her chest, tears filling her eyes. How had she gotten so lucky to have another thoughtful man in her life who knew her so well? "I love you," she said.

"And I love you. Shall I read to you?"

"Yes."

He opened the book but stopped when his cellphone buzzed. Before Sloane could see the number on the screen, he stood and walked away. He typed something, then came back over.

"Sorry, darling, it's Fred. He's moved tomorrow's meeting up to today."

Sloane felt her mistrust rise, wondering if it was Fred or Madelyn on the other side of the text. She was not suspicious by nature, but Madelyn's words still echoed in her ears. Especially the part about Sloane not knowing Whit at all. She didn't really believe Madelyn, but the old adage *where there's smoke there's fire* gave her pause. She sat up straighter. This was exactly what Madelyn wanted—to create tension between Sloane and Whit. She smiled at him.

"Of course."

After he left, Athena brought her lunch. She looked at the packages surrounding Sloane.

"Is it your birthday?"

Sloane shook her head. "No, Whit picked up some things to cheer me up."

Athena gave her a thin smile. "How nice. Would you like me to move all this so you can have lunch here?"

Did Sloane detect a tone of resentment in the woman's voice?

She arched an eyebrow. "Actually, I'm going downstairs after I finish my tea. I'm sick of this bedroom. Please take my lunch back down, and I'll meet you there."

"Sloane, I'm not trying to be difficult, but the senator said you had orders from your doctor to stay in bed."

Sloane had to get out of her room, if even for a little while. "He said until I felt better, and I do."

Athena gave her a skeptical look, but nodded. "Why don't I take the tray down and come back and help you?"

"I'm perfectly capable of getting myself down the stairs."

"Okay. Whatever you say."

Was the woman patronizing her? The way Athena said it sounded like a dare and gave Sloane just the extra boost she needed to rise from the chaise and walk to her bedroom door. By the time she reached the bottom of the staircase and walked into the sunroom, she felt a hundred times better. "I'll have lunch in here," she said to Athena, and sat at the small table by the Palladian window. How therapeutic to have a change of scenery. She needed to do this every day.

Athena set the tray down. "Can I get you anything else?"

"No, I'm fine. Thank you."

"I'll be in the kitchen if you need me."

Sloane picked at the poached mackerel and spinach and ate a few blueberries before pushing the tray away. She sat for a while, cheered by the sound of birdsong and the warmth of the sun. Later she decided to spend some time in her office going through mail and checking in with Brianna. It couldn't have been more than two hours before all the activity took its toll and Sloane, ready for a nap, went back upstairs to her room. Before she got into bed, Athena walked in carrying a drink.

"I brought you a protein shake. You didn't really eat much of your lunch. You need to keep your strength up."

Sloane accepted the glass and sat down in the love seat, taking small sips. "What's in this? It tastes a little bitter."

"I added some greens. I'm sorry if it's not good. Do you want me to make a new one?".

Sloane shook her head. "It's fine." She finished it and gave the glass back to Athena. "I'm going to rest for a bit."

After Athena left, she fell into bed and slept.

Now, glancing at the clock on the nightstand, she saw that it was almost four o'clock. A wave of nausea made her draw her knees up to her chest as she breathed in and out. Sweat broke out on her forehead, and she stumbled from the bed and ran to the bathroom, where she vomited. Afterward, she splashed cool water on her face and waited for the dizziness to pass. Looking in the mirror, she spoke aloud: *You will get through this.* The woman looking back at her, the one with the dark circles under her eyes and the swollen face, didn't appear to be convinced.

Returning to her bed, Sloane lay back in exhaustion, but an all-consuming thirst forced her to rise to a sitting position, her arms shaking with the effort. Reaching over to pick up the glass of water on the table, she grasped it tightly and brought it to her parched lips. She tried unsuccessfully to return it to the bedstand, and it went crashing to the floor. Beads of sweat again dotted her forehead, and she fell back against the pillow, exhausted by the effort. As a new wave of nausea overwhelmed her, she inhaled deeply in an attempt to keep it at bay. She finally reached next to her and pressed the button to summon Athena.

"Are you all— Oh my." Athena surveyed the hardwood floor and the broken glass scattered there. "I'll be right back with something to clean this up."

Athena came back, sweeping up the mess and then setting another drink on the nightstand—a plastic tumbler with a lid and straw. "Here you go, this one won't break."

Sloane sat up and pushed herself to the edge of the bed. "I don't need a sippy cup, Athena. Glasses break sometimes." The nerve of this woman. Sloane wouldn't be treated like this. She picked up her phone and rang for Doris.

"Doris, would you please bring me a ginger ale. And some saltines. Thank you." She turned to Athena. "I don't know what you put in that smoothie, but it made me sick."

Athena looked at her in surprise. "You vomited?"

"Yes!"

"I'm sorry. I don't think it was the smoothie. Maybe some of the meds?"

Sloane waved a hand, wanting to be rid of her. "I'll be better once Doris brings me the ginger ale."

"Okay. Hopefully later you can eat some dinner. I made lemon chicken soup. You're due for your last dose of prednisone, and you don't want to take it without food and upset your stomach again."

Suddenly, Athena's face changed, and her teeth grew long. They became pointed fangs. She leaned in to smooth the covers and Sloane shrank back. Athena's entire face morphed into that of a snarling monster, with thick saliva spewing from her mouth. Sloane blinked, and slowly Athena's face returned to normal. She clutched the cover in front of her, terrified.

"Are you okay?" Athena asked.

Sloane took a deep breath. What had just happened? "Um, yes, I'm just tired. You can go."

"You rest now. I'll come back in a few hours with the soup and your meds."

Sloane nodded her assent. Had she just had a hallucination? She thought of some of the stories she'd heard at her support group of people who had brain involvement. But surely she had just imagined it all. She was still trying to process it when she heard Whit call Athena's name.

"How's she been today?" she heard him ask Athena.

"I think she's getting worse."

"It seems that way to me too."

The voices were just outside her room, Whit's deep and sonorous, and Athena's soft and lilting.

The talking continued, but muffled, so it was difficult for her to make out what they were saying. Sloane shifted in the bed, moaning as a bolt of pain shot through her body. Fighting sleep, she opened her eyes and watched the two of them through the crack of the slightly ajar door. Whit's tall frame bent toward Athena, and then his hand rested on her shoulder as they spoke in hushed tones. Sloane's eyes grew weary, and just before she closed them, she saw Whit reach out and close her bedroom door. *Had Athena reached up and stroked his face? And had he smiled at her the way he used to smile at Sloane? She must have imagined that too.*

25

ATHENA

On the evenings Whit was home, he carried Sloane's dinner tray upstairs and sat with her while she ate. His own meal was then served in the dining room by around eight thirty. But earlier that morning, Athena had requested they dine together so she could update him on Sloane's progress, and now she took a seat across from him at the inlaid wooden table. It was set as if for an elegant dinner party, with bone china server and bread plate, crystal glassware, and sterling silver cutlery. She wondered if he had specifically requested the graceful array since they were having dinner together or if he ate this way every night.

"Thank you for allowing me to dine with you tonight. I thought it would be good to have a chance to share some concerns I have without Sloane overhearing."

He frowned. "Concerns?"

"You asked me when I first started to let you know if I saw any signs of a decrease in her mental acuity. And I'm sorry to say that I have."

"Go on."

"There's been a marked difference in her memory from when I started just four weeks ago. She's forgetting things I tell her, and at times she stubbornly insists on doing things that are contraindicated with her condition. She pushes herself, and there have been times when she seemed to be . . . sort of not there. Really zoned out. I'm very concerned."

Whit's eyebrows rose. "Sloane does have a tendency to push herself. It's one of the reasons I wanted to bring you on. I'll have a talk with her. Tell her she needs to allow you to set the pace for her."

"Thank you. I appreciate that."

"I know you thought you'd be out of here in a few weeks, but now with Sloane's flare it's turned into over a month. We really need you here. I hope it's not a problem. I imagine it can be difficult being away from home."

"It's perfectly fine. I've come to care about Sloane and am happy to be here as long as necessary. I'm quite used to adapting to new surroundings as a home healthcare worker, although I must say they're usually not as beautiful as this."

"Good. So you're comfortable, then."

She gave a slight laugh. "I think 'comfortable' might be an understatement, Senator. The room is not only comfortable, but sumptuous, and the art on the walls is exquisite. I find myself studying the paintings as if I'm in a museum."

Whit looked intrigued. "Really. Which ones in particular?"

"I absolutely love the one of a New York street scene by Florine Stettheimer. I'd never heard of her, but when I looked her up, I was impressed."

"That's one of Sloane's favorites. We often talked about art at dinner. I miss that," Whit said, giving her a sad smile. "I'm glad you suggested having dinner together. It's nice to have company."

"I know how hard it is when someone is ill. But hopefully, Sloane will be well enough to join you very soon."

Whit frowned, his forehead etched with worry lines. "I hope so. I know she's been through this in the past, but it seems worse this time, especially with what you're telling me now."

"Sometimes this kind of flare can take a long time to resolve, and the surgery certainly hasn't helped. It's an assault on the body even if you're in good health, but with lupus it's worse. She's been reluctant to take the stronger pain medicine, but I'm trying to convince her otherwise. The stress caused by the pain isn't good for her."

"Maybe I'll say something to her. She's always believed in a stiff upper lip, but if you think that could compromise her recovery . . ."

Athena nodded. "Normally I would advise a patient to avoid taking opioid painkillers—they can be very addictive. But the pain from her hip surgery, coupled with the lupus flare, is too much for anyone."

He took a sip of water and put the goblet on a sculpted coaster, then lifted the linen napkin, dabbing the corner of his mouth. "My wife's a trouper. She's been dealing with this disease for a long time, but I take your point. Maybe if she realizes the sooner she gets better, the sooner she can get back to work, then she'll consider taking the pain meds."

Athena forced a sympathetic expression on her face. "It's very hard for her not to work right now. I'm doing my best to take care of emails and admin things for her, but she keeps asking Brianna to send her updates every week. I heard her talking to Brianna about being worried that some of the shelters will suffer if she's not able to disburse funds." Athena often eavesdropped on Sloane's conversations by hovering outside her door. But when she'd tried to find out more from Brianna, the woman had stonewalled her.

Whit waved a hand. "I'll talk to her about it. She needs to focus on getting better, not worrying about the foundation right now. There are some projects that need her sign-off for funding. She's the only one who can disburse money right now."

"Can't she give you the authority to act on her behalf? It would be one less thing for her to worry about."

"I'll talk to her about doing that. I'm sure she appreciates having you look after her so well. I knew when I married Sloane that she was ill. Robert, her first husband, was a good friend of mine. He would confide in me how much he worried about her. He used to have to remind her to take it easy during her flares. I need to do the same."

Athena wanted to know more. She'd read all about the shooting tragedy two years ago, but she wanted to hear the details from him. "It must have been very hard on you . . . what happened . . ." Her voice trailed off.

Whit stared at her for a long moment. " 'Hard' is an understatement. You can't imagine the guilt I have to live with, knowing that Robert died saving me."

She looked down at her plate and twisted the napkin in her lap, hoping to appear ill at ease. "You're right. I can't imagine. I didn't mean—"

He put up a hand. "No, it's okay. It's awkward. Most people don't know what to say. I want you to understand that Peg was a very troubled woman."

Athena leaned forward.

"Such a terrible tragedy. And to lose your best friend as well as your wife. Was Sloane close to your late wife?"

"We were all close, but Peg put up a lot of walls. We vacationed together and spent a lot of time at their various homes. But she didn't know how bad Peg's drinking had become."

"That must have been so difficult for you. Had your wife always had a problem?"

"She liked her drink. It got worse as the years went on, but I never would have dreamed this was how it would end. I still have nightmares about it," he said with a frown. "I would give anything to go back to that weekend and change things."

"I understand. We all have moments in our past we'd like to go back and change."

He looked at her with interest. "Do you have a moment like that?"

She considered the best way to answer. "Doesn't everyone? But then new people and new opportunities come into our lives. You know the old saying: When a door closes, a window opens."

"Very true."

Athena gave him a sympathetic smile. "You've been through a lot, but it's time to look forward. I'm here to support both of you. People are always worried about the sick one, but it's equally tough on the caregiver. Sloane is very lucky to have you. I'm sure she must tell you how much she appreciates the way you look after her."

"That's very kind of you to say, Athena. I know I can never replace Robert, but I try my best to take care of her the way he would want me to. It was hard to convince her that it was okay for us to be together. I'll admit it was a bit awkward initially, since I'd been married to Robert's cousin. But when Sloane realized that my marriage had essentially been over for years, I think that made our union easier. The one thing I didn't really count on, though, is how much she still misses Robert." Whit gave her a sad look. "When I proposed, she said no at first. I think she felt guilty for wanting to be happy. I know I'll always be second best in Sloane's eyes, that she'll never love me the way she loved Robert, but I've tried to make peace with that." Whit looked up and stopped talking as a young woman in uniform brought in their dinner—baked salmon, baby white potatoes in a butter sauce, and cooked spinach. Athena thought how nice it must be to have someone serve you your dinner each night and take care of all the cleanup when you were finished.

Once they were alone again, he tasted the fish, nodded in approval, and then continued. "I hope I can take care of both Sloane and Emmy in a way that Robert would approve."

"I'm sure you will. It seems obvious to me that you care very much about them both. They're lucky to have you." She thought about the emptiness of her own life and took a large sip of wine, forcing her thoughts back to the present.

"Sloane told me she's always worried that one day she'll be confined to bed. She said that she wouldn't want to live that way," he said.

"Yes, that would be a terrible existence. For both of you," she added.

Whit looked past her into the distance. "You know, I grew up in a small town in Virginia. My parents were hardworking, honest people who did everything they could to see that I had a fine education. They weren't alive when I was elected to Congress, and I regret that bitterly. I never dreamed I would be where I am today, and all I want is to be able to share it with someone." He shook his head. "I don't know. Maybe that's just not meant to be."

"Some people believe that our lives are preordained. The three Fates in Greek mythology are said to assign destinies to humans at birth." Athena's eyes met his. "But I believe we make our own fate. You live the life you choose."

Whit leveled his gaze at her. "I want that to be true, Athena. I want very much for that to be true."

Things were falling into place much more quickly than she'd anticipated. Athena suppressed a smile.

26

ROSEMARY

Rosemary was looking forward to Faye's visit, and she hoped that her old friend would help her figure out the wisest course of action. Faye had known Robert well and, as a longtime congress-woman, had worked with both him and Whit. She should be able to shed some light on what Mac had found concerning Whit's meetings with Horner and Peterson, since she had been in attendance at one of the meetings.

She still had a couple of hours before Faye was due to arrive and she opened her laptop to see if Mac's final report was there. Scanning her email, she spotted it and clicked it open. She read through it twice. No new information on anything related to the shooting of Peg and Robert. Mac had been able to interview some of Peg's former neighbors, but they had nothing but good things to say about Whit. It was the last paragraph of the report that had her on high alert. Mac had turned up new information on Athena Karras. Her LinkedIn page showed her history of home healthcare work and told one story. But using facial recognition software, he'd found a picture on someone's Facebook page that she'd been tagged in, but the tag had a different name and didn't connect to her current Facebook page. His email asked if she wanted him to investigate further. She composed a reply asking him to keep digging.

Rosemary picked up the house phone and dialed Sloane. It went straight to voicemail.

"Sloane, darling, it's Rosemary. I need to talk to you. It's a long story, but I came across some information that indicates your Ms. Karras isn't who she claims to be. Please call me as soon as you get this message." She put the phone down, frustrated, then thought of something Emmy had told her: No one listens to voicemail anymore. She stood and went to her desk, where she kept the cellphone that Camille had insisted she take with her when driving. It was a basic model, not a complicated smartphone, which Rosemary had no use for. She was not going to allow herself to become like all the zombielike people glued to their phones at every idle moment. She powered it up and sent a text to Sloane.

> I have info on Athena Karras— She isn't who she claims to be. I don't think Athena Karras is her real name. Please call me as soon as you see this!

She put the phone down and went into the kitchen to prepare a tray and put on a pot of coffee. Earlier that morning, she'd had Matilda prepare some homemade pumpkin muffins—Faye's favorite. The doorbell chimed, and she went to the hallway to greet her friend.

Faye embraced her tightly. "Rosemary! So good to see you. It's been far too long."

As they took their seats next to each other in the living room, Rosemary picked up the folder in which she'd put Mac's report. "I've put a pot of coffee on. In the meantime, take a look at this." Handing the folder to Faye, she pointed to the part about the meetings at the St. Regis.

"Why would they be having secret meetings? And doesn't it seem strange that they always coincide with when the vice president happens to be having dinner there? Is it possible he's involved with them in something?" Rosemary asked.

Faye shrugged. "It could just be a coincidence."

"What about the fact that the three of them met with the VP on at least three occasions that were recorded on the public visitor logs. On the occasion that you met with them, what was the purpose of the meeting?"

Faye hesitated. "I'm not really supposed to discuss government business, but I can assure you it was nothing untoward."

Rosemary was getting frustrated. "Okay, well, what about the fact that they were at all those HUD ribbon cuttings with Dominic Peterson? He's in charge of one of the largest lobbying firms in DC. What interest does he have in public housing? His company is public; I looked up their client list and did some more research. All his major clients do construction on private commercial properties. I'm going to have Mac compare the client list to the contractors on the three projects where they attended the ribbon cutting. See if there's a connection."

"You're turning into quite the armchair detective. I really don't think there's anything worrisome going on. Maybe Peterson is just trying to curry favor because some of his clients want to get into the public housing game." She reached out and patted Rosemary's hand. "Listen, I know how hard it's been for you to see Sloane re-married, and so soon. But do you think maybe you're looking for shadows where there are none?"

Rosemary suppressed an annoyed sigh. "No. I know that something's going on. Are you sure nothing seemed fishy at the meeting you attended?"

"Not at all, but I will say the old-boy network likes to keep their secrets. That said, I really don't think you have anything to worry about. But I'll make some discreet inquiries. See what I can find."

"Thank you. Mac said he may be onto more evidence but needs more time. I'm not going to let this go."

"How is Mac? Still living in the same place?" Faye asked. "It's been ages since I've seen him."

Rosemary nodded. "Yes, he loves that old house. I keep telling him the neighborhood's not safe anymore, but he refuses to move."

Rosemary stood. "Coffee should be ready now. And your favorite—pumpkin muffins baked this morning. Be right back."

As Rosemary picked up the tray from the counter, she heard the doorbell ring and the chime of the front door. She frowned. That was strange, she thought, but then maybe Faye forgot something in her car and the driver had brought it. With the tray in her hands, she walked into the hallway.

"Faye, is someone here?" she called. As she rounded the corner, she saw a hooded figure and Faye splayed out on the floor, her eyes closed. She froze.

"Who . . ." It took a moment for her brain to register what was happening. Rosemary's hands tightened on the tray as she tried to decide what to do. Before she took another step, everything seemed to move in double time, and she dropped the tray as her hands went up to try to remove the ones gripping her shoulders. She felt herself being roughly pulled forward. The last thing she saw was the marble floor as her head came crashing down to meet it.

27

SLOANE

Whit had been working late the past week, and Athena had asked for the night off tonight. Even thought it was still early, at a little past seven, Sloane decided to turn in for the night. Her head felt like it might explode, and her stomach was so upset she'd barely touched her dinner.

After she washed up, she went to plug her phone into the charger, but couldn't find it. She could have sworn she'd put it on her nightstand when she'd come upstairs earlier, but she couldn't face going up and down those stairs again. She was on her own since Whit was still at the office and Athena had already left. He was working late nights more and more often lately, but she pushed her concerns away. Crawling into bed, she pulled up the covers and was out in minutes.

The next morning, an insistent tapping at her door woke her and she sat up.

"Yes?" she called.

Athena's voice came through the door. "Sloane, I'm so sorry to disturb you, but there's a call for you on your cell. I wouldn't have answered, but it kept ringing. It's Camille."

Sloane glanced at the bedside clock: 7 A.M. "Just a minute," she said, moving slowly from the bed to a standing position and taking hold of the cane. She went to the door, opening it a crack. "Where was my phone?"

"On the kitchen counter." Athena cleared her throat, handing the phone over. "She sounds pretty upset. You'd better take the call." Sloane took the phone and shut the door. "Camille?"

Camille's voice came over the line, breathless and shaky. "Sloane! I'm at the hospital. I've been trying to reach you all night!"

"I'm sorry, I left my phone downstairs. What's wrong?" She and Robert had dispensed with a house phone a few years ago.

"It's Mom."

Sloane's heart began to beat faster. "What about her?"

"She was attacked! I got a call last night from Lawrence, her caretaker. He went back to the house unexpectedly when he heard a storm was brewing. Had to bring the furniture in. Anyway, the door was ajar when he got there, and someone pushed past him and ran away as he entered. Faye Chambers was visiting, and when Lawrence got there they were both on the floor. Someone had assaulted them."

"Oh my God! That's terrible. Are they okay?"

"Mom's in surgery now. Faye's conscious but they're checking her out. I've been at the hospital all night. They don't know if Mom's going to make it."

"We're on our way. You're at Sibley?"

"Yes."

Whit walked into the room. "What's going on?"

"We have to get to the hospital! Rosemary's hurt. She's in surgery now." Sloane swung around, wincing in pain at the sudden movement.

"Here, let me help you. I know you're upset, but rushing and hurting yourself won't do any good." He put an arm against her back, steering her to the bathroom. "Are you sure it's a good idea for you to go to the hospital? You know the steroids suppress your immune system."

"I have to go. I'll wear a mask."

"Okay, then tell me what to grab from your closet for you while you wash up."

"Thank you," she said, grateful for his calm steadiness.

Twenty minutes later, they were in the car and on their way. In

one hand Sloane held the smoothie Whit had asked Athena to prepare; in the other, her phone. Sloane felt numb, her mind racing.
Her cheeks were wet with tears as she continued to repeat a silent
prayer that Rosemary would recover. "Should I call Emmy?" she
asked Whit.

"Not yet. Let's wait until we have more news. There's nothing
she can do from California. It will only worry her."

"I guess you're right."

Sloane noticed she had a text message. She swiped and read.

"Whit, she sent me a message last night."

He turned to look at her. "Who?"

"Rosemary. Something about Athena not being who she says
she is."

"What? That makes no sense."

"I have a voicemail too."

Sloane listened to it with growing concern. "Again, it's about
Athena. She said that's not her real name." A thought seized her.
"Whit, do you think Athena could be the one who attacked Rose-
mary? She was off last night."

"Sloane, come on! That's crazy. Let's wait and see what Camille
says when we get there."

When they reached the waiting room, Camille sprang up and
ran to them.

"How is she?" Sloane asked her, breathless from the walk down
the long hallway.

"Still in surgery." Camille wiped her eyes, looking drawn and
pale.

"I'm so sorry! I can't believe this. Do the police know anything
yet? Do they have any idea who did this?" Sloane asked, Whit at
her side.

Camille shook her head. "Both Lawrence and Faye said they
saw a figure in black. Neither of them got a good look. The police
said whoever it was jammed the house security cameras."

"How did they do that?" Sloane asked.

"I don't understand it. But something about a Wi-Fi jammer, and nothing got recorded."

"Was it a robbery?" Whit asked.

"Nothing was taken from the house. It looks like a random attack. She was struck on the head several times, but that's all they know. The detective left me his card. Said he'd be in touch."

"This is unbelievable," Sloane said. "What did the doctor say about her condition?"

"The blows to her head caused a bleed—and the Coumadin made it worse. When you're on a blood thinner, any head trauma can be deadly. They said after the surgery there would be brain swelling, so they'll keep her in a medicated coma, then do another CT scan to monitor her. She'll be on a ventilator." Camille began to cry again.

Sloane squeezed Camille's hand. "Your mother is strong, and we need to be strong for her as well. Come, let's sit down." As the four of them sat, an older woman with silver hair was escorted out the double doors, and Sloane realized it was Congresswoman Faye Chambers. She had a bandage on her forehead. She rose to greet her.

"Sloane, dear. So sorry to see you under these circumstances."

"Are you all right?" Camille asked.

Faye nodded. "They did a CAT scan to be sure, but it's just a bump on the head. The doorbell rang, and like a fool, I didn't think, I just opened it. Someone dressed in black with a mask on rushed in and pushed me. That's the last thing I remember until Lawrence was standing over me." Faye pursed her lips and looked at Camille. "I was going to call you, Camille. The reason I went over there was to discuss some concerns your mother had, but I also wanted to check on her. She's not been herself lately. Confused at times. Even paranoid."

Sloane was shocked. "What do you mean?"

"She's missed quite a few of our garden club meetings, and when

I've called to inquire after her, she says she's forgotten. Over the past year she's often called me with theories about conspiracies." She looked at Sloane and sighed. "I'm afraid she's quite suspicious of your husband. I think Robert's death hit her much harder than we all realize."

Sloane was incredulous. It sounded like they were talking about two different women. Granted, due to Rosemary's antipathy toward Whit, Sloane hadn't seen much of her in the past six months, but when she'd come to visit Sloane after the hip surgery, she seemed perfectly fine.

Camille nodded. "There have been little things, but then again, we all forget things sometimes. She's misplaced her cellphone a few times lately, and she occasionally tells me something that she's already told me. Occasionally she can't recall someone's name. But I've been telling myself that it's not that unusual. Robert's death hit her so hard she's become obsessed trying to prove it wasn't an accident. What if there *is* something wrong and I've ignored it?"

The congresswoman patted Camille's hand. "Now dear, you can't blame yourself. The doctors will get to the bottom of everything. Let's not borrow trouble."

Sloane thought again about Rosemary's urgent message saying Athena wasn't who she claimed to be. But then she considered Rosemary's continued suspicion and accusations against Whit— even Camille thought they were over the top. Was all of it some part of a paranoid delusion on Rosemary's part?

Finally, a figure in a white coat came toward them. It must be the doctor, Sloane thought. Her expression was grim.

They all stood at the same time.

"How is she?" Camille asked.

"Out of surgery, but I'm concerned about the swelling in her brain. I may have to go back in at some point and put in a shunt to monitor her intracranial pressure if it doesn't resolve." She paused. "She suffered what's called an intraparenchymal hemorrhage to the left side of the brain. That causes blood to pool in the brain.

This stops the flow of blood and causes a buildup of pressure. Her right side will be affected, but we won't know what kind of deficits she might have until she's awake again and off the ventilator. She's got a fight ahead of her over the next few weeks, and a longer road after that."

"Is there a chance she might not make it?" Camille asked.

"I wish I could tell you that she'll recover, but there's no way to know at this point."

"Is there anything we can do?" Sloane asked.

"There's nothing to do but wait. And if you're a praying person, pray."

28

WHIT

Whit rose early the next day and left the house for a five-mile run. He needed to clear his head after the events of the past two days. Emmy had flown in last night and would be staying for the weekend. The run did him good, and by the time he returned to the house, Emmy and Sloane were up. The smell of bacon floated in from the kitchen.

"Morning," he called as he walked in, forcing cheerfulness into his tone.

Sloane, sitting at the kitchen table, looked up and smiled at him. "How was your run?"

"Good."

She inclined her head toward Emmy, who was cracking eggs into a bowl. "As you can see, Emmy's rustling up a grand Saturday morning breakfast for us."

"Fantastic. I'm starving. I'll grab a shower and be back down." He stopped in the doorway and looked at Sloane. "What are you two up to for the rest of the day?"

"Emmy's going back to the hospital after breakfast. I wanted to go with her, but Dr. Porter forbade it. So I'll just be here."

"I'm glad you're listening to him. The last thing you need is to pick up an infection," Whit said. He headed upstairs.

He was halfway up the stairs when he heard Emmy call his name from the bottom of the staircase. He walked back down.

"Whit, I want to talk to you privately. Can we go into my father's study?"

He stiffened. He didn't like the fact that she still referred to it as her father's study, even though it had been converted into a home office for him. "Sure."

She took a seat in one of the leather and chrome Barcelona chairs facing his desk.

"I'm worried about Mom." Emmy paused, shifting in her seat. "She had that steroid shot weeks ago and she's no better. In fact, she seems worse. And now with Gram in the hospital she's even more stressed out. What's the doctor saying?"

Whit pressed his lips together, gathering his thoughts. "He's monitoring her meds and he said it takes time. You know as well as I do that the flares are unpredictable." He drummed his fingers on the table. "Athena has been a big help. From what I've seen, she's been very attentive and has instructed the kitchen staff on what foods are good for inflammation and what aren't. She's even shown me how to make some herbal teas with healing properties."

Emmy nodded. "That's good. Just impress upon Athena the importance of Mom getting her rest. I'll talk to her as well, but I'm the absent daughter who flew in for the weekend, so I think it'll have more impact coming from you, don't you?"

"Of course."

Later that evening, Whit went upstairs to check on Sloane. Emmy was back at the hospital visiting Rosemary. As he entered the bedroom, he had to admit that she did look ill. He hadn't noticed until now just how drawn her face was, and how sallow her color. So different from her usual glowing skin and bright eyes. Rosemary's attack wasn't helping any. Sloane was reclining in the chaise longue, her book open on her lap.

"Emmy is worried about you," Whit said. "To be honest, so am I. I've noticed you're still doing too much work from home. That's why we have Athena. You need your rest."

Sloane sighed in what sounded like exasperation. "Athena is a big help, but she can't interface with potential donors. They want to hear from me. And besides, I'm the only one with the authority to release funds and approve invoices."

"But if you don't allow your body to heal, you're going to be down much longer. Please take it easy until this flare is under control. Let me help. What if you add me as a temporary trustee on the foundation? Then I could handle those approvals until you're back on your feet."

She blew out a breath. "You've got enough on your plate. Are you sure it's not too much?"

He was quiet for a moment. "I'm already on the board and have brought donors to the foundation. You know how much I believe in the work, and I'm familiar enough. And besides, Brianna's excellent; she can tee up everything for me."

She nodded. "That's true. It would be a load off my mind." Sloane looked past him and rubbed a finger across her upper lip for a few seconds. "Okay," she finally said. "I'll have the lawyers draw up the papers. I need to close my eyes for a few minutes."

Soon the sound of even breathing signaled that she'd fallen asleep.

Emmy was right. Sloane was getting worse every day. He made a mental note to make sure that she took care of making him a trustee as soon as possible.

29

SLOANE

Despite Camille's and Faye's assertions about Rosemary's declining state of mind, Sloane could not bring herself to completely disregard her warning and was determined to find out as much as she could about the woman living under her roof. After Whit left, she summoned Athena. She'd put together a list to keep her away from the house for a while.

"I need you to go to the foundation to pick up some files for me and print some project reports out."

"Of course. How is Mrs. Chase doing? Any updates?"

"No change, I'm afraid. Hopefully Emmy will bring back some good news when she gets home from the hospital today."

"Let's hope," Athena said.

"I was so exhausted the night it happened I went to bed early. Of all nights to leave my phone downstairs. Did you hear it ring, or were you out late?"

"Not too late. I had dinner with a friend at Kramers and then went to my apartment to pick up a few more things. Some books and clothes. I got back around eleven. So what do you need me to do at the foundation?"

"Here's the list. Brianna can let you in my office."

"Okay, thanks. I'll see you in a little while."

"Hold on. Why don't you take the Mercedes? It's not fair for you to be putting miles on your car when you're doing work for me."

"Oh, okay. Thank you."

When she left, Sloane went to the window and waited until she saw Athena pull away in their spare car. She called Brianna to let her know that Athena was on her way.

Now it was time to do some investigating. She got up and walked to Athena's room. Reaching out, she closed her hand around the knob and turned it. The room was immaculately tidy, she saw as she walked in and looked around. The bed was made, three books were stacked neatly on the nightstand, and no clothing was strewn about, not even a pair of shoes. She opened the nightstand drawer and saw a leather Bible. Shutting it, she went to the closet and opened the door. A sexy red dress was the first thing she saw. She was tempted to rip it from the hanger and throw it into the trash.

Sloane moved to the desk. Methodically, she opened and closed drawers, but found nothing out of the ordinary. Next, she went to the dresser. The first drawer had precisely positioned rows of underpants and bras. Sloane closed the drawer, opened the next one, and saw neatly folded uniform pants and tops. A large blue stone caught her eye. She recognized it as the "evil eye," so popular in Greece.

Sighing, she looked around the room again, then picked up the books on the nightstand, thumbing through each. Nothing.

As she approached the bedroom door to leave, she stopped to wipe the perspiration from her upper lip. Repositioning her hand on the cane, she saw something on the floor. A string of dental floss. Maybe Athena wasn't as neat as she appeared.

She was getting tired, but she had one more thing to do. Navigating carefully down the stairs, she opened the front door and stood in front of Athena's car, then snapped a photo of the license plate with her phone. By the time she returned to her bedroom, she was out of breath, and she sat on the edge of the bed, trying to quell the nausea rising up. After a few minutes, she regained her equilibrium. She had a phone call to make. The head of the Investigative Services Bureau was a good friend of Robert's and hers. She dialed his cell, and he answered on the first ring.

"Hi, Jim, it's Sloane Montgomery."

"Sloane, what can I do for you?"

"I have a favor to ask. Could you run a license plate and check it against CCTV and tell me if this car was spotted near Kramers Bookstore between 7 and 9 P.M. two nights ago?" She read him the plate number.

"What's this about?"

"The car belongs to my home healthcare worker." Sloane didn't want to tell him about Rosemary's message just yet, since it was possible that she'd dreamed everything up. "It's a little embarrassing. Both she and Whit were out that night. I just want to make sure they weren't at the same place. That's why I need your discretion." She felt bad about the light in which this placed Whit, but Jim was trustworthy, and she knew it would go no further.

"I can check the cameras around Dupont Circle, but you know how limited the metered parking is, so even if she was at the bookstore, her car could be anywhere. The parking garage in the Dupont Circle Hotel is a possibility too, but to be honest it's all a long shot. And then viewing footage from the cameras is pretty tedious. Takes some time."

"I understand. Is it possible to track where the car has been? It seems like there are cameras at all the traffic lights in town."

"No, the VDOTs are live. They show traffic in real time, but they don't record traffic camera footage. I'll see what I can do on the CCTV cameras, Sloane, and get back to you."

"Thanks, you're a doll."

She ended the call and closed her eyes. She knew from her own security cameras that Athena had left the house at 7:15 and returned at 11:05. What she'd done between those hours was the question.

30

ATHENA

Athena was on her way to the foundation in the Mercedes that was kept at the house for when Emmy visited. It was a smooth ride, and she loved driving a car that was so much more luxurious than her own. As she rubbed her hand over the leather steering wheel and took in the sleek console, she couldn't help the sense of distaste she felt that a gorgeous vehicle like this just sat around for the occasional visit. It was a staggering example of conspicuous consumption.

When she arrived at the foundation, Athena parked the car, and as she entered the building, she thought again about the items that Whit had given Sloane, just for the heck of it. The halter dress was gorgeous and obviously expensive. She hadn't been prepared for the price tag, though: over five thousand dollars for a dress! The most Athena had ever paid for a dress was four hundred dollars, and even then she'd felt guilty for splurging. You had to make serious money to throw it away on something so frivolous, and there was no way Whit pulled that in on a senator's salary alone. She knew from her research that Whit hadn't grown up rich. So was he using Sloane's money to buy gifts for her? She wondered, not for the first time, if he'd married Sloane for money or love. If it was the former, that could work in her favor.

Putting a bright smile on her face when the elevator doors opened on the seventh floor, Athena greeted the receptionist and went directly to Brianna's office. She tapped on the open door and walked in. "Good morning. I have a few things to take care of for Sloane. She said she was going to let you know I was coming in this morning."

"Yes. I spoke to her a half hour ago. You can go right in, I unlocked her office," Brianna said, looking up from her wheelchair.

"Great. Thanks." Athena turned to leave.

"Oh, one more thing," Brianna said. "I have some papers that need her signature. Could you stop by my office before you leave, and I'll give them to you?"

"Sure. No problem."

This was the first time Athena had been at the foundation without Sloane. She shut the door, sat down behind the desk, and slowly swiveled the chair, surveying the room at her leisure. When she'd first visited the foundation with Sloane, she'd been surprised. Sloane's office was smaller than she'd thought it would be. In fact, all of the offices were fairly modest, considering the foundation's enormous endowment. It was a pleasant room, though, filled with books, photographs, and memorabilia. On the desk was a framed quotation that read: *Only What We Do for People Will Be Left Here.* She looked away and was tempted to browse the bookcases and take some time to examine the framed photographs on the walls, but she resisted. She didn't have all day, and there were more important things to do. Who knew when she'd have the next opportunity?

She decided to take care of everything on the list before doing her own sleuthing. She began with the list of video calls she needed to schedule for Sloane. After an hour, she'd checked off everything on the list and placed all the reports in her bag. She logged in to the desktop with the code Sloane had given her and printed off the financials on the shelter project Sloane had requested. Now she could poke around Sloane's computer and see if she could get into the financial files. She methodically clicked through each project folder for a quick view, but there were no spreadsheets or ledgers. A photo icon caught her eye. Why did Sloane have a lone picture of Emmy on the desktop? She clicked on it and laughed. Voilà! A balance sheet with all the deposits over the past six months. Did Sloane really think this was a secure method for hiding a file? Athena printed it off. She then printed the accompanying disbursement ledgers for the foundation's most recent projects. It wouldn't tell the entire story, but it would give Athena a truer picture of what the foundation's assets were. While everything printed, she opened each desk drawer and looked through, although her search didn't yield anything of consequence. There was a key in the top drawer, however, one that looked like it could be for a small safe. She scanned the room again but saw nothing resembling a safe. She rubbed the key between her fingers, thinking. Perhaps inside the credenza or behind a photograph, as James Bond as that sounded?

Rising from the chair, Athena crossed the room and opened the credenza, but the shelves inside were filled with scrapbooks. She picked up the first one and flipped through, seeing photos of a new shelter opening. Quickly scanning the rest, she saw that they were similar mementos from each new shelter the foundation had sponsored. She closed the cabinet doors and looked around once again, then moved to the wall of photographs and began to look behind each one. On the tenth picture she found it: a safe built into the wall. Her breathing became rapid with excitement, until she saw the combination lock. The key she held was useless, so she returned it to the drawer, and she sat, wondering if the combination might be written down somewhere. She looked up as she heard the door open.

"I'm going into a meeting, so I thought I'd bring you the paperwork for Sloane." Brianna handed her a folder.

"Thank you. I'm finished with everything Sloane asked me to do, so I'll be on my way, then." Athena hoped she sounded as innocent as she was trying to appear. She grabbed the papers from the printer and turned it off.

Brianna pivoted the chair and hesitated a moment as she faced the wall. Athena followed her gaze to the picture hanging crookedly over the safe. Dammit. She'd been careless. It was a stupid mistake. She knew better.

"Tell Sloane I asked about her," Brianna said before turning the chair and wheeling away.

Athena exhaled, castigating herself again. She didn't need Brianna harboring any suspicions about her or taking those suspicions to Sloane. She'd have to be more careful, try and ingratiate herself the next time she was here. When Athena reached the ground floor and walked out of the building, the tension in her shoulders finally eased. She made her way back to the house so she could drop everything off with Sloane before taking the rest of the day off. When she looked in on Sloane, she saw that she was sleeping. Tiptoeing into the room, she put the folders down on the nightstand and retreated. She stopped by her room to freshen up her makeup. She opened the door to her bedroom and looked down. The dental floss. Someone had been in her room.

31

WHIT

Whit took the stairs to the vice president's office in the Eisenhower Executive Office Building. Built in the 1800s next to the White House, the enormous structure, with over five hundred offices, had been called the ugliest building in America by Mark Twain. Whit disagreed, thinking the French architectural style amusing in a city filled with neoclassical federal structures. He checked his watch as he reached the landing, seeing that he was early for their ten o'clock meeting.

"Morning, Shelly," he said cheerily to Vice President Bishop's secretary as he entered the outer office. "I'm a little early."

"Good morning, Senator. You can have a seat here. He should be finished any minute."

"Thank you." Whit sat in one of the blue-and-gold silk chairs. Picking up a copy of the *Congressional Record,* he began leafing through it.

After a few minutes, the door to the inner office opened, and Whit saw that Frank Horner, a congressman from Louisiana, was already seated. Whit nodded to him.

"Whit," Bishop thundered, extending his hand. "Come in, come in."

Whit followed him into the elegant room with its floor-to-ceiling windows and Oriental rugs. The vice president took a seat behind the historic Roosevelt desk, motioned to a chair for Whit, and picked up the ever-present unlit cigar that he constantly rolled between his thumb and forefinger.

Whit got right to the point. "Peterson found a new contractor to work on the HUD housing projects. After that idiot caused the fire that killed all those people two years ago, Peterson made sure to really vet the new contractor."

"I hope that's true, Whit. We're way behind schedule because of all this. Fred Sawyer's been badgering me, and that son of a bitch can badger like no one else," Bishop said.

"Tell me about it. But after all, this has got to be made right. We can't let it all come tumbling down. We have to rebuild. And we will," Whit responded.

For the next half hour, the three of them discussed a strategy and a backup plan, until they were satisfied with what their next moves would be, which would have to take place at a later date and in a more secure location. Whit rose, leaned over the desk, and shook Bishop's hand. "Good meeting, Mr. Vice President. Thank you." He and Horner walked out together, but Whit stopped at the secretary's desk. "By the way, Shelly, I have tickets for four to *Hamilton* at the Kennedy Center and thought you might like to have them. I remember your saying how much you enjoy the theater. Take a few friends." He removed an envelope from his inside pocket and handed it to her.

"Oh wow, Senator. Thank you so much."

"You're welcome. Enjoy."

Whit got back to the office in time for his meeting with Fred, who was waiting when he arrived. He reached out to shake the older man's hand. Whit appraised Fred, his eyes resting on the bulging flesh hanging over his crocodile Hermès belt, making him look nine months pregnant. The bald head and pallid skin were dotted with brown age spots, and Whit thought he'd rather be dead than ever look like that. Madelyn often joked that Fred hadn't been able to set eyes on his flaccid penis in years. She also bitched about the erectile dysfunction drugmakers that forced her to service her repulsive husband. Oh well, she certainly made up for it by spending his money, Whit thought. "Hey, Fred, how are you?"

"I've been better," Fred growled.

"Why don't we sit over there?" Whit said, leading him to a small round table with six chairs around it. "Can I get you a drink?"

Fred took off his coat and threw it onto a sofa. "Diet Coke," he said, taking a seat.

Whit grabbed one of the dozen cans of Diet Coke he always had stocked in the minifridge for Fred's visits, even though it obviously had no effect on his weight. Fred grabbed the can, popped the tab, and took a long, gurgling swallow, ignoring the glass Whit had placed on the table for him.

"Look." Fred belched and then went on. "If you say we can fix this, then fine. But if not, your campaign war chest is going to go to shit. I only back winners. You should know that by now."

Whit was doing his best to contain his fury at this old bastard whose money and power could instantly make or break anyone's political fortunes. If voters knew who the real power players in Washington were, they'd see that representing the people mattered little to their elected officials.

"There's nothing to worry about, Fred. I met with the vice president this morning, and he's working on it too."

"Bishop's getting dotty. He can't remember what he had for breakfast. Should have never accepted the vice presidential position at his age."

Whit found Fred's comments amusing, seeing as he was at least six years older than the VP. "I haven't seen that at all, Fred. The plan he outlined to me this morning was cogent and well thought out. I think you're underestimating him."

Fred's lips puckered. "All right. You've never let me down in the past, so if you say it's all under control, I'm going to trust you on that." He chugged the rest of his soda, glanced at his watch, and rose from the chair. "You keep me posted. I want to know about any, I mean *any*, developments. You hear?"

"Of course, Fred. I hear you."

"Good." Fred grabbed his coat and walked to the door, stopping just before turning the handle. "Gotta run. Dinner date with my wife, who seems uncharacteristically distracted lately."

32

SLOANE

Sloane's phone rang and she saw it was the captain calling her back. "Jim, hi."

"You got lucky. I found your girl's car on the first camera reel. Parked right in front of Kramers if you can believe it. The film showed her parking at 7:45 and leaving at 9:00."

"That's great, Jim. I was being paranoid for nothing. I hope you'll forget about this."

"Of course."

She made a note to send Jim and his wife tickets to the symphony. So, Athena was nowhere near Rosemary's house in McLean that night. She suddenly felt foolish for thinking that Athena could have done something so violent and horrible. Poor Rosemary. Maybe something *was* wrong with her. She hoped it wasn't dementia. Sighing, she turned her attention to the file she'd asked Athena to bring home from the foundation. It was one of her pet projects and near completion. The domestic violence shelters accounted for most of the foundation's work, but Sloane had come to realize that as vital as they were, they were only the first step in helping individuals get back on their feet. Their newest initiative combined temporary living accommodations with skills training, résumé preparation, and career planning, as well as assistance in securing long-term living arrangements. The first of such facilities was near completion in Richmond, Virginia. The ribbon cutting would be in sixty days, and Sloane was determined to get better and be there to do it herself. Whit had taken a special interest in the project and suggested there might be some synergy between the new program and HUD housing projects and Section 8 apartments that he and his political allies had supported with legislation increasing their funding. She would pursue that further, once she was feeling good again.

Her door opened, and Athena came in with a tray.

"I brought you some chicken noodle soup. Hungry?"

She wasn't, but she knew she should at least try to eat something. She put the folder down on the bed and nodded. She was going to suggest she go over to the love seat, but suddenly felt drained. "You can set the tray here, thanks."

Athena picked up the folder and put it on the nightstand. "How's everything going with the project?"

"Looks like it's all on schedule. I'm very excited about it."

"Everyone at the foundation is. It's such a terrific program. You must feel so gratified to be helping so many families."

"I am. Robert and I both always felt it was our calling. He would have been thrilled with this."

"It must feel good to be able to continue to honor him."

Sloane felt the familiar anger return. "It does. He should still be here, though. Peg was always troubled, but I had no idea how out of touch with reality she'd become—that she would actually try to kill Whit, and that Robert would be caught in the crossfire. I'll never understand it."

"Peg and Robert were cousins, weren't they?"

"Yes. Robert was very protective of her." Sloane looked past Athena. "Too protective."

"Were you close with Peg too?"

"Not really. I tried, but she was hard to know. The only person she truly opened up to was Robert. I think that's why she took her life. She couldn't live with what she'd done. She told me that she and Whit were having problems, but I was used to Peg making mountains out of molehills. I wish I'd taken her more seriously now."

"What kind of problems? Do you think he was unhappy with her?"

Sloane was taken aback by Athena's brashness, then berated herself for opening the door to the subject. "It's inappropriate for us to discuss this. I shouldn't have told you all that."

"I'm sorry, I didn't mean to pry."

Sloane closed her eyes. "I think I'll rest a little now."

She heard Athena quietly leaving the room. She took a minute to gather her thoughts, then had a few spoonsful of the soup, even though she wasn't really hungry. She needed her nutrition, so she made herself finish half the bowl. Putting the spoon down, she picked up the tumbler with the pumpkin spiced iced coffee she'd asked Whit to pick up on his way home last night and hadn't yet drunk.

She missed Emmy, sad that her daughter now lived so far away. She missed her friends too, and working, and being with people. Sloane was lonely, but it had been foolish to pour her heart out to Athena as if she were a friend. She'd allowed her to become too familiar, and now the woman was asking questions that were probing and too personal. They were employer and employee, and as such, should have defined boundaries. Sloane would talk to Whit about it as well. The casual interaction she'd witnessed between him and Athena disturbed her. Why did they have dinner together every night lately? Why didn't he bring his own dinner up with Sloane's and have dinner with her? Did he prefer Athena's company to hers?

She grabbed her phone from the bedside table and tapped in Brianna's number.

"Sloane, hi. How are you?" Brianna's voice came over the line.

"I'm okay, Bri. Can you do something for me?"

"Of course. Anything."

"Will you lock my office door, and keep the key in your office?"

"Sure. No problem. Do you want me to give Athena a key?"

"No. I don't want her using my office anymore. I want you to give her any files she needs to bring home, and if she has any work to do there, she can use one of the intern offices. No one goes into my office unless you're with them, understand?"

"I do. I'm glad to hear that. I was going to call you, but you beat me to it."

"What do you mean?"

"The other day when she was here working in your office, it seemed to me like she was snooping around. The picture in front of your safe was crooked. She must have looked behind it. Maybe tried to open it."

"Seriously?"

"Yes. I might be reading more into it than there is, but . . ."

"Hmm. Keep your eye on her for me. And don't let her near my office, okay? As an added precaution, change the password on my desktop."

"I'll take care of it."

"Thanks, Bri." Sloane ended the call. Thinking about what Brianna had told her, an idea came to her. She picked the phone back up and called Brianna again.

"Sloane?"

"On second thought, disregard what I said about letting Athena use the office. The only thing I want you to do is change the computer password."

"Ooookay." Brianna didn't press her for an explanation even though it was clear she was surprised. That was a trait that Sloane valued in Brianna. She knew when to ask questions and when not to.

Next, she called the security company that monitored the foundation offices and instructed them to put video surveillance cameras in her office so she could access them from her phone and view her office from all angles. As an added precaution she told them to do it after hours when the offices were empty. She didn't want anyone knowing they were there. She'd send Athena back in a few days to pick something up and watch what she did. Feeling better about that, she took a deep breath. She hoped Athena would prove her wrong. She needed to get this flare under control. Get well enough so she didn't need Athena anymore. Athena should have been gone already, after Sloane had recovered from the hip operation. And she had to get well enough to visit Rosemary at the hospital. The doctors were still not sure if Rosemary was going to regain consciousness. Taking a deep breath, she sat up again and rose on unsteady legs. She wasn't ready for a marathon, but her new hip was working well, and she could build her strength back up by walking up and down the hallway.

But by the time she reached the bedroom door, her forehead was damp with perspiration, and she was breathing hard. She turned the knob and continued. One step in front of the other. She ignored the burning sensation in her feet and the cramping muscles in her arms and legs. *If I can just make it up and back,* she thought.

Suddenly, magically, the weariness lifted, and she felt her body grow wings. A feeling of euphoria washed over her. She was weightless. She could fly! Sloane threw out her arms and wrapped her fingers around the railing, peering down the two stories to the hall below. She didn't have to use the stairs; she could fly, she thought giddily, laughing out loud as she leaned over the railing and prepared for takeoff.

33

ROSEMARY

When Rosemary opened her eyes, the room slowly came into focus. She looked around in confusion. This wasn't her bedroom. Where was she? It took a moment for her to realize she was in a hospital room. Feeling around the bed, she found the call button and depressed it. A woman in scrubs walked in.

"So glad to see you're awake, Mrs. Chase. I'm Sophie, your nurse. You're at Sibley Hospital. We've been very worried about you."

Rosemary tried to speak but was able to emit only a grunt. She cleared her throat again. "What happened?" The words came out in a hoarse whisper.

"You've suffered a head injury. You've had surgery. Let me get your doctor to explain."

Rosemary's mind raced as she absorbed this news. A head injury? What had happened?

"Hello, Mrs. Chase. I'm Dr. Makris." An attractive young woman approached the bed. "How are you feeling?" She held a flashlight and examined Rosemary's eyes, then had her follow her finger up, down, and side to side.

"You've been in the hospital over three weeks. We had to operate when you were brought in by EMS. Your CT scan showed a brain bleed. We've been monitoring the swelling in your brain and have had you in a medicated coma until five days ago. You've been in and out of consciousness since. Fortunately, your latest scan was normal."

Rosemary tried to remember what had happened, but everything was a blank. The last thing she remembered was waiting for Faye to come to her house. "How . . . what . . . ?"

"You were brought in by ambulance with severe head trauma."

"Home. Now?" Rosemary tried to make it sound like a question but was unable to add an inflection.

"We'll run some more tests, and then we'll see. You're also going to need rehab. Your daughter's been here most of the time. I'll give her a call and tell her you're awake. She can explain what happened."

Rosemary nodded and closed her eyes, exhaustion overtaking her.

It was dark outside when Rosemary woke up and saw Camille sitting in the chair by the window. Camille jumped up and came to the side of the bed.

"Thank God you're awake! I've been so worried."

"What hap— happened?"

Camille took her mother's hand. "You were assaulted."

Rosemary shook her head. "Who?"

"We don't know. Faye was at your house and said the bell rang. She opened the door, and someone attacked both of you." Tears fell from Camille's eyes. "I've been so scared."

Rosemary couldn't remember. She struggled to think. Something had been bothering her. But what?

"You should rest. Don't tax yourself. I need to call the detectives and let them know you're awake. They'll want to talk to you. Do you remember anything?"

"No . . . something . . ." What had she been worried about? Mac. She'd called him. Whit. Something going on.

She pointed to the cup of water set on the hospital tray, and Camille brought the straw to her lips. She took a few sips, cleared her throat, and took a deep breath.

"Listen," she commanded, shocked by how gravelly her voice sounded.

"What is it?"

"My friend . . . Mmmac Sllllade." She stopped again to catch her breath.

"From Philly, that Mac?" Camille asked.

Camille had never met Mac, only heard stories about him.

Rosemary nodded. "Call Mac." There was something she'd wanted to tell Sloane. Why couldn't she remember? Everything was one big jumble. She sighed in frustration.

Camille's eyes grew troubled. "I don't understand. But I'll call him. I don't have his number."

"Address book."

"Okay, I'll call Matilda and have her look for it."

"Now. Worried . . . Sloane," Rosemary insisted.

"What about Sloane?"

"Worried," Rosemary repeated, out of breath.

Camille leaned over to kiss her cheek. "It will be fine, Mom. Don't worry. I'll call her now." She took out her phone. "I have no reception in here. I'll run outside for a minute."

After she'd gone, Rosemary closed her eyes and tried to summon any memories of the night of her fall. She slowed her breathing and used the techniques she'd learned in her yoga class. Deep breath in, cleansing breath out. The sequence of events was coming back to her now. She remembered letting Lawrence and Matilda off early and waiting for Faye. Mac's report was in a folder in the living room. She was going to get coffee and then discuss the report with Faye. That was the last thing she remembered from that night. How did she fall? Suddenly, a flash of something came to her. Hands on her shoulders, pulling.

"Good evening, Mrs. Chase. I'm here to check your vitals." A nurse walked in, breaking her concentration. She sighed in frustration.

"All good. Try and get some sleep now," the nurse said as she switched off the light.

Rosemary's mind was racing, nerves pulsing in fight mode. She couldn't rest until she knew the truth. Even so, the pull of sleep became irresistible. She finally began to drift off when a noise from the doorway startled her. It was too dark to see anything except a large shadow.

"Hello?" she called out, her voice barely a whisper.

The figure crept toward her, silent, and stopped when it reached her bedside.

What are you doing? she tried to say, but no words would form.

She watched in terror as a syringe was pulled from the figure's jacket and a hand moved toward her IV.

34

SLOANE

M rs. Montgomery! What are you doing?" a voice screamed.
Sloane felt arms grab at her, squeezing viselike around her
waist and pulling at her body. She looked over the railing, confused
and swooning in dizziness at the long drop. She turned to see that
the arms belonged to Doris, who was holding on to her with an
iron grip. Sloane opened her mouth, but no words came out.

"Mrs. Montgomery, are you okay? What were you trying to do?"
Doris loosened her hold and led Sloane away from the railing.

"I . . . uh . . . I'm not sure." Sloane felt a tear slide down her
cheek, and she searched Doris's face. "What did it look like?"

"It sounds crazy . . . but it looked like you were trying to fly."
Doris was staring at her. "I was in the hallway when I heard you
laughing, really loud, almost hysterical. That's why I ran up to see
what was going on."

Sloane closed her eyes and remembered the feeling of freedom,
as if she could fly. As if she had wings. A hallucination. She shud-
dered at what that meant. Her brain was being affected.

"You're white as a ghost. I'm going to call Senator Montgomery," Doris said.

Sloane shook her head. "No, please. Don't. I'm okay. Just let me
catch my breath, then help me back to my room. I got dizzy. Probably because I hardly ate anything today."

Athena's door opened and she ran over to them. "Sloane, is
everything okay?"

"No, everything's not okay," Doris yelled, glaring at Athena.
"Mrs. Montgomery almost fell! Where were you? Didn't you hear
her?"

"Oh my gosh, I'm so sorry. I thought Sloane was asleep." She looked at Doris. "I can take it from here."

"Hmph, can you? If I hadn't been here, Mrs. Montgomery might be lying on that marble floor below."

"All right, all right, it's okay, Doris. Let's not make this a bigger deal than it is." Sloane was humiliated.

"Do you want me to stay?" Doris asked.

Sloane shook her head. "Thank you, Doris. I'm fine."

Doris gave Athena another long look, then went back downstairs.

Athena helped Sloane back to the bedroom and got her settled under the covers. "What happened?"

Sloane sighed. "I just got confused for a minute."

"Sloane, Doris said it looked like you were about to fall over the railing. What were you confused about?"

"I thought I could . . ." She sighed. "I don't want to talk about it."

Athena cleared her throat. "I just want to say . . . well, if it was something like a hallucination, we need to call your doctor and tell him what happened. In fact, it wouldn't hurt for you to be seen. If you think it was one, that is."

Sloane wasn't ready to hear that the lupus was invading her brain. She put up a hand. "No, I'm fine. I just got a little ambitious about improvising with my physical therapy."

"I really think we should call the doctor."

"I'm fine. I just want to forget about it. I'd appreciate it if you didn't mention it to my husband either."

Athena merely nodded.

"I have a follow-up with Dr. Porter in two days. I'll tell him about it then."

That seemed to placate Athena. "Hopefully you'll get some more answers after you see him."

"I'm sure we will." Why was the woman always asking her questions, wanting to know more? She wasn't a doctor. Her job was to help Sloane recover from her surgery. She wasn't even supposed to still be here.

"We could try some meditation," Athena suggested.

Sloane gave her a tight smile. "I'll think about it." She changed the subject. "Listen, I've signed the papers Brianna sent home. The folder's on my dresser. Can you take them back to her?"

"Of course." Athena retrieved the paperwork, then stopped by the bed again. "I enjoy being at the foundation, getting a view of all the important work it does. You must be very proud."

"Yes, I am."

"Senator Montgomery has been there a lot lately. Will he continue working with you when you've recuperated from your surgery and are back full time?"

"Probably not." Sloane cut the conversation short, annoyed by Athena's constant questions.

Athena glanced at the half-empty bowl on the night table. "I'll just take that away."

"Fine, Athena. That's all," Sloane said, weary of her.

"You'll call me if you need anything?"

"Yep."

"You'll think about the meditation, won't you? I mentioned it to the senator, and he thought it was a good idea." Athena took the bowl and left the room, closing the door behind her.

I mentioned it to the senator . . . Sloane mimicked in a singsong voice after Athena had gone. What were they saying about her while she lay in bed and they had dinner together? Would she tell Whit about the hallucination? Athena wasn't naïve, and she certainly hadn't bought Sloane's ridiculous explanation. And she was nosy, wanting to know things that were none of her business. Sloane was determined to do a little more looking around in Athena's bedroom the next time she took a day off. She wanted better insight into the woman. If only she could be privy to those dinner conversations.

She frowned, remembering how real it had felt. It was truly

terrifying how real. She bit the inside of her lip and reluctantly picked up the sheaf of proposals Athena had left on the bed for her. She might as well do something useful and read through them while she was still lucid, she thought wryly.

Sloane made notes here and there, but her eyes began to tire after twenty minutes. Then she blinked, rereading an item that seemed odd: a shelter in Ohio proposing a grant for expansion in the amount of $150,000. When had they opened a shelter in Ohio?

35

WHIT

Whit opened a bottle of pinot noir and poured two glasses. Athena came into the dining room, wearing a short red dress that accentuated her curves in all the right places, along with sexy high heels.

"You look lovely tonight. It's nice to have such a charming dinner companion."

She smiled at him. "Thank you. It's nice to get dressed for dinner, especially in such elegant surroundings."

If any of the household staff thought it unusual that he and Athena dined together every night now, their expressions never reflected that, although just this morning he'd heard Doris mention it to Sloane. The first time Athena joined him for dinner, he'd been surprised at how striking she looked. He was used to seeing her in scrubs, but she had worn a short black dress and high heels.

Athena took a seat across from him. "I'm worried about Sloane. I'm pretty sure she had a hallucination earlier today."

He raised his eyebrows. "What?"

"Yes, Doris and I heard her laughing in the hallway. Doris came upstairs at the same time I ran out from my room, and Sloane was perched over the railing, her arms waving like she was trying to fly. I wanted to call you, but she was very insistent that I not. I'm really not sure what to do about this. I mean, if we hadn't been there, who knows what could have happened?"

Whit wrinkled his brow. "She could have killed herself!"

Athena blew out a breath. "That's what Doris said. In fact, if I may say, she was pretty rude about it. She tried to blame me. I can't sit in Sloane's room 24/7. I mean, I wouldn't mind, but Sloane wouldn't stand for it. It's clear that we need to do something to make sure she's safe."

"I'll speak to Doris. She's been with Sloane a long time and can be a bit overprotective."

"We do need to do something, though. We can't very well lock her in her room, but maybe we need to put an alarm on her door or something to alert one of us if she's out of her room. I also think you need to get her in to see her doctor as soon as possible," Athena said.

"I agree," Whit said. "She has an appointment in two days, but I'll call in the morning to ask if he wants to see her sooner."

"Good idea."

"I'll contact the security people about adding a door sensor to Sloane's room. But she's not going to like it," Whit said.

"I can tell she's getting frustrated. And she's been upset, with so much on her mind, worrying about her former mother-in-law."

"Apparently, Mrs. Chase regained consciousness. I let Sloane know earlier," Whit said.

"That's good news, isn't it?"

"Yes, very."

"I hope it made her feel less discouraged with everything." Athena paused. "I don't know if I should mention this, but I think I may have upset Sloane. She was telling me about the day that . . . everything happened."

Whit put down his glass and looked at her. "What did she tell you?"

"That she feels guilty for not realizing how bad off Peg really was. She mentioned that Peg was drinking a lot, and that you and she were having problems."

Whit was annoyed. What was Sloane doing discussing his prior marriage with Athena? "What did you say to upset her?"

Athena looked sheepish. "I asked her if you were unhappy in your marriage, and she told me that was an inappropriate question. I apologized, but I hope that she isn't still upset with me. I would hate for her to feel that she didn't want me caring for her any longer."

"Don't worry, I'll smooth it over." He took another sip of wine and scrutinized her for a moment. "For the record, I *was* unhappy. Can I confide something in you?" he asked.

"Of course," she said, her eyes wide.

He tented his hands. "It's something I never told anyone. It was too humiliating. Well, for the last several years of our marriage, Peg was drinking heavily, spending her evenings at bars. She . . ." He shook his head.

"What is it?" Athena asked.

"I found out from one of our neighbors that she was bringing random men home. I begged her to get help; told her that if she continued, I would leave her. She'd promise and for a while she'd stop drinking, but then the cycle would start all over again. The day it happened . . . I had told her I thought we should separate. I had a golf obligation with the mayor that I couldn't get out of. When I came home, she had Robert there to try to talk me out of it." Whit took another sip of his wine.

"Her infidelity must have been painful."

"You have no idea. I tried to get her help, but she wasn't interested. It even became too embarrassing for her to accompany me to social events here in DC. I can't tell you the number of times I had to practically carry her out of a party."

Athena shook her head. "It would be so amazing to go to those kinds of events. It's hard for me to imagine someone not doing everything they could to maintain that privilege. She must have known what was expected of her as the wife of a prominent senator. What a shame she couldn't manage it."

He went on. "Exactly. I needed a wife I could be proud to have with me. In the last few years, the only time we could socialize as a couple was with Robert and Sloane. They understood that she was having problems and didn't judge."

"What a terrible way to live. It sounds like Senator Chase was a good friend. Were he and Sloane happy?"

"Very. As I've told you before, I'll never be able to measure up to him in Sloane's eyes." He gave Athena a sad look. "Don't get me wrong. I understand that just because someone is gone doesn't mean you stop having feelings for them." He raised his wineglass and swirled it around, then sighed. "But is it so wrong to hope that your wife will put you first in her heart? I mean, I really hoped that after being so hurt in my first marriage, this one would be different. Not that Sloane is anything like Peg, but I sometimes wonder if I'm going to have to give up hoping for the deep connection I'm seeking with another person. Do you think that's terrible?"

"Of course not. Any man would want the same. You deserve to be loved and appreciated."

"It's so nice to be understood. Sloane and I have been through so much. I just hope that one day we can leave the tragedy behind and appreciate what we have now. I'm doing my best to be patient and kind. Especially with her health issues."

Athena's eyes were warm. "The tragedy seems to have made you more compassionate. Sloane's lucky to have such a wonderful husband to care about her."

"Well, she's also lucky to have such a compassionate caregiver."

She looked down at her wineglass. "I appreciate that, Senator. And I know how difficult it is for you to see her so ill. And now she's hallucinating. I can't imagine what you're going through."

"You have no idea how wonderful it is to have someone to talk to. I worry so much, but I would never tell Sloane that, and I really don't want to upset Emmy any more than she already is. But now, with you, it's different."

"I'm here for all of you, so please don't ever hesitate to talk to me about your concerns," she said.

"Sloane has belonged to a lupus support group ever since she was diagnosed. She's made strong bonds with many of its members over the years. I went to a meeting when we were first married."

Here he paused and cleared his throat. "There's a man—Harold—that Sloane befriended. His wife has lupus. Sloane told me that a few years ago she went to visit Harold and his wife. Harold took Sloane to his wife's room. The woman lay in bed, practically comatose. Sloane said she was a bag of bones, her face wrinkled and etched with pain. It sounded horrible."

"That must have been an awful thing for her to see," Athena said.

"Yes, it was. I met Harold at the meeting, and Sloane told me his story. When we got into the car, Sloane put her hand on mine and stopped me from putting the car in drive. *Look at me*, she said. *Don't ever let me get like that. Promise me!* I could hear in her voice how terrified she was. We talked more after that, about what a toll his wife's illness had taken on Harold, and how she had no quality of life whatsoever. Sloane told me she didn't ever want to live that way. And she didn't want me to see her like that—a lifeless shell that I felt honor bound to care for. She said I'd grow to resent her, and she couldn't stand that." Whit finished his wine and wiped his lips. "Sloane said that there comes a time when patients can't carry out their own wishes. She made me promise I wouldn't let her end up like Harold's wife—and now she's hallucinating. I'm so worried."

"She said something similar to me when we had lunch. Said she's seen what this can do, and for her to live that way is unthinkable. Now I understand."

Whit took a moment to gather his thoughts. "Sloane is a very proud woman—independent and strong. She's made it very clear to me that it would be intolerable to reach a point where she could no longer take care of herself. There's a very real possibility that the lupus will affect Sloane's brain permanently. And I'm wondering if she's had other incidents that we don't know about. I need you to be vigilant."

"Thank you for telling me that. Of course I'll let you know if I see any more evidence. But—"

His phone buzzed and he looked down. A text from Madelyn. "Would you excuse me? Something's come up. I'll be back as soon as I can."

"Of course," she replied.

"If Sloane asks where I am, tell her I had to take care of something back at my office before my meeting with the vice president."

"That sounds exciting. What's he like? I saw him at the party here, but of course I didn't get a chance to meet him."

Whit shrugged. "A little full of himself, but I guess that's what happens when you're a heartbeat away from the presidency."

Athena tilted her head. "Maybe that'll be you one day. But president, not vice president."

Whit chuckled. "Well, well. Maybe I should hire you as my campaign manager."

"Now, that's a job I could learn to love, Senator," she said, teasing.

"Say, if you're not too tired, why don't you wait up? We'll have another drink when I get back. It would be nice to have something to look forward to."

She nodded. "It's a plan. I'm not tired at all."

"And by the way, don't you think it's time you called me Whit?"

36

ROSEMARY

The sound of approaching voices spooked the skulking figure, and they ran from the room. Rosemary's heart was beating so hard she felt like it was going to burst. She recognized Camille's voice and looked over to see her standing in the doorway.

"I have permission to be here after visiting hours. Someone tried to kill her, I'm not leaving her alone. It should be in her chart!" she heard Camille say to someone.

A nurse Rosemary had never seen before, her face red, shook her head. "No one told me," she said with an exasperated sigh.

"Call Sophie, the supervising nurse. She'll tell you," Camille insisted. "When I'm not here, we've hired a private nurse. She's not to be left alone."

The nurse shook her head again. "I'm not going to call this late. Whatever. Just be quiet. Patients are trying to get some rest." She left the room, muttering under her breath.

Rosemary attempted to speak but found it impossible to form the words. She tried to calm her breathing. She had to let Camille know that someone had been in her room. She wasn't safe here.

"Mom, sorry for the ruckus. But I called Mac and got his girlfriend." She grimaced. "She gave me some very bad news. Mac was found dead a few days ago."

Rosemary's eyes widened. "How?" she managed to croak out.

Camille swallowed. "An overdose. Alcohol and drugs."

Rosemary shook her head. "No."

Camille took her hand in her own. "I know how upsetting this must be, but—"

"No," Rosemary said more adamantly. Sighing, she pointed at the pad next to the bed. It was too hard to talk.

Camille read the words she'd written. *AA, past 10 years.*

Camille frowned. "That's what his girlfriend said. Do you think he fell off the wagon?"

Rosemary swallowed, then pointed at the cup of water. She drank a few sips as Camille held the cup.

"His report. Faye. I think I told Faye about it when I called her." This was torture!

Camille shook her head. "Faye said that you told her about some kind of conspiracy but insists that she couldn't find any evidence of that. Just rest. You need to rest. Your mind needs to heal. You've been through a lot."

She didn't need rest. She needed answers. Rosemary tried to tell her about the person in her room, but her eyes began to close of their own accord. "Someone . . ." She tried to get the words out, but it was as if a dark curtain closed over her mind as she took a deep breath and descended into the darkness.

37

WHIT

Whit was not looking forward to the conversation he needed to have with Sloane. He'd rearranged his meetings at his Senate office so he could have time with her this morning. She was sitting on the love seat in their bedroom, reading a book, when he walked in.

"Good morning," he said, smiling as he approached her and kissed her on the lips. "Athena brewed you a cup of green tea, so I brought it up for you. I thought we could have some time together this morning."

"How nice." She patted the cushion next to her. "Come sit."

"How are you feeling?"

"Better. I told Athena I want to take a stroll outside after breakfast. I can't sit in this room all day staring at the walls. I'm going crazy."

He squeezed her hand. "I know, but your joints are so swollen. Don't push yourself. Actually, I wanted to talk to you about something."

Her forehead creased, and she looked at him with suspicion. "What?"

Whit sighed. "Athena told me about what happened yesterday. In the hallway. Sloane, you could have been killed."

Her shoulders sagged, and she looked down at her lap. "I told Athena to keep that between us!"

"It's her job to make sure you're safe, and honey, you're not. Tell me what happened."

Her hands tightened into fists at her sides. "It was nothing. I was just looking over the railing, and all of a sudden Doris came running up the stairs and grabbed on to me for no reason."

"Sloane, come on. We both know that's not what happened."

She squeezed her eyes shut and rocked forward. "Oh, Whit. It was scary, but strange and wonderful at the same time." She took a deep breath. "Suddenly, I was infused with all this energy, and I thought . . . just for a minute . . . well, I thought I could fly." She sat up straight and looked at him, her eyes brimming with concern.

Whit put his arm around her, pulling her close to him, and she leaned her head against his shoulder.

"I'm frightened," she said.

"I know, I know. But we have to be proactive. We've always known that hallucinations are possible with your kind of lupus. What if Doris and Athena hadn't come out in time? Have you thought about that?"

She nodded. "I've thought of nothing else. I'm going to call Dr. Porter's office today."

"I already have. He's upped the steroids again and will see you at your appointment the day after tomorrow."

"Okay."

"Until then, we need to make sure you don't leave your room unsupervised."

"What do you mean?" Her tone was guarded.

He took his arm away and faced her eye to eye. "You just admitted you thought you could fly! The alarm people are coming later this morning to put a sensor on your door that will alert Athena and the staff when it's opened."

"You're treating me like a child! It's humiliating."

"No, I'm treating you as someone I love and am worried might hurt herself without knowing it. And it's only until we get to the bottom of things. We can't risk another incident like this. Be reasonable, Sloane. What other solution is there?"

She slowly nodded. "Fine. But only until after we see Dr. Porter and get this resolved."

He could hear defeat in her voice. "Of course, sweetheart." He stood. "I'm going to stop by the foundation and sign some checks for Brianna. Then I've got back-to-back meetings this afternoon, so I'm not sure how late I'll be."

"Okay."

He leaned over and kissed her. "I'll see you tonight."

Athena was in the kitchen when Whit walked in to grab a cup of coffee for the road.

"Did you speak with Sloane?"

He nodded. "Yes, she took it as well as can be expected. Alarm Systems will be here around ten."

"Okay, that's good. I'll stay upstairs until then and keep an eye on her. What did Dr. Porter say?" she asked.

"He's concerned, of course, but this type of brain involvement has always been a possibility. He's upping her steroids for now, and if that doesn't work, he may add some new meds to her regimen—possibly a different immunosuppressive to reduce the inflammation of the blood vessels. I really hope something works. I can't stop thinking about all the possibilities. What if she has a stroke?"

Athena patted his arm. "You can't think like that. One day at a time. You're doing everything you can for her, and it won't help anyone to ponder all the what-ifs."

"You're right. Thanks for keeping me grounded."

She smiled at him. "That's what I'm here for. Well, I'd better go check on Sloane."

"See you later." As he watched her walk away, Whit thought again how her presence had made such a difference. She was much more than just a home care worker. She was ministering to both of them with her care of Sloane and her willingness to be a sounding board for him. He'd only thought about what he needed for Sloane when Athena was hired, not realizing that he would benefit too. His thoughts were interrupted by Doris's sudden appearance.

"Excuse me, Senator. I was hoping I might have a word."

"Of course, Doris. What is it?"

She opened the kitchen door, looked out, then came back in, her voice lowered. "It's Miss Karras. I'm concerned that she's not taking proper care of Mrs. Montgomery."

Whit's brow furrowed. "What do you mean?"

"Forgive me for saying so, but it hasn't escaped my notice that Mrs. Montgomery has gone downhill ever since she arrived. She's always mixing strange things into her food, and when I ask what they are she tells me it's different herbal remedies."

Whit was annoyed. He didn't have time for these petty jealousies. "I know you care deeply for Mrs. Montgomery, and I assure you she is getting the best possible care. In fact, Ms. Karras is so concerned with Mrs. Montgomery's safety that we're having an alarm installed on her door. Ms. Karras's references are impeccable, and she's been a great help to us both."

Doris looked as though she wanted to say something else but hesitated. Finally, she nodded. "Yes, I can see that she's been a comfort to you as well."

Before Whit could reply, she spoke again. "Forgive me for bringing it up. I'll take my leave."

Whit was fuming as she walked out. How dare she insinuate that something improper was going on between him and Athena! Sloane was already suspicious of Madelyn; he didn't need Doris fanning the flames and making her jealous of Athena too. He'd have to keep a close eye on Doris. She might be a longtime employee, but she was by no means irreplaceable.

38

ATHENA

Athena kept her distance while the alarm company outfitted Sloane's door with the new sensor. Now a chime would ring through the house anytime Sloane opened the door. That would make it much easier for Athena to move about the house unobserved by Sloane. It was almost time for lunch, so she walked down to the kitchen.

"Hi, Doris. Is Mrs. Montgomery's lunch ready?"

"Yes, I made her a nice chicken pot pie. She's getting rail thin. I hope you can get her to eat something."

"I'll do my best. Can you take it into the sunroom? I'll eat with her there as well. She said she wants to start coming downstairs again for her meals, and I don't want her to eat alone. Hopefully that will cheer her up."

Doris nodded in approval. "I like the sound of that."

Athena knew that the effort of walking up and down the stairs would use up the little energy Sloane had, but she could see that Sloane was getting depressed being stuck in her room all day. She didn't want Sloane to shut down before Athena had accomplished what she came here for.

When she reached the bedroom, Sloane was asleep on the love seat, her book on her lap, her head back. Athena debated whether to let her sleep but decided that Sloane couldn't afford to skip any meals. She walked over and gently touched her shoulder.

"Sloane?"

Sloane's eyes fluttered open, and she looked at Athena in confusion, then seemed to get her bearings. "I must have dozed off. What time is it?"

"Close to one. I thought you might like to go downstairs for lunch. Doris made her special pot pie. I'd love to join you if that's okay. I asked her to set us up in the sunroom. You mentioned that it's your favorite room in the house." Athena was doing her best to regain the sense of companionship they'd enjoyed when she first arrived. Sloane had become wary around her, and that wouldn't do at all.

"That sounds nice."

She followed behind Sloane as she made her way gingerly down the stairs. Athena could tell she was in pain by the way she winced each time her foot came down on a step. By the time they reached the sunroom, Sloane's color was ashen, her upper lip dotted with sweat. Doris had already put their plates and silverware on the table, and they both took a seat. Sloane's hand trembled as she reached for the napkin and placed it on her lap.

"Are you okay?" Athena asked.

Sloane nodded. "Fine." She pointed to the empty glass in front of her plate. "Would you mind pouring me some water?"

Doris had left a glass pitcher on the table.

"Of course." She reached over and filled Sloane's glass, then her own.

They began to eat, and after a few minutes Athena looked over at Sloane. It was time to address the elephant in the room. "Sloane, I just want to tell you that in my experience, what you're going through is temporary. I had a lupus patient a few years ago, and she also experienced hallucinations. Once her medicine was modified, the hallucinations stopped. I know it's scary, and I'm sure it makes you uncomfortable to discuss. But that's what I'm here for. There's no need for any embarrassment on your part. I just want to help."

Sloane sighed, and her eyes filled. "It's easy for you to say. You're healthy. Can you imagine what you'd be feeling if you couldn't trust what your own eyes and ears were telling you?"

"I would be terrified. I'm not trying to minimize what's happening, but we both know that it's because of the lupus. It's only been a day since Dr. Porter increased your steroids. Whit told me that Porter said if that doesn't help, he'll introduce some new meds. But you need to give the steroids time to work and get that inflammation down."

"I guess. But it's not just the hallucinations. I'm forgetting things. Chunks of time," Sloane said.

Athena was gratified that she was opening up to her. "It's going to be okay. You're getting the best medical care there is, and I'm going to take care of you while this gets figured out."

"I appreciate your trying to cheer me up, but I've seen what this disease can do when the central nervous system is involved. I do my best to stay positive, but the idea that my brain could suffer damage that would change my personality or render me comatose is unthinkable. I wouldn't want to live that way."

Athena put her fork down and looked at Sloane. "You're right. It *is* unthinkable. But the reality is that no one knows what tomorrow brings. An accident, any sudden illness, an injury—all of those things can change our lives in an instant." Athena knew this firsthand. "My mother always said worry is like paying interest on money you don't owe."

Sloane nodded. "Your mother sounds like a wise woman."

"She was. She'd also tell you that you need your strength, so eat up." She pointed to Sloane's dish. When they'd finished, they headed back upstairs.

After Athena got her settled, she sat in the corner of the room with a book until Sloane was asleep. Going out to her car, she took the phone from the glove compartment and sent a text to Clint.

She's beginning to trust me again. Caution is still necessary. When I was at her office, a staff member noticed that the picture over the wall safe was crooked. I'd neglected to make sure it was straight, and she seemed suspicious. This situation is trickier than the last one. Let's keep communication to a minimum and not meet for a while—I don't think I'm followed when I leave the house, but you never know. The payoff will be worth every ounce of planning and stress. Don't reach out. I'll contact you.

39

ROSEMARY

Rosemary had never been happier to be on her way home. The hospital finally released her after five more days, and Camille had stayed with her every night. The detectives had come to the hospital, but Rosemary still couldn't remember anything. They had no leads whatsoever at this point. Camille arranged for a hospital bed, round-the-clock nursing care, and physical and speech therapy at her home, to help her regain her strength after being immobile for weeks in the hospital. The doctors were amazed at her recovery thus far, and said it was truly a miracle that she was talking and able to move so well.

She felt her mood lift as the familiar Stonefield sign came into view. Through the graceful iron gates onto the long tree-lined drive, they passed the stables and riding ring before the house came into view. Even after all these years, the sight of the beautiful stone dwelling comforted her. She smiled at her daughter, seated next to her, as her driver pulled up to the front. She waited while Anthony opened the wheelchair and then helped her into it from the back seat. Her eyes wandered to the tennis courts. She sighed, wondering how long it would be before she was playing on them again.

"Do you want to rest?" Camille asked once they were inside.

Rosemary shook her head. "Porch."

Camille wheeled her into the screened porch with her chair facing the windows. The sun felt good on her skin. She needed to let Camille know about the report Mac had brought her. She remembered now: the vice president, Congressman Horner, Whit, and Peterson all going to those housing projects. Secret meetings.

She needed to show the report to Camille. It must be in the house somewhere.

She cleared her throat. "Living room. Find report."

Camille left the room but was back in a few minutes. "I couldn't find anything. I asked Matilda if she'd seen a folder, but she said no."

"Call . . . Faye," she told her daughter.

Camille walked to the desk and retrieved Rosemary's address book. "This number?" she said, pointing.

"Yes."

Camille waited for an answer, then spoke. "Good morning. This is Camille Chase. I'm calling for Congresswoman Chambers. It's personal."

Camille pulled the phone from her ear and whispered, "On hold."

After several minutes, Camille nodded. "Good morning, Faye. Yes, she's home now. Okay if I put you on speaker?"

Camille put the phone down on the desk, and Faye's voice came over the speaker.

"Rosemary! So glad to hear that you're home. How are you?"

Camille spoke for her. "She's better. Hard for her to talk. Listen, I know when you came to the hospital, you said that Mom was upset about something she'd found out. At the time I was so worried about her condition we didn't really get into it."

"I'm sorry, Rosemary, but Camille has to know that I've been worried about your state of mind for a while."

Rosemary frowned, not liking the tone of her friend's voice.

Camille continued. "Well, the thing is, there was a man named Mac Slade that Mom asked to look into Whit. Unfortunately, he recently passed away. He brought a report that Mom said she showed you. Some meetings with the VP, Whit, and another congressman. Mom remembers asking you to look into it and said that's why you were coming to see her that night. Were you able to find anything out?"

"There were some meetings, yes, and I looked into them. They were all perfectly legitimate. Whit's spearheading a wonderful project to build low-income housing. That's all they were meeting about. I was in attendance at one of them and I told Rosemary that it was fine, but she kept pushing, even trying to get me to give details of private meetings. I've been concerned about Rosemary's fixation on finding fault with Whit. I understand it's been hard to see Robert's widow married, but it's time to let it go. She's become obsessed."

"Thanks for your time," Camille said, and ended the call.

Rosemary shook her head. "No, no. Not true." Her fists were clenched so tightly that her fingernails bit painfully into her palms.

Camille took her mother's hands in hers. "It's okay, Mom. You have to admit, you have been determined to discredit Whit since Sloane married him. It's not healthy. You've got to move on. I really think you need to get on an antidepressant. There's no shame in needing some help. Depression can cause memory loss and confusion. We'll figure it out."

The look of pity and dismay she saw in Camille's eyes pierced her to her core. Her own daughter was questioning her judgment, but she was wrong. Rosemary wasn't obsessed with Whit, she was obsessed with finding out the truth. She felt her body grow cold. She now knew who her enemies were. She had no doubt that they would stop at nothing to shut her up. But there was no way in hell Rosemary would allow herself to be silenced.

40

WHIT

Whit stood in front of the mirror and straightened his tie as he mulled over whether or not to let Sloane know that Madelyn was joining Fred and him for dinner tonight. It was, after all, an invitation he couldn't just shrug off. Whit wasn't under any illusions. Fred would be fine with Whit canceling the date due to the gravity of Sloane's illness, but Madelyn would never stand for that. And Madelyn had a cunning way of manipulating facts. He had no doubt that she would somehow convince Fred that Whit was exaggerating and must have another reason for opting out. It would be foolish of him to anger Fred.

Whit exhaled, turned out the light, and left the room, hesitating only a moment as he reached the second-floor landing and Sloane's bedroom. No, he thought as he continued descending the stairs to the first floor. It would only upset Sloane to know that Madelyn would be there too. He'd gone straight up to see her when he got home earlier, and she hadn't looked good. In fact, the desiccated shell of a person had no resemblance to the vivacious, beautiful woman he'd married seven months ago.

He felt in his pocket for the car keys as he headed to the kitchen and garage. Athena stood at the counter, her back to him, stirring something on the stove.

"I'm leaving now," he said. "I shouldn't be too late."

Athena turned to face him. "Okay. I'm making something for Sloane. She barely touched her dinner, and she's eating less and less lately. I was hoping this might appeal to her." Athena touched the pot handle.

"What is it?"

"It's a sort of pudding I'm making with milled chia seeds, coconut milk, and blueberries. I'm hoping she'll enjoy the taste. Something different, and it's full of things that are good for reducing inflammation and blood sugar."

"Sounds great. Well, gotta run."

"Good night . . . Whit," she said a beat after.

"Good night, Athena." He opened the door to the garage, chuckling in amusement. It was obvious Athena was still a little in awe of him. No matter how careful he promised himself he would be, it felt good to be admired by such a beautiful woman.

Whit drove the short distance to Cafe Milano, parked the car, and went into the restaurant. He spotted Fred and Madelyn at a table by the windows, but it took him almost ten minutes to get to them by the time he finished greeting friends and associates at other tables along the way. As usual, the place was filled with Washington insiders.

"Fred, Madelyn," Whit said when he reached their table.

Fred reached up to shake Whit's hand, while Madelyn barely looked at Whit, uttering only a frigid "Hello." Great, Whit thought as he sat. This had all the makings of one shitty evening.

"What are you drinking?" Fred asked, raising his hand to their waiter, who was there in an instant.

"I'll have a Jefferson's straight up," Whit said, glancing at the other drinks on the table. "How about you two? Are you ready for another?"

"We're good," Fred said.

Madelyn had yet to say another word or even look at him. Whit regarded the two of them, fascinated as always by their unlikely union. Even in the obviously custom-made suit he wore, Fred managed to look sloppy and coarse, his face beefy red like raw meat, his reptilian eyes disappearing into fleshy cheeks. Madelyn looked smashing in an emerald-green dress that hugged her body, her raven hair swept back in a bun and her makeup flawless. It was almost comical to imagine them having sex, although he knew they both found their pleasure outside of the bed they shared.

In minutes, the waiter set Whit's drink before him and withdrew.

"Cheers." Fred lifted his glass and drank, smacking his lips in satisfaction. "Before we get on to the reelection committee, let's talk about the other properties coming up. They've been checked out? Is Peterson sure this won't happen again?"

"Everything's under control with Peterson. Don't worry." Whit took a long swig of bourbon and leaned toward Fred. The man spoke in rapid-fire bursts, in a long-winded summation of what he expected in return for his weighty support. Whit had heard it all before. Every senator and congressman had. No one was going to give millions to your campaign and get nothing in return; that wasn't how it worked. His mind wandered as Fred droned on. He almost jumped when he suddenly felt something push against his crotch but managed to maintain his composure. It was Madelyn's foot, warm and teasing. He gulped. When he looked at her, she smiled, licking her lips seductively.

Whit sat back, trying to distance himself. What the hell was she doing? This was the last thing he needed right now, especially with Fred sitting inches away from him. From the corner of his eye, he could see Madelyn's mocking expression.

"Gotta hit the head." Fred grunted as he pushed his chair back from the table. He pointed to his empty glass. "Order me another, won't you?"

As soon as he was out of earshot, Madelyn spoke. "I thought he'd never leave." She looked around the crowded restaurant. "If we were somewhere more private, I'd use this time to give you a little handy, but I guess this will have to do for now." She pulled out her phone and tapped. Whit heard the whoosh of an incoming text on his phone. He glanced down. A video.

"Play it. There's no sound. Fred will be a while. His prostate doesn't make peeing easy." She made a disgusted face.

"Madelyn, this isn't the time . . ."

"Don't make me make a scene."

She was nuts. He hit play. It was Madelyn, although you couldn't see her face. But he knew her body. He watched in fascination as she stripped, then opened her legs and began to touch herself. Heat spread to his face, and he became aroused. He had to turn it off. When he looked up at her, she licked her lips slowly. "Watch till the end, lover."

"Madelyn, please."

"Put your damn cellphone away." Fred's voice boomed behind him.

Whit swiped quickly and put the phone into his jacket pocket.

Fred shook his head. "I'm so sick of those damn things. All everyone does is stare at those tiny screens all day long. Worst invention ever. I'm starving. Let's order."

"Darling, I'm not feeling so well. I'm getting a migraine. Would you mind if I had Derek take me home?" Madelyn smiled sweetly.

"He's running an errand for me. I told him we'd be here at least two hours." Fred grabbed a roll, buttered it, and stuffed it into his mouth, then pointed at Whit with his knife. "Let's eat and then you can run her home. I have to meet someone later anyway."

Shit. What the hell could he say? He was sick and tired of being Fred's errand boy, but now was not the time to assert his independence. "Sure, Fred."

They made small talk until dinner arrived, and after they were finished, Fred nodded toward Madelyn. "Why don't you drop her home now." He waved his hand in dismissal.

Madelyn kissed Fred on the cheek and stood. "Thanks, baby doll. See you at home."

As they exited the restaurant and rounded the corner to Whit's car, Madelyn gave him a seductive look. "My headache's gone, surprise, surprise."

He bit the inside of his cheek, trying to remind himself of everything at stake. Madelyn never made things easy.

41

SLOANE

Sloane opened the app on her phone and watched in anticipation. She'd sent Athena to her office after lunch, ostensibly to pick up three files. She'd reminded Brianna to give Athena unfettered access and to leave her in the office alone. Athena would need to open the file cabinet to retrieve the files, and Sloane wanted to see if she would complete the task and leave, or if she would nose around. She watched as her office door opened and Athena entered. She flicked on the light and walked to Sloane's desk, then opened the bottom drawer. Interesting. Athena shut the drawer right away and looked over to the file cabinet. She moved to the bookcase against the wall and stopped, leaning down to look at the books on the bottom shelf. What was she doing? Sloane wondered. Athena crouched down and took two books from the shelf, but Sloane couldn't see which ones. She pinched the screen to get a close-up. Athena put the books back, but in reverse order. Sloane couldn't help but laugh. Sloane had arranged the titles alphabetically and those two were in the wrong order. Next, Athena turned back to the filing cabinet, opened it, and pulled out the three files, one by one. She flicked off the switch and shut the door. Sloane's shoulders slumped. How anticlimactic. But good, she supposed. She closed the app, put the phone down, and picked up the newspaper when she heard the chime ring.

The bedroom door opened, and Emmy stood there. "Are you up to a visit?" She smiled, closing the door behind her.

Sloane felt her spirits rise instantly. "Emmy! What are you doing here?" She held out her arms to her daughter. "How wonderful. Come give me a hug."

"I took the red-eye. I can only stay a day, but I wanted to see you. FaceTime wasn't cutting it." Emmy walked over to the love seat where her mother was doing a crossword puzzle and embraced her before settling herself next to Sloane. "What's with the alarm sensor on your door?"

"Oh, that." Sloane waved her hand dismissively. "Whit insisted on it as an extra precaution since he's been sleeping in a guest room. I'm on so much medication, he wants to make sure I don't sleepwalk or something."

Emmy frowned. "I still don't understand why he's not sleeping in here. Aren't you lonely?"

Sloane was, but she didn't want to upset Emmy, so she shook her head. "I'm so restless at night, and he needs his sleep. He's doing so much between his job and helping with the foundation." She sighed. "And taking care of me. Anyway, enough about me. Have you eaten? There should be some stew in the fridge from dinner. I just came upstairs."

"I'm good, Mom. I grabbed something at the airport. Whit said that the doctor upped your steroids. Is it helping?"

Sloane shrugged. "The swelling in my legs has gone down, so that's good. And my bionic hip is great!" She didn't mention her constant exhaustion or the host of other troubling symptoms plaguing her. Especially not the terrifying hallucinations. Emmy would be beside herself.

"Do you want to finish your tea?" Emmy picked up the mug and then stopped, her brows knitted. "What's this white stuff floating on top?" She handed the mug to Sloane.

Sloane raised the cup to her nose and inhaled, but there was no discernible scent. "Maybe it's stevia. I guess it's been sitting too long," was all she said to Emmy, but she would show it to Doris later and see if she knew what it was. She had no intention of drinking it and placed it on the table next to her.

Emmy tilted her head. "How is Athena working out? Are you happy with her?"

She wasn't pleased with how much time Athena was spending with Whit, but she *was* relieved that she'd found nothing about Athena's past to raise alarm bells thus far. Rosemary's suspicions were probably her imagination, but Sloane was not ready to completely dismiss them. None of these things was something to burden Emmy with, however. "She's been a great help to me."

"Okay, well, you know I'm always just a phone call away."

Sloane smiled at her daughter. "I know. And *you* know I don't want you worrying about me. I'm well taken care of."

Emmy nodded, but Sloane could see from her expression that she was still worried. Sloane wasn't about to let this disease steal her daughter's peace of mind. She was careful to keep her voice even. "Athena is terrific. I'm really glad she's here."

"I hate that I'm so far away," Emmy said.

Sloane reached out and stroked Emmy's face. "The next time you're home, I'll be up and around, making all your favorites."

The smile on Emmy's face was evidence enough that Sloane was doing the right thing to keep any reservations about Athena to herself. Truthfully, Athena *had* been doing a good job, no matter how much she sometimes aggravated Sloane with her intrusiveness. It couldn't be easy, though, caring for sick people and living in someone else's home. But soon enough, Sloane would be on her feet, and Athena's presence here nothing more than a fading memory.

It was after eleven by the time Emmy went to bed, and Whit still wasn't home. Sloane wasn't ready to get back into bed yet. She picked up her phone and opened Instagram. Ever since Madelyn's bitchy remarks at the donor party, Sloane had been uneasy. She hated the fact that Whit had to have anything to do with her.

She navigated to Madelyn's Instagram page, which was public. She'd heard Madelyn call herself a social media influencer, and with over three hundred thousand followers, Sloane conceded that she was. She rolled her eyes as she reviewed the posts from the past few days. Didn't the woman have anything better to do than catalogue every moment of her life for public consumption? A picture of her manicure with the caption: *Zelda is the best #junglered.* Next, a picture of her with Fred, Madelyn in a figure-hugging turquoise sheath, Fred looking droll in a plain tuxedo with a sour expression on his face. Caption: *Charityworks Dream Ball #breakthecycle.* Post after post of her fabulous life with all the accoutrements of wealth—at the DC Film Festival, Wolf Trap, Hillwood Mansion. Sloane knew that Madelyn was a narcissist, but this was over the top. She saw that Madelyn had recently added a story. It was a selfie of Madelyn in a limo with a man's arm around her shoulder. He was out of the frame, but part of his arm was clearly visible. What caught her attention was his wrist. The nickel-sized burn that had scarred Whit from an old fireworks accident. Was he with her right now? She felt the heat spread to her face and adrenaline rush through her body. That bitch had intentionally posted this, hoping Sloane would see it. But wouldn't Fred also see it and become suspicious? Then again, Fred probably didn't even use social media. All thoughts of sleep evaded her now. Had Peg been right about Whit? And if so, was history repeating itself? She texted him.

Come see me when you get home. We need to talk.

42

SLOANE

Sloane had struggled to stay awake until Whit got home last night, but by midnight she was unable to keep her eyes open any longer. She had no idea what time he'd finally gotten in. Emmy woke her at ten, bringing in Sloane's breakfast tray.

"I'm sorry to wake you, Mom, but my flight's at two, so I need to leave for the airport soon."

"Oh, Emmy, you should have gotten me up sooner so we could have spent more time together. I'm sorry I slept so late."

"No, no. You need your rest. I'll be home again soon. I had some time with Whit before he left for the office. He and Athena were having breakfast together when I went downstairs. Do they do that every morning?"

Sloane felt her face grow warm. "I . . . I usually don't sleep this late. Athena has breakfast with me." But lately she *had* been sleeping late. The truth was, she had no idea if they were together in the mornings.

"Anyway, tell me more about the work you're doing. I want to hear everything before you leave."

After a tearful farewell an hour later, Emmy left for the airport. As soon as she was gone, Sloane called Whit and asked him to get home early so they could talk. His late hours were becoming more and more frequent, and she couldn't help but wonder if Madelyn had anything to do with it. Especially after that picture from last night. And why the hell was he having breakfast with Athena this morning? It was inappropriate of him and unprofessional of Athena. She thought back to last night's tea and the white crap floating in it. Was it really stevia, or was it something else?

All these things kept rolling around in her head as she swung between paranoia and reason. Once again, she thought of Peg and how they'd all accused *her* of paranoia. One thing was for damn sure: She wasn't going to discover anything lying in this bed. The first thing to do was get up and get dressed.

It took all her effort to shower and dress, but she had to admit that she felt more powerful out of bedclothes. For the first time in she didn't know how long, she applied a tinted moisturizer, lip gloss, and mascara, then brushed her hair until it lay loosely on her shoulders. She faced the image in the mirror and saw the changes. Illness was taking its toll. She rang for Athena, and moments later, her door opened.

"Sloane, how are you . . ." Athena's expression turned to surprise as she took in Sloane's appearance. "You look very nice. Are you going somewhere?"

Sloane might have been dressed nicely, but the mirror didn't lie. She'd taken great pains to do her hair and makeup, but the increased steroid dosage had made her face swell, and no amount of concealer could hide the bags under her eyes. She felt worse than ever, and it had been a gargantuan effort to put herself together. But she wasn't about to have the conversation she planned to have with Whit sitting in her bed, feeling helpless.

"Whit and I are having dinner together tonight, so I'm afraid you'll have to make other plans." She took pleasure in the shocked look on Athena's face.

Athena quickly recovered. "That's wonderful, Sloane."

"Yes, well. I didn't want you to come running when you heard my door open. Also . . ." She hated having to ask. "I could use your help on the stairs. My legs are not feeling too steady."

"Of course."

Athena helped her navigate to the living room. "I'll wait here until Whit gets home. Why don't you take a break for a while?" Sloane said.

"Are you sure?"

"Yes. You deserve it." Sloane didn't want her skulking around, overhearing their conversation.

"It's nice to see you feeling better," Athena said.

"Thank you. Can you hand me my phone? I'd like to check to see if Emmy's flight has landed."

Athena walked over to the table and brought it to her. "Here you go. I know you must be happy that she was able to come see you, since she won't make it back for Thanksgiving."

Sloane froze. *How did Athena know that?* Emmy had called a few days ago to tell her she wasn't going to make it back for the holiday. Was Athena somehow listening in on her calls? Or maybe she'd somehow tapped into Sloane's cellphone. Was that even possible?

Athena cleared her throat. "Whit mentioned that she wasn't coming. Didn't mean to bring your mood down."

"It's okay," Sloane said.

"Well, I'll be going, then. Be back in a few hours. How about if I bring you an iced tea before I go?"

"Thank you," Sloane said absently.

After Athena had gone, she picked up the glass of tea, checking for anything floating in it before taking a sip. As she drank, she rehearsed what she wanted to say to Whit until she heard the front door chime announce his arrival at five thirty.

"I'm in here," she called out.

Whit walked in, a surprised look on his face. "Well, this is a treat! You must be feeling better. You look wonderful."

His tone was oversolicitous, almost patronizing, she thought testily. "Amazing how grown up one feels to actually get dressed and leave the bedroom."

"Is everything all right?" He went over to the bar and poured himself a bourbon. "Can I add some ice to your tea?"

She handed him her glass. "Sure."

He turned back to the cart and added three ice cubes. "Here you go," he said, and then took the chair across from her. "You seem angry."

"You're very astute. There are a few things I'd like cleared up. First off, what time did you finally come in last night? I waited up until after midnight."

He took a sip and studied her before answering. "I'm not too crazy about your tone. You know I had a meeting with Fred. We had a lot to cover. We went back to my office and worked until around one."

She arched an eyebrow. "Do you really expect me to believe that? I saw the picture. I know you were with her."

"With who?"

"Don't play dumb! With Madelyn."

His eyebrows shot up. "What picture?"

She pulled out her phone and went to Madelyn's Instagram page. "I saw a picture on her story last night. In her limo. Your arm was around her. I could tell because of the scar on your wrist." She frowned as she scrolled through, but the picture was gone. "She must have deleted it." She berated herself for not having taken a screenshot. She looked up at Whit. "It was there. I . . ." She couldn't have imagined it, could she?

"I don't know about any picture. But look, it's not what you think. Yes, Madelyn came to dinner. I didn't want to tell you and upset you. She had a migraine coming on, and Fred asked me to drive her home, which I did. Then I met him at his office."

"You should have told me she was there. Can't you see how it looks when you keep things from me?"

"You're right. But you've been so sick. I didn't want to do anything to upset you. I'm not doing anything wrong. It didn't seem important to tell you."

"You swear you just took her home and dropped her off?"

"Yes! That must have been a picture from a couple of years ago from a charity event. Fred was in that limo too. In fact, he took the picture. Madelyn likes to put everything on social media. Last night I drove her home; we weren't in her limo. I don't know why she'd post a picture like that."

Sloane sighed. Maybe Madelyn was just trying to goad her into fighting with Whit. She had played right into her hands. She was still feeling suspicious, but what else could she say? "Okay, I believe you. But you can't keep things from me anymore. All right?" She was tempted to bring up the matter of breakfast with Athena this morning, but now didn't seem like the right time.

He nodded. "Yes. Shall we go have dinner now?"

As she leaned forward to rise, the room began to blur, and Sloane gripped the arm of the sofa. She could see Whit's mouth moving, but the words were unclear. The birds on the wallpaper slowly began to move, opening their wings and peeling away from the walls. She could hear them chirping as they began to fly around the room, the swirl of colors so beautiful. The breeze rushed across her face as they whizzed past, their wings flapping madly. She reached out to try and touch one, but it dipped up and down, its wings fluttering, and eluded her grasp. They were everywhere now, flying all around the room. Smiling at her as they came close to her face and then swept away. So beautiful! "Look at them!" she cried. "They're everywhere." A large red-winged blackbird turned and flew toward her. The orange and yellow, so pretty. It came closer and closer until its beak nearly touched her face. It was going to peck at her eyes. "Stop!" she screamed, sinking back against the cushion.

"Sloane, Sloane!" Whit's voice broke through, and the bird disappeared.

"What happened? Where did the birds go?" Slowly it dawned on her. She'd had another hallucination.

Whit picked her up and carried her upstairs while she tried to make sense of what had happened. She'd experienced bad flares before but had never hallucinated. All of this had started after Athena moved in. She thought of the white stuff in her drink. It wasn't stevia. Was the woman drugging her?

43

ATHENA

As soon as the words left her lips, Athena could have kicked herself. Hopefully Sloane hadn't realized that Athena was lying when she told her that Whit had mentioned Emmy's canceled Thanksgiving plans. She'd had Clint talk her through how to install an app on Sloane's phone to tap it and she listened to her conversations every evening. Prior to her visit, Emmy had phoned to tell Sloane that she wasn't going to be able to come for Thanksgiving after all. That was another sloppy mistake. Sloane was catching on.

Since Sloane had told her to take a break, she left and drove back to her apartment. She wanted to pick up a few more items of clothing. Despite her decision to keep some distance between her and Clint, she wanted to let him know that Sloane was not someone to be underestimated. She called him from the car on her way.

"Sloane's sharper than we gave her credit for," she said as soon as he answered.

"What are you talking about?"

"When I listened to the calls she made yesterday, I discovered she had cameras installed in her office to see if she could catch me doing anything wrong. She sent me on an errand there to test me."

"And?"

"I made it look a little fishy at first. Going to her desk instead of the file cabinet. Then I rearranged two books on a shelf that were out of alphabetical order."

"What? Another freak who arranges books that way?" He laughed.

"The point is, she'll think that Brianna was overreacting. I passed the test."

"I don't like it. We need to get things wrapped up soon. Maybe we should rethink our strategy."

Athena regretted calling him. "No. I've got it under control. I'll check in with you later. Gotta go." Athena inhaled deeply. She wasn't about to listen to another lecture from Clint. She was beginning to think that their differences were too great. Clint had no real appreciation for everything that she'd been through, the losses that she'd suffered. She was the one putting her life on hold, unable to form any authentic attachments, while he went home to his family every night. He didn't have to live with the regrets and guilt that she did. She'd learned all she could from him, she realized now. She didn't need him anymore.

A new resolve filled her. She would amend the plan and do things her way. Clint would be pissed, but he'd eventually get over it. It would be her swan song—her greatest achievement yet. It was time to up her game. The only potential problem was Sloane. She was beginning to get suspicious, and that wasn't good. Athena wasn't about to let a jealous wife get her fired. She was going to have to be proactive. As they say, the best defense is a good offense.

44

SLOANE

The morning sun was streaming into the room when Sloane opened her eyes. She was in bed and in pajamas, the clothes she'd worn last night thrown across the back of a chair. When had she changed? Her eyes traveled to the far end of the room, where Whit sat by the window reading the paper.

"Whit?"

"Ah, you're awake. How are you feeling?" he asked, folding the newspaper and putting it down.

"Confused. What happened?"

He went to the bed and sat next to her on the edge. "You don't remember?"

She sat up and rubbed her temples. "Why does my head feel so fuzzy?"

"I gave you a sleeping pill. You were so upset. You don't remember what happened in the living room before dinner?"

A vague memory came to her. Something about birds flying around. The knot in her stomach grew. "I had another hallucination, didn't I?"

He nodded. "You thought the birds on the wallpaper were real. Dr. Porter wants you to see a neurologist. His office is going to call me back today with some names. Hopefully we can get you in very soon."

"What am I supposed to do in the meantime?"

"This is why I had that alarm put on your door. I don't think it's good for you to be alone. He did say that the steroid increase could take a little while to do the trick. But we can't take any chances while we wait."

She felt a roiling in her stomach as the bile rushed to her throat. "I'm going to throw up," she said, pushing Whit aside and standing on unsteady feet. He put out an arm to help her, but she shook it away and walked by herself as quickly as her swollen feet would take her to the bathroom, where she lifted the lid of the toilet and vomited her guts out. Two hallucinations in only a few days? What was next? How was she supposed to go on when she wasn't even safe from herself? Stumbling over to the sink, she splashed water on her face and looked at herself in the mirror.

"This is no life," she said to the swollen woman staring back.

She returned to the bedroom and fell onto the mattress. "I don't care if you have to call every neurologist in a hundred-mile radius. I want to be seen as soon as possible. I can't do this anymore."

Whit gently pushed the damp hair from her forehead. "It's going to be all right. I'm taking the day off. Getting you seen right away is my top priority."

She stared up at the ceiling, fear gnawing at her.

"I'm sorry to interrupt," she heard Athena say. She was standing in the doorway holding something.

"What is it?" Sloane said.

"I picked up your iron supplements," Athena said, coming into the room. "They're best taken on an empty stomach, so I wanted to give them to you before breakfast." She handed her the pills and a glass of water. Sloane hesitated a moment. She wanted to make sure they were really iron supplements but needed an excuse to explain why she felt the need to look them up.

"You know, the pharmacy made a mistake once and gave me the wrong medicine, so now I always check."

"These aren't prescription. See?" Athena showed her the bottle with the name Proferrin on it.

Sloane shrugged. "There can also be manufacturing mistakes. I like to check everything on Drugs.com," she said, and picked up her phone. There was no way she was taking Athena's word for it that these were iron pills. She saw a look pass between Whit and

Athena but continued anyway to a search bar and typed in *Proferrin*, then clicked images. It was a green pill, just like the ones in her hand. They were both staring at her with skepticism. She swallowed the pills while Athena stood over her, watching.

Whit patted Sloane's shoulder. "Good. Athena is going to spend the day with you."

"Yes, I'm so sorry that you had another hallucination. We're not going to leave you alone," Athena said, taking the glass from Sloane.

Sloane wanted to spit at her. She couldn't stand the look of intense watchfulness on Athena's face.

Whit stood. "I almost forgot, I have something for you."

"Another present. Aren't you the lucky one?" Athena said.

Could she sound any more insincere? Sloane thought, feeling waves of impatience. "Athena. Would you mind giving us some privacy? My husband will let you know when he's leaving, and you can come back and babysit me then."

Athena gave her a curt nod and withdrew from the room.

Whit returned with a crystal vase filled with white roses. "I thought these would cheer you up."

"Thank you," she said woodenly. What good were flowers when she was losing her mind?

"It must have been nice to see Emmy, even though it was a short visit."

"It was wonderful." She cleared her throat. "Listen. I don't want Emmy to know about these hallucinations. Until we know exactly what's going on, there's no need to worry her."

Whit nodded. "Whatever you want."

She sat up straight, regaining some equilibrium. "I've been thinking about the foundation. You're going to have a lot to juggle, now that I'm temporarily out of commission. Are you sure you're okay handling all the disbursement requests? Maybe I should ask Camille to help out in the meantime."

"No, of course I have time. You need to get well before you go back to work, and I take my responsibility as trustee very seriously. Our work at the foundation is just as important as my work in Congress. The foundation is our legacy."

Sloane was stung by his words. The foundation was the legacy of Robert and her, but Whit talked as if Robert had never existed, as if he wanted to erase him from Sloane's past. Until recently, Whit had never expressed much interest in the foundation's projects and initiatives, and the notion of its being his legacy felt offensive.

She held her tongue, trying to talk herself out of her resentment. In the end, she really did want Whit to feel ownership now that he was a trustee. Together they would advance the work, and she would make sure that they kept Robert's memory alive.

"I'm glad you want to be such an integral part of the foundation," Sloane finally said. "By the way, Brianna said we had a large cash contribution. Who was it from? The only info she had was that it came from a Triad III LLC, and the company didn't designate to which specific charity the money should go."

Whit shifted in his seat. "I thought we just agreed that you'll go back to work when you're well. This is not the time for you to worry about what's going on at the foundation."

"But I'm just asking who they are—"

"Stop," he interrupted. "You need to focus on getting better. End of discussion." He picked up her laptop. "As a matter of fact, let's give this a rest for a few days."

"What are you doing?"

"How are you ever going to get better if you keep working and worrying about the foundation? We have it under control. Besides, what if you start hallucinating in the middle of a video call . . ." He let the implication dangle.

She went warm with humiliation.

"But . . ."

"No buts." He rose abruptly and said, "I'll come back up later with your pomegranate juice. Read to you if you like."

Sloane wasn't used to being ordered about, but she realized it would do no good to argue with Whit. After he left, she'd have Athena retrieve her laptop.

Her gaze swung restlessly around the once-luxurious bedroom with its cozy seating area by the fireplace. Now it was merely a sickroom, with pill bottles, medical devices, and bare wooden floors that were once covered with Oriental rugs, now removed so she wouldn't trip on them. She couldn't let Whit treat her like someone who could no longer think, however. How dare he refuse to answer her question about the donor, as if it were all too much for her poor muddled mind! There was a reason for these hallucinations. Inflammation in the blood vessels in her brain. Once that was resolved, she would be fine. She had to be. And right now, she didn't feel at all confused.

Raising her phone again, she began a detailed text to Brianna regarding the new shelter in Ohio—the one she'd never heard of—and the large donation from an unknown donor. She asked Brianna to email her any details she had. Her phone dinged immediately with a text from Brianna, reminding her that she was in closed-door meetings with the auditor for the next two days, and asking if she could look into it after that. Sloane responded that it could wait.

She grabbed her reading glasses from the nightstand, went to a search bar on her phone, and typed in *Triad III LLC*. The page was populated with numerous companies by the same name in different states and in various industries—medical, automotive, investments, and more. She needed to know in which state they had filed. She sent another text to Brianna and asked her for that information as well when she was out of her meetings. Sloane put the phone down and closed her eyes. Was she being paranoid? She should be thrilled that they had a new donor. But she wasn't used to being out of the loop. Even though she'd placed her confidence in Whit and made him a trustee, she wasn't going to stop until she had the answers she sought.

45

WHIT

Sloane hadn't had another hallucination since the birds three days ago. Whit left her asleep and walked down the hall to knock on Athena's bedroom door.

"Oh, hi. You're back. You were lucky Dr. Porter was able to get Sloane into the neurologist so quickly. How is she?" Athena asked.

"Out like a light," he said. "Take a drive with me. I'll fill you in on the appointment, so no one will overhear our conversation. I don't want the staff to know yet."

"Sure."

"Meet me in the garage."

Twenty minutes later, he was driving through Georgetown with Athena next to him in the Porsche's passenger seat. He'd seldom driven it after Sloane's hip made it too painful for her to get in and out, using the Bentley for all their outings instead. It felt good to be behind the wheel again. He'd forgotten how nice it was to have someone attractive, young, and interested in the seat next to him in this sporty car. They rode in silence until he pulled into a parking lot, stopped the car, and turned off the engine. Turning to face her, he began. "I'm afraid the doctor didn't offer much hope."

"What did he say?"

Whit continued. "He's ordered a brain MRI. Hopefully, they can get her in before the end of the week. He feels it will only confirm what he already believes—that these latest symptoms are indicative of inflammation in the brain. Possibly even organic brain syndrome, which would account for the hallucinations, headaches, dizziness, blurry vision, and memory lapses. The MRI will show whether there's damage."

"Are they optimistic?"

Whit looked down. "Dr. Porter will need to review the MRI and suggest next steps. But it looks pretty dire. The neurologist did some basic cognitive tests, and she didn't do well. It was horrible. I felt so bad for her. I'm afraid the progression is only going to get worse."

"This is so awful," Athena said.

He ran his hand along the steering wheel, then dropped it to his lap. "It won't do any good to foster false hope. Sloane has central nervous system involvement. You've seen yourself what she's going through. She's suffering greatly."

"Now it makes sense."

"What?"

Athena sighed. "I wasn't sure if I should say anything, but Sloane's been saying some things that are concerning. She's having some paranoid delusions."

"Like what?"

"She thinks you're cheating on her. First it was Yvette. Then she mentioned Madelyn Sawyer. I'm afraid she's even accused *me* of being after you."

"Why didn't you tell me this sooner?"

"I've seen it before. It doesn't mean anything. We just have to take it with a grain of salt. If she insists on firing Yvette because of it, you just have to ignore it."

Whit shook his head. "I knew she was having issues, but I didn't realize it was this bad. I guess I should have known. When we got back from the doctor, she asked where we'd been. She didn't even remember seeing him. She's even worse than I thought. I hope she's not mistreating you."

"It's fine. She can't help what's going on."

Whit was quiet for a few minutes, then finally spoke again. "I went to see Harold yesterday. His wife had another stroke and is now completely paralyzed."

Athena's hand went to her mouth. "That's so sad."

"There's nothing they can do for her now. She's going to live like that for years. God only knows whether or not she's aware of anything. It's inhumane."

Athena shook her head. "You're right. It *is* inhumane."

"There's more . . ." His voice trailed off. He hesitated, then leaned toward her. "I wasn't going to tell you this. I promised Sloane I wouldn't; she has so much pride." He sighed. "Yesterday, she forgot who I was."

Athena's eyes widened. "What?"

"Yes, she had this look of total confusion in her eyes that terrified me. She asked what I was doing in her room. But then a moment later, she was back."

Athena turned away and gazed out the window. "I'm so sorry. That's terrible," she said.

"It is. Like the person you love has disappeared." He stopped a moment, letting the gravity of his words sink in. "Athena, I need to ask you something."

"What is it?"

"I'm sure it's no surprise that I look into everyone's background before bringing them into my home. I am, after all, a public figure."

She waited, saying nothing.

"Your husband. He died of a brain injury, right? A motorcycle accident?"

She nodded.

"But he didn't die right away, did he?"

She took her time answering. "No. He was on life support. I hoped he'd recover, but . . ."

"So you must have gone through the same experience. The person is there in body, but you know that in every way that matters, they're gone."

"I . . ."

"Tell me you understand. Because I'm suddenly feeling very guilty about my feelings. My wife is alive, but she's not really living. I'm losing her, but I've found you. It feels like fate; like some divine intervention brought you into my life for a reason."

"I know beyond a doubt that I was brought into your life for a reason," she said in a hushed voice.

"You understand what I'm going through. It's so good to have someone to talk to who's been through something similar. Oh, Athena." Whit placed his hand on the back of her neck. He leaned toward her and pulled her close, but Athena drew back.

"I'm sorry," he said, dropping his hand. "I lost control. Please forgive me."

Athena touched his arm. "There's nothing to forgive, Whit. I understand, but we need to have restraint. As long as Sloane is alive, you're still a married man. But as you said, I've been there. I know what you're going through."

Whit covered her hand with his. "I had no right to make you dredge up painful memories."

"My husband was brain-dead. There was no activity. But still . . . it was the hardest decision I've ever had to make. It still haunts me." She gripped his hand. "No one should have to be faced with that kind of decision."

"Sometimes the decision is made for you," he answered. "It would kill me to see a vital, independent woman like Sloane reduced to nothing but a shell. Can you imagine living that way?"

"No, I can't."

"Thank you for helping me. I'm traveling this road without a map. I don't know what I'd do without you, Athena. And I hope I never have to find out."

46

WHIT

The next day, Whit left his office at six. The short drive to Madelyn's was a familiar one to Whit's driver, whose discretion was a major point in his favor. With everything going on with Sloane, a visit to Madelyn's house was not something he was looking forward to, but he had to get her signature on these bank cards. At least there would be the safety of Fred's presence while he was there, since Whit had insisted that the visit be combined with catching the live TV coverage of the vice president.

"You can wait on the street. I don't know how long I'll be," Whit said as he got out of the car in front of the Sawyer residence. He strode briskly to the grand bronze entry doors and rang the doorbell.

"It's open," he heard Madelyn call. As he entered, he smiled, amused by the curving marble staircase that dominated the entrance, picturing the scene from *Sunset Boulevard* where Norma Desmond descends the stairs. He and Madelyn had sampled each other in every one of the ten bedrooms, and the sex had risen to new heights in the sauna and Jacuzzi.

"There you are." Madelyn came waltzing into the hall. She looked luscious in a black lace lounging gown. What was she playing at? And where the hell was Fred?

"Your attire is not fair play. How am I supposed to concentrate on business with you looking like this?" He forced a flirtatious tone.

She threw her head back and laughed, then spun around in a pirouette, her long hair billowing around her. "You never used to complain. Only the finest from Bordelle," she said, eyeing him coquettishly.

"You should put some clothes on."

"Party pooper." She pouted.

"What kind of game is this, Madelyn? Where's Fred?"

"Fred's out."

"What do you mean, Fred's out? Where is he, and when will he be back?"

"Who knows?" she said, glancing at her watch.

With a determined look in her eyes, Madelyn took his hand and led him to the living room sofa, pushing him onto it. A framed photo of Madelyn and Fred stared back at him from the end table. "I want you right now," she said, straddling him as she unbuttoned his shirt.

Whit grew uneasy, panicked at the thought that Fred could walk in at any moment. But then it occurred to him that Madelyn already knew precisely the time he'd be home. She was far too shrewd to take chances.

She continued to caress Whit and suddenly made a face when she felt the small box in his pocket. Pulling it out, she opened it and looked at the sapphire and diamond earrings. "Are these for her?"

Shit. Why hadn't he left those in the car? They were a pair from Tiffany that Whit had bought for Sloane. "Have some compassion. She's sick. I wanted to cheer her up."

"Maybe she'll do us both a favor and die," she said, putting on the earrings. "These are mine now." She climbed from his lap and walked to the mirror on the wall, tucking her hair behind her ears as she examined the new studs.

"Fine, keep them. Enough talk about Sloane," he said. He rose from the chair, buttoned his shirt, and opened his briefcase, pulling out the signature cards. "You need to sign these, and I'll take them to the bank."

She grabbed the pen from him and scrawled her signature, then held out the cards. As he reached to take them, she pulled her hand back, still holding on to the cards.

"Not so fast." She unzipped the one-piece outfit she wore and let it drop to the floor, standing naked before him. "I may not be able to force you to pleasure me, but if you want these back, you'll have to watch a little show."

Her hands moved to her breasts, and she fondled herself while he watched, feeling like he was going to erupt. "Stop," he whispered. "I'm leaving."

"You've been a bad boy. Don't you dare move."

She continued to explore her body while he stared, unable to tear his gaze away, until she moaned in ecstasy. He stood open-mouthed, watching her perfectly rounded ass as she walked toward the staircase, the signature cards still clutched in one hand. "I'll go change. Fred's car should be pulling up about now. I'll be back with these," she said, waving the cards. "And then we can have a cozy threesome and watch the veep do his thing."

Madelyn reached the top of the stairs just as the front door chimed "The Yellow Rose of Texas." Fred changed the music according to his mood and the season, Madelyn had once told him. The man had some bizarre quirks.

"Mr. Senator," Fred bellowed as he came lumbering through the door and into the grand foyer. "Ready for Bishop's little show tonight?"

"Been looking forward to it all day," Whit replied.

Fred shrugged out of his coat and threw it onto a low bench in the hall. "C'mon." He motioned for Whit to follow him into the living room. "Sit. I'll make drinks." Fred went to the bar cart and poured two bourbons. "Where's Madelyn?" he asked, handing Whit a glass and plunking down onto the sofa.

"Here I am, darling." Madelyn's voice dripped with honey as she waltzed into the room, dressed in flowing silk pants and top. She planted a kiss on the top of Fred's bald head. "Where's *my* drink, lovey?"

Fred huffed breathlessly as he got up and went back to the cart, and Madelyn took the opportunity to sit so she would be between the two men. She gave Whit a flirtatious smile and squeezed his thigh.

"It's almost seven," Whit said, trying to ignore her. "We should turn on the TV, Fred."

"Yup." Fred picked up the remote and settled into the sofa cushions. From that moment, they stayed glued to the screen.

Vice President Bishop stood before a ten-foot bronze sculpture memorializing those who had perished in the horrific fire that ravaged a Section 8 apartment building two years ago. The statue depicting men, women, and children holding hands was backed by a granite wall inscribed with the names of those who had died. Bishop expressed his condolences to the families of those who'd lost their lives and asked for a moment of silence in remembrance. "We have put measures into place to assure a tragedy like this never occurs again," he began in conclusion. "This was a failure not only on the part of the contractor and the building inspectors but on the part of our system. We are introducing legislation that would require that the wiring on the buildings is checked, and triple-checked. We have also inspected all the buildings constructed by the same contractor and have been assured that the wiring is safe."

"Bishop kept his word. The contractor really got thrown under the bus," Fred said.

"As he should have! What kind of an asshole uses copper terminals with aluminum wiring? He should have waited for the proper terminals to come through, but he was in a hurry to get paid, so he used what he could get his hands on. He put us all in jeopardy," Whit said.

"Not to mention all the lives lost," Madelyn added. "Doesn't that bother either of you?"

Fred rolled his eyes. "That's not our fault. Won't do no good to cry about it now."

The last news item showed a clip of the vice president making a short farewell speech and boarding Air Force Two for the trip back to Washington. Oozing sincerity, he looked sorrowful, and spoke with heartfelt poignancy.

Fred clicked the remote, and the screen went dark. "Bishop had another meeting with the new contractor before he left Chicago. Enough time has elapsed since the fire for us to form a new LLC with him and get things rolling again."

"Sounds good." Whit downed the rest of his drink and rose. "Well, I need to get going. I told Sloane I wouldn't be late." He hadn't, but Whit was ready to leave.

"How *is* Sloane? Madelyn says she's not doing too well."

"She's having a rough time, but she's going to get through it."

"Give her my regards. She was a mighty fine catch, Whit." Fred's eyes twinkled with mischief.

"I'll walk you to the door," Madelyn said, taking Whit's arm. When they reached the front door, Madelyn dug her fingernails into his arm. "Are you rushing home to be with that trash-bag health aide you hired?" she said with petulance.

Whit felt his impatience surging, but he knew he had to be careful. He looked at Madelyn again, seeing the lust in her eyes. "There are other things more important than giving in to temptation."

She reached out and grabbed him by the balls, squeezing. "After Peg died you told me we'd be together, but then you went and married that stuck-up bitch. I'm running out of patience. Maybe I should look for a new candidate to back." She let go and shoved him away from her.

He was still fuming on the ride home. She hadn't given him the signed signature cards. Madelyn was totally out of control. He needed to be free of her clutches sooner rather than later.

47

SLOANE

reakfast already?" Sloane said as Athena came in with her tray. "I'm not very hungry."

"You don't have to eat right away. The fruit and granola will keep. I'll put the yogurt in the refrigerator. At least have your tea. It's ginger and will settle your stomach." She handed Sloane the mug. "Would you like me to stay for a little?"

"Actually, I want you to do something for me. Whit took my laptop. I know he thinks I'm working too hard and tiring myself out, but I'd like it back," Sloane said.

"I'm sorry, but I don't know where he put it."

"It's probably in his office. Can you check?"

"Sure. Remember I need to swing by the care agency this morning. I'll do it when I get back if that's okay. But Sloane, you really shouldn't be working. I thought you were going to take it easy."

Sloane tried to tamp down her initial irritation. "I know my husband is only trying to protect me by keeping my laptop away, but it can be frustrating. You understand, don't you?"

"Yes, I do. But Emmy's also worried about you doing too much. She called me just last night and asked me to make sure you're taking it easy."

"I don't want Emmy worrying about me. What did you say to her?"

"I told her you were following doctor's orders and getting the rest you need. And I'm sure she'd be glad to hear that your husband took your computer away. And not very happy to hear that you want it back."

"I know what my limits are, and I'm certainly not going to do anything that will jeopardize my recovery." Sloane raised the cup to her lips, and then put it down without taking a sip.

"But that's just it; you keep pushing your limits. There's no reason why you can't take time off from your work. With Brianna's help, I can handle things. It's not forever. The place isn't going to come crashing down because you miss a week or two."

Sloane stared at her, shocked by her impertinence. Who was Athena to assume that she could handle things at the foundation after helping out for only a few weeks? "You have no idea what will or will not come 'crashing down,' as you say, because of my absence."

Athena had the grace to appear sheepish. "Of course you're right. I didn't mean it that way. It's just . . . I want you to get better, and the only way that's going to happen is if you rest completely. I'm only here to help."

Sloane looked at her with suspicion. Why was Athena so anxious to keep Sloane down? Maybe she wanted to help herself to Sloane's life, but she'd be damned if she was going to let that happen.

"I'll look for your laptop, but in the meantime, please try to rest so you'll get well."

"Get well? I've seen where this can lead," Sloane said, resting her head against the pillow.

"Are you talking about Harold's wife?"

"What do you know about her?" Sloane asked sharply, sitting up.

"I've heard a little about her from Whit. From what he's told me, she's a rare case, Sloane. Look at all the others who don't end up like that." Athena bit her lip, then continued. "I know that the support group is a good thing, but I really wish Harold hadn't let you and Whit see what has happened to his wife."

Sloane bristled at Athena's familiar reference to Whit. What had happened to "Senator Montgomery"? Had she taken it upon herself, or had Whit invited her to be more intimate? "I'm not really comfortable with my husband discussing such personal things about me with you."

Athena appeared crestfallen. "I can't seem to say anything right today. I'm sorry. Really. But, Sloane, I don't think it's good for you to focus on what-ifs. Harold's wife's case has nothing to do with you."

"I'd like to be alone for a while," Sloane said.

"Of course. I'll go now," Athena said, rising. "Please try to eat a little granola. I know you're not hungry, but at least finish your tea—it's good for you." She picked up the tray. "When I get back, I'll look for your laptop, okay?"

Sloane watched her leave the room, seeing her the way her husband might. Athena was stunning—a woman any man would be thrilled to have on his arm. No man was immune to feminine charm and beauty, and he and Athena were spending a lot of time together. And what woman wouldn't be attracted to Whit, so handsome, charming, and at the top of his game? It hadn't escaped her notice that he enjoyed the admiration of attractive women, Athena included.

She sat up and took the mug of tea, examining it, then bringing it to her nose to smell. A slightly acrid scent rose from the mug. Athena was always pushing tea and smoothies on her, not satisfied until Sloane had drunk every last drop. And how coincidental that her hallucinations always occurred after Athena had brought her something to drink. Hope swelled in her. It wasn't the lupus making her hallucinate—it was Athena. She would prove it. These past few weeks the hallucinations had lowered her credibility in Whit's eyes. She needed to prove that she wasn't imagining things. But in the meantime, she'd be careful. No more drinking anything Athena brought to her. But she wouldn't let Athena know that. She would take it to the bathroom and pour it down the drain before Athena returned. From now on, the only things she would drink were beverages in a sealed container that she herself opened or water from the bathroom tap.

Sloane waited a while before calling down to the housekeeper. "Doris," she said over the intercom. "Has Athena left yet?"

"Yes, about five minutes ago. Can I get you something?"

"Yes. I need you to have some things picked up for me and run an errand. Please come up."

"Of course, ma'am."

Sloane made a list instructing her to purchase a small refrigerator and fill it with bottles of spring water and various juices.

"What can I get for you, Mrs. Montgomery?"

She handed Doris the list and the mug of tea. "Put this in a container with a lid and take it to the foundation and give it to Brianna. And make sure no one sees you do it."

"Yes, ma'am."

She called Brianna. "Doris is going to bring you a container with our tap water. I want you to take it to Carlson Labs; I'll text you their address. I've already called them. I'm concerned about heavy metals and they're going to test it. Don't take the lid off the container, it needs to stay pure."

"Of course. I'll take care of it right away."

Sloane disconnected. She didn't want Brianna or anyone else to know what she suspected—she didn't need others thinking she was paranoid. The company told her they could have results to her in two or three days, and then she would know if she was being poisoned. In the meantime, she'd only pretend to drink anything Athena brought to her.

She inched her body to the edge of the bed and swung her legs over the side. She took her smartphone from the nightstand and went to the security company app. What Whit failed to realize was that she knew the alarm system better than he did. She didn't need the control panel or any of the portable remotes to deactivate it. Punching in the code, she disarmed the alarm. With some effort, she managed to shift her body from the bed, and then stood still a few minutes as she caught her breath. She slowly walked out of her bedroom and down the hall to Athena's room. She wanted to conduct a more thorough search to see if Athena was hiding poison somewhere. As she was turning the knob on Athena's door, she heard heels on the steps and the unmistakable cadence of Athena's walk. Her heart pounding, she turned around and walked back to her room as fast as she could and shut the door quietly. She grabbed a book from the nightstand and sat in the chair by the window. She heard Athena's hand on the door. The door alarm! She grabbed her phone and stabbed at the keys, but her nerves made her type in the wrong passcode. With a shaking hand she tried again and failed. The knob began to turn.

48

ATHENA

Athena had taken the morning off to take care of some personal matters, not to go to the agency as she'd told Sloane: a
trip to the post office to retrieve her mail from a PO box, a stop
at the pharmacy, and last a return to her condo to transfer items
from her phone to the computer she kept there. Upon her return,
Athena headed straight to Whit's office to retrieve Sloane's laptop.
The thing was, she knew before even trying that she wouldn't get
in. She'd tried enough times while Whit was away and Sloane slept
to know that it would be locked, and she was right. If she'd been
able to pick the lock, she would have done so already, but Clint had
informed her that the Bowley was unpickable by anyone but an
expert. It wasn't even possible to have a duplicate key made without authorization from the company. Athena smiled. Now she had
a perfectly plausible reason to ask Sloane for the key. In her mind,
she composed the text she would send to Clint to let him know of
the opportunity that had fallen into their laps. Maybe that would
calm him down and keep him off her back.

Sloane was not in bed but sitting in a chair when Athena entered the room. She hastily tucked her phone between the cushion
and the arm of the chair, as if she were trying to hide it from
Athena. A book sat on her lap.

"Interesting book?" Athena asked.

"What?" She glanced down to her side and then back at Athena.
"Oh. Yes." Sloane frowned. "I don't see you holding my laptop. You
didn't find it in my husband's office?"

"I couldn't get in. His office is locked."

"Oh, for heaven's sake. This is getting more annoying by the minute. There's a set of keys in the brown box on the high dresser. Would you bring them to me, please?"

Sloane took the ring of keys and removed one, holding it out to Athena. "This is the key to the office. Please bring my laptop to me as soon as you find it."

"Of course. I'll go down right now," she said, taking the key in her hand. She held on to it as if it were a priceless diamond as she hurried down the stairs. Standing in front of the office door, she looked around, feeling suddenly foolish for being paranoid. She had every reason to be standing here with a key to unlock Whit's office door. There was nothing to be afraid of. She inserted the key into the lock, but it didn't fit. Not only would the key not turn, but it didn't even go in all the way. She pulled it out and put it in again. Same thing. She wiggled it around as much as she dared, trying all sorts of configurations, but the door remained locked. Obviously, it was the wrong key. Damn! She wanted to stomp her foot in frustration.

Back upstairs and in Sloane's room, she handed the key to her. "Are you sure you gave me the right key? This one doesn't work."

Sloane examined the key, turning it over in her hand. "Yes. It's the right key. It should work."

"Well, it doesn't. I tried it every which way. It doesn't even go in all the way. I was afraid it would break in the lock if I kept trying."

Sloane's face was pinched, her jaw clenched. Athena could see the wheels turning.

"Do you think he changed the lock?" Athena asked her.

"Of course not. He would have told me."

Athena thought of the times Sloane had forgotten something she'd told her. "Do you think maybe he told you and it slipped your mind?"

She saw a flash of anger cross Sloane's face, but in an instant a mask of composure replaced it. "No. But I'm sure there's a reasonable explanation."

"Shall I put the keys—"

"I'll take care of it," Sloane said, interrupting her.

"Okay. Is there anything else you need right now?"

"No. Thank you."

Athena moved to the door. "I'll be in my room if you need anything."

Athena could hardly contain her anger at the missed opportunity. But the fact that Whit had found it necessary to change his office lock without telling Sloane, or presumably any of the staff, meant he had something to hide. If only she could have gotten in, she might have discovered something that would make Whit's financial standing clear to her . . . whether it was all tied to Sloane, or if he stood to gain independence if anything happened to her.

49

SLOANE

Sloane closed her fist around the keys in her hand, feeling the sharp edges bite into the flesh of her palm. Had Whit changed the lock on Robert's old office? And if so, why? It didn't make sense. Maybe Athena was lying about the key not fitting. But that didn't make any sense either. Opening her hand, she looked at the keys once more and then put them in her night table drawer. She sat pondering when the chime of her bedroom door startled her. The door opened and Camille leaned her head in. Sloane felt a small leap of happiness.

"Camille!"

"Hey," she said as she walked in. "How are you? I've missed you, sweetie."

Sloane's eyes filled with tears. "I've missed you too. I'm so glad to see you." She held out her arms to her friend. As they embraced, Sloane breathed in the fresh citrus scent that Camille had worn forever. Camille sat on the edge of the bed.

"How's your mother?" Sloane asked, seeing the tension in her friend's face.

"She's improving. Physically, that is. But I think her injuries have impacted her memory."

"What's going on? Is she forgetting things?"

Camille shook her head. "She can't remember anything from the day of the attack. And she keeps insisting that Whit is involved in something shady despite Faye's assurances that he's not."

"What do you mean?"

"It's no secret she's continued to harbor resentment toward Whit, but I think it has turned into an obsession. Mom claims she had her friend Mac looking into Whit and that he found some-thing suspicious."

Sloane felt concern mix with dread. "What?"

"I tried to call Mac, her lawyer friend, but unfortunately, he died."

"Wait . . . She thought she spoke to a man who's actually dead? It does sound like the fall's left her confused."

"No, Mac died *after* she claims to have spoken to him, appar-ently from a drug overdose. I think he fell off the wagon. It doesn't sound like he was in any position to be doing investigating. And this all happened *before* she was attacked. I don't know what to think anymore. She says Mac brought her a report, but it's nowhere to be found. I wouldn't burden you with this right now, but I'm afraid she might call and bother you with all of this. I just wanted you to know what's going on."

Sloane frowned. "It seems impossible that your mother would be imagining this, but on the other hand, it does sound strange." She reached out and squeezed Camille's arm. "I'm glad you told me, though. You know how much I love your mother. Please keep me in the loop. And give her my love."

"I will. You take care of yourself. I want to see you out of that bed. Whit said that the doctor increased your prednisone. Is it help-ing?"

Sloane gave her a weak smile. "A little," she said, lying. She didn't want to tell Camille about the hallucinations or forgetful-ness. She loved Camille, but sometimes her take-charge personality was overbearing. Sloane didn't have the energy to deal with it right now.

"Well, you know I'm a big advocate of getting a second opinion. I know a great rheumatologist—"

Sloane put up her hand. She appreciated Camille's concern, but Dr. Porter was one of the best. She'd lived with this disease long enough to know that there was only so much the doctor and the medicine could do. "Thanks, but I'm sure this will pass."

She slumped back against the pillow once Camille had left, more worried than she'd let on. Could Rosemary really have imagined a report that never existed? It seemed awfully coincidental that Mac turned up dead. Sloane sighed. What she needed to do was talk to Rosemary and hear what she had to say. She chewed on her lower lip as she tapped the number into the phone, listening as it rang several times and went to voicemail. Sloane would call her later; maybe then she'd get some answers.

Next, she tried Emmy, but it went to voicemail. Between the three-hour time difference and Emmy's busy schedule, they hadn't spoken in several days. She reread last night's text from her daughter:

> Miss you so much! Sorry I wasn't able to take your call. New client with nonstop meetings. Remember to text me on this number. Since my company provides a cell, I got rid of my old number. I'll try you later tonight. Love you.

Maybe it was just as well they hadn't spoken. Emmy would be able to pick up on Sloane's distress and would be worried sick. Until Sloane knew what the MRI results were, there was no point in scaring her daughter. Besides, it was clear that Athena was skulking around listening in on Sloane's phone conversations. She didn't need the woman knowing how afraid she was. She already felt vulnerable enough.

Sloane sat up slightly, adjusting the pillow behind her as Doris came in with a dinner tray and set it on the bed—clear broth with a few pieces of chicken floating in it, a glass of water, and six saltine crackers. She wanted to enjoy food again, to savor a glass of wine while relishing the hearty meal to come. This was something that might be offered to a nursing home patient who had a case of flu. She sighed and picked up the soup spoon.

"Thank you, Doris. And please thank Yvette as well."

Sloane saw pity in the woman's eyes. "I wish it were more appetizing, Mrs. Montgomery, but I guess she has her orders from your doctor." Even though Doris had been with them forever, she still insisted on the formality of using honorifics like Miss and Mrs.

"Yes, of course. No worries," Sloane said with a smile she didn't feel.

"Well, if there's nothing else, I'll be heading downstairs. The senator and Miss Karras will be needing dinner soon." Doris shut the door behind her as she left.

A flash of resentment filled Sloane. Even though she knew she hadn't meant it that way, Doris's phrasing made it sound like Whit and Athena were a couple. She ate a few bites, then pushed the tray aside and rose, walking to the window. She flushed with anger when she saw Whit and Athena strolling along the back gardens. They were walking close together, and Athena shivered. Whit stopped, took off his scarf, and wrapped it around her neck. Fuming, Sloane called downstairs to Doris.

"Please ask Senator Montgomery to come see me."

In a few minutes, the bedroom door opened. "Everything okay? Doris said you wanted to see me."

"No, everything's not okay. Can you explain why you and Athena were out walking together, and why you felt the need to give her your scarf?"

Whit sat down on the bed and spoke calmly. "We were just getting some fresh air. We're both so worried about you, we just needed to walk it off. It was cold out, and I took it off and lent it to her."

Sloane pressed her lips together, anger still burning in her chest. Yet what else could she say without sounding like a jealous shrew? "Whatever. Listen, I want my computer back. I asked Athena to get it, but your office lock has been changed. Why did you do that?"

"I told you. I had them changed before Athena moved in. I didn't want to take the chance of a stranger going through work I bring home. There are sensitive government documents in there."

Sloane was stunned. She didn't remember that. "When did you tell me?"

"Right before your surgery. You said it was a good idea."

Sloane bristled. He had never said any such thing. Was he trying to gaslight her? There was no reason to change the original lock, and besides, she knew he kept anything sensitive at his Senate office. It was clear that he was lying, but she wasn't going to get anywhere by confronting him.

"Oh, that's right," she said, playing along. "Can you please give me a key to the new lock?"

"I already did, but I'll give you another set."

She suppressed the urge to tell him he was full of shit. Instead, she smiled sweetly. "Thank you. Until you do, will you please bring me my computer now?"

Whit furrowed his brow. "What? No. Look at you. You're too sick, and if you start working again, you'll get even worse."

"It's not up to you to decide what I can and cannot do. You're my husband, not my doctor. Whether I work or not is my decision, not yours."

"Okay, listen. How about we compromise? You rest tonight. Get a good night's sleep and I'll bring it back in the morning. What do you say?" His tone was conciliatory.

Sloane clenched and unclenched her fists. "No. I want it now," she insisted.

"Come on, Sloane. You're just being bullheaded. It's too late to do any work tonight. Why can't it wait till tomorrow?"

"Because I want to have it now."

"All right, you win. I'll bring it up to you later." He gave her the famous Whit smile, but something in his expression told her the laptop wasn't going to appear anytime soon. Why was he so intent on keeping it from her?

"Oh, by the way, I saw Brianna today and she said you asked her about a new shelter in Ohio and the grant for $150,000. You remember, we agreed to fund the expansion of an existing shelter in Cleveland. I'd even found a large donor to contribute to the project at the time. Anyway, Brianna and I got it all straightened out. Nothing for you to worry about."

Brianna had already gotten back to Sloane with the same information. But as for the new donor, Triad III, Brianna told her she had no information. Whit told Brianna he was still reviewing the file. "Yes, she told me. What about Triad III? Who are they?"

"Sloane, why are you interrogating me? You've asked me to step in for you, and I have. But I have to say, being questioned with suspicion is something I don't appreciate. Would you prefer I not be involved anymore?" His eyes were hard.

"No, of course not."

"Well, then please stop second-guessing everything I do. Focus on getting better. Any other questions?"

"No," Sloane said, still wound up.

She glanced at the phone on her nightstand. It was a poor substitute for her computer, but at least she had internet access through it. The downside was that the small print tired her eyes, and the words on her phone began to blur after just a short time.

"By the way," Whit's voice broke into her thoughts. "Athena said Camille was here earlier. You didn't tell me."

"Maybe Athena should mind her own business."

"You're being silly, Sloane. You *are* her business. So why didn't you tell me Camille was coming over today?"

"I didn't know she was. But why are you making a big deal out of it?"

"I'm not. I just would have liked to ask her about Rosemary. See if maybe she can talk to her about coming over when she's better, for a family dinner. I've been feeling bad, actually, that I've not tried harder to heal the breach between us."

Sloane looked at him in surprise. "Really?"

"Really. My parents are gone. So are yours. Rosemary and Camille are our only family. We need to pull together and be there for each other. I'm going to see that it happens."

Sloane felt suddenly remorseful for the tone she'd taken with Whit. "That's wonderful. I'm glad you feel that way."

"Well, you look tired. I should let you get some rest." Whit kissed her cheek. "Good night, sweetheart," he said, and left the bedroom.

Sloane stared at the closed door, turning things over in her mind. She felt trapped and defenseless, unable to trust those around her. "You can trust yourself," she said out loud. That would have to be enough.

50

ATHENA

Athena was exhausted. Now that Sloane was so sick, it felt like she was working around the clock. She opened her laptop and typed in her notes from today.

> Sloane slept fitfully last night, up at least five times. This has been the pattern the last few days. Muscle tone weaker. Mild confusion upon being awakened for dinner. Ate two crackers and one ounce of chicken. Must increase protein shakes. Speak to Whit about having new labs done to check for anemia.

Because Athena was not a nurse, her job requirements didn't involve direct communication with Sloane's doctors, so she relied on Whit to report back to her.

Once she finished her notes, she changed into her nightgown and brought the laptop into bed with her, replaying tonight's dinner conversation with Whit. Their talks had become more intimate, their walks in the garden a nightly ritual. She knew that Whit was coming to depend upon her to bring some relief and lightness to his burdens. Athena did feel a little guilty for keeping Clint in the dark about her developing relationship with Whit. If he knew that she was having dinner with Whit on a regular basis, she'd get a lecture that that wasn't part of her job, that she was letting the lines blur, blah-blah-blah.

She knew it was important that she maintain Whit's trust. She had to tread lightly, but it was her hope that Whit would begin to include her on the medical decisions.

She shut the laptop and got up, slipping on her robe. She should check on Sloane again before turning in for the night, although if the last few nights were anything to go by, she wouldn't be getting much sleep. The hall was dark, and as she approached Sloane's bedroom, she saw that no light shined from below her door. Deactivating the alarm with her remote control, she slowly turned the knob and crept into the room. Sloane was out cold. Athena shut the door behind her and walked to the foot of the bed, staring at the woman as she slept. She moved to the nightstand, turned on the lamp, and waited. Sloane didn't awaken. She picked up Sloane's cellphone and tapped in the password she'd watched Sloane enter the day they'd gone to lunch together. Athena smiled as the phone opened. She scrolled through the list of recent calls, then went to the texts and read through those. Glancing at Sloane to make sure she was still out, she opened up the email. She forwarded two emails that Brianna had sent to her own email, and then put the phone back. She turned back to the sleeping figure. Her breathing was shallow, and Athena watched as her hand jerked to the side in a spasm. She was definitely getting worse.

51

SLOANE

The next morning, Sloane woke up and looked in confusion at the nail scissors next to her pillow. Then she saw the hair scattered across the sheet. It took a minute for it to sink in. She lifted her hand to her head and screamed. Her hair! It was all chopped up.

Whit came running into the room. "Sloane, what's wrong?"

When she lifted her head, his mouth dropped open. "What happened?"

Sloane was so unnerved she could barely speak. She held up the small pair of nail scissors. "These were on my pillow. And all my hair." She pointed. "Can you get me a mirror?"

Whit took the hand mirror from her dressing table and handed it to her.

"My God, what have I done?" she moaned, turning her head from side to side as she examined her likeness. "This is impossible! I don't remember anything! How could I have done this?"

Whit sat on the bed and took Sloane's hand in his. "We're going to figure this out. But is there anything you haven't told me? There's no shame here. I need to know. Have you been blacking out, or forgetting things?"

Sloane didn't answer right away. Blowing out a large breath, she hesitated. She thought about her confusion at times, and about how she seemed to keep forgetting little things like the fact that Whit had told her about changing his office lock. Just the other day she'd had trouble remembering the name of Doris, the housekeeper who had been with her for over twenty years. "A little. I, um, sometimes I can't think of words. But this . . . this is horrible." Sloane touched her head again, and her face flushed pink. "What's happening to me? I feel like I'm losing my mind. It's been almost a week. When are we going to have the results of the MRI?"

"I called Friday, but they didn't have them yet. I'll try again tomorrow."

"Call Dr. Porter. See if he can rush the report."

"Absolutely. Why don't I get you something to drink, and then I'll call."

Sloane nodded absently, and Whit withdrew from the room.

The door opened again, and Athena entered holding a large mug. "Whit asked me to bring up your tea." She placed it on the table. "I'm so sorry that you're going through this. Would you like me to try and fix your hair?"

Sloane was too humiliated to place a call to her own hairdresser. She nodded mutely, then watched Athena work. "You're pretty good with those scissors."

Athena stopped for a moment. "Say, would you like to drink some of your tea before it gets cold?"

"I'm fine. Keep going." No way was she drinking anything Athena gave her. "By the way, I'd like you to put my medicines on my nightstand. I will resume managing them myself."

"Um, I'm not sure that's such a good idea. You're not exactly yourself right now. What if you get confused?"

Like a thunderbolt, it struck her that Athena must have snuck in and cut her hair in the middle of the night to make her think she was losing her mind. And to make her look ugly. It *had* to have been her.

"It's not open for discussion, Athena. I want it done immediately. Do you understand?"

Athena raised an eyebrow and took her time answering. "I understand. I'll mention it to Whit. I wouldn't be doing my job if I didn't let him know my concerns."

Sloane's mouth dropped open at the woman's audacity. Before she could respond, Athena left the room.

Were the two of them in on it together? She was going to find out. It would be a tricky dance going forward if that was true. She'd need to stay one step ahead of them. She texted Whit and asked him to come back upstairs.

"Sweetie, what is it?"

Sloane studied his face, recognizing that something in his demeanor had changed over the last days. He was not as rushed; he was more solicitous of her, staying with her for longer periods. Did his newfound hovering mean that he'd given up hope of her recovering and was doing everything he could to make her comfortable until the end? He never failed to bring up Harold's wife in conversation, ignoring Sloane's entreaties to stop. Was he identifying with Harold? Expecting that she would meet the same fate as his wife? She didn't even know the poor woman's name—as if her entire identity could be summed up by being the comatose wife of Harold.

"Whit," she said, her voice filled with determination. "I'm not paranoid, no matter what you say. Athena has become disrespectful, and I don't want her here anymore. I insist that you fire her."

"She's been a godsend, and you want me to fire her? Who's going to take care of you?"

"I'll call the agency. Get someone new. I'm sure Doris won't mind filling in until we find someone."

Whit exhaled heavily. "Doris isn't here any longer."

"What do you mean, she isn't here any longer?" Had something happened to her? Was she ill?

"I had to let her go," Whit said.

Sloane stared mutely at him; her mouth opened in shock. "You *what*?" She felt a hot stab of fury in her chest.

"I'm sorry, Sloane. I hated to do it, but she stole something. From Athena. I didn't believe it at first, but we found Athena's missing Greek evil eye necklace in Doris's room. We can't have a thief in the house." He put his head in his hands. "Sloane, I told you this two days ago. You don't remember?"

He had never told her! Adrenaline coursed through Sloane until she felt she would explode with suppressed rage. Athena was lying. And what about Whit? Were he and Athena working together to get rid of her? She swallowed and told herself to remain calm. Whatever was going on, she needed both of them to believe she trusted them. If they knew she had any suspicions, she was doomed.

"I'm sorry to hear that about her. Of course, you were right to let her go," she said. "You must be right; I'm not in my right mind. I'm sure the new medicine will help. Please don't mention to Athena that I asked you to fire her." Was Yvette next? They must be planning to isolate her here with just the two of them. She'd be completely at their mercy.

"I'm glad you understand. I know it's difficult. She's been with you a long time. I'm so sorry, Sloane."

She had to get help. She could call Brianna and tell her, but then she realized how ridiculous that would sound. If Whit and Athena were trying to make her seem mentally incapacitated, she'd be playing right into their hands. She'd left two more messages for Camille, and still no return call. She would try Emmy again and tell her what was going on. As much as she wanted to protect her daughter, it was Sloane who was in need of protection now.

"I'd like to sleep now," she said to Whit.

As soon as he left, she redialed Emmy. It went right to voicemail again. "Emmy, it's Mom. Please call me back. I'm in trouble here. I need you."

She hung up, terror vying with desperation in her mind.

WHIT

The following afternoon, Whit went upstairs to see Sloane. As he tiptoed into her room, he saw that she was shifting restlessly around the bed. He crossed the room and lightly shook her shoulder. "Sloane, wake up."

Her eyes opened halfway and closed again. "Sloane," he repeated.

"Hmm. What?" Her eyes were open now.

"How are you feeling?"

"Uh . . . I . . . I don't know. Okay, I guess."

She looked like hell, he thought. "The doctor is worried. Do you remember what he said?"

"The doctor? What?"

"What he told you today. About your condition."

Her eyes were clouded with confusion. "The doctor was here today?"

Whit gave an exaggerated sigh. "Oh, Sloane. We went to his office this morning. Remember when he called back last night, he insisted on seeing you today? He prescribed a new medication to reduce the inflammation. You don't remember?"

A tear ran down her cheek, and she turned her head away from him.

"Never mind, sweetheart. We can talk about this later." He rose from the edge of the bed. "You rest again. I'll bring your dinner up later."

He went back downstairs to have a drink before dinner, and saw that Athena was sitting outside on the back terrace. Putting down the bourbon, he went to the wine rack to pull out a Cabernet and walked outside.

"Mind if I join you?" he asked, sitting before she could answer, holding the bottle and two glasses.

"Please do," she said.

He poured wine into both glasses and handed her one. She closed the folder in her lap and placed it beside her on the bench before accepting the long-stemmed glass.

"Thanks."

"You're welcome. Work from the foundation?" he asked, looking at the folder.

"Yes. Just a little. Everything seems well under control. There are a few things for you to look at. Nothing urgent."

"Good." He held up his glass to hers. "Cheers. To fall evenings."

Their glasses touched, and he watched her take a small sip.

"Soon it will be too cold to be outside without a heavy coat. We used to live most of our lives outdoors in Greece," she said, pulling her sweater more tightly around her.

"You must miss it. This is beautiful, but nothing compared to the scenery there."

She sighed. "Yes, I do. There's really no place quite like it."

"Tell me about it."

"Hmm," she said. "You might be sorry. I could talk all night about Greece."

"I love hearing you talk. Go on. Talk all night."

She laughed and took another sip of wine. "Most people on the islands live rather simply. A lot of the houses are modest and unpretentious. From May until October, everyone spends most of their time outdoors. I barely ever watched television when I was there. Everything was lived in the moment. Lots of company, what the Greeks call *parea*."

"What does *parea* mean?" Whit asked.

"A group of friends who share life experiences. You're never lonely there. Everyone is very social. It's so different from life here."

"Sounds wonderful. Will you ever return?"

She hesitated before answering. "It's hard. After my husband . . . it was just easier to come back here. Too many memories."

"It's very hard losing someone you love."

"I guess I believed that when you've had the love of your life, it wouldn't be likely that you'd find another. Maybe I was wrong."

Whit took a long swallow of his wine. "I once thought that myself. Do you believe in the concept of soul mates?"

She looked surprised by the question. "Soul mates?"

"You know. Someone you're destined to be with."

"Yes. I do."

"I do as well. But you know what I'm discovering?"

"What?"

"Sometimes the person you thought was your soul mate is just a way station for your real one."

He sipped his wine and let the words hang between them.

"Do you think Sloane is your soul mate?" Athena finally asked.

"I thought so at one point, but I don't anymore. Can you truly be soul mates if it's one-sided?"

"What do you mean?" she asked.

"Robert was her true soul mate. I don't think she's ever really let him go. She's pulled away from me with her illness and talks more and more about him and how much she wishes she were with him. I wish I knew what he used to do to comfort her."

"You're doing the best you can."

"I hope so, but I don't even know what to say anymore. She didn't even remember going to the doctor this morning."

"Really?"

"Yes. No memory of it at all. The prognosis is not good, I'm afraid. Just more suffering."

Athena was quiet.

Whit skimmed the back of his hand across her cheek. "You know, I hate that it was Sloane's illness that brought you into my life, but I can't help but be grateful I found you."

"You shouldn't say things like that."

"Why not? It's the truth."

"It might be true, but it's not the right time."

"I wish we could put all of this behind us and leave together," he said. "That we could drink wine together in the country where the grape is grown. That you could show me the Greece you love."

"That sounds like an impossible dream," Athena said, raising an eyebrow.

He lifted his glass. "To impossible dreams," he said. "And soul mates."

"To soul mates," she said, and they drank again.

"This is nice," he said quietly. "Been so long since I've felt happy. Thank you." He reached out and took her hand in his, his thumb rubbing the top of hers. "This could be our life together," he whispered. "Wouldn't that be amazing?"

She turned toward him, her eyes shining. "Don't make promises you can't keep."

53

SLOANE

Sloane took a long sip from the bottle of celery juice next to her and closed her eyes, breathing deeply as she tried to stop the wild thumping in her chest. Lately she'd noticed more episodes of her heart beating erratically, like she'd been running, and then seconds later it would go back to normal. She wondered if she'd mentioned it to Dr. Porter when she'd seen him yesterday. Sloane remembered getting into the car with Whit, but that was it. Maybe she should call his office and ask for a recap, without admitting that she had no recollection of seeing him yesterday. Leaning on her elbow, she took the phone from her night table. His reception-ist answered on the second ring.

"Hello. This is Sloane Montgomery. I wonder if I might speak to Dr. Porter."

"Hello, Mrs. Montgomery. I'm sorry, but he left this morning for a few days off. He'll be back next week. Do you want me to leave a message for the doctor on call?"

"I'll call you back." She hung up before the woman could re-spond.

Had she really completely forgotten a whole chunk of her day? She tried to concentrate and think this through. Maybe Whit had discussed the doctor visit with Emmy. When she tried Emmy's cell, the call went straight to voicemail. "Emmy, give me a call when you get this message. It's important."

It had been three days since she sent the tea for testing. She should have an email by now with the results. She picked up her phone again and dialed Carlson Labs.

"Carlson Labs, how may I help you?" a man's voice came across the line.

"Hello, this is Sloane Montgomery. I've been waiting for a report on a sample I sent in a few days ago."

"Just a moment, Mrs. Montgomery. I'll look it up."

Sloane nervously drummed her fingers on the nightstand while she waited.

"Here we go. It was emailed to you yesterday," he said.

"What? I never received an email from you. Can you give the results to me over the phone?"

"I'm sorry, I don't have access to that, but I can leave a message for the lab manager to call you back."

"That would be great. Thank you." She clicked off the call and opened her email, scanning everything from yesterday. There was nothing from Carlson Labs. Could she have deleted it by accident?

She decided to read for a bit, to take her mind off her troubles. She went to grab her book and took a last sip of the celery juice. Picking up her book, she began to read, but her eyes started to blur. She blinked, trying to clear her vision, but it was no use. She threw the book onto the bed, exasperated. Now she was being denied even the simple pleasure of reading.

Suddenly, the book stood up on its own and began to dance in the air. Clashing cymbals rang in her ears as a discordant song began blaring. Where was that coming from? She put her hands over her ears. "Stop, stop!" The woman on the cover of the book leapt off the page, and her face came within inches of Sloane's. "What do you want with me?" the woman yelled at Sloane. "Leave me alone!"

Sloane screamed, trying to push her away. The woman grabbed her arms, pinning them to her sides.

"Get off of me!" Sloane yelled.

"Sloane, Sloane, it's me. Athena. Calm down."

She opened her eyes. Athena was standing over her, her expression inscrutable. "What happened?"

Sloane swallowed. She pointed at the book—which was now just a book again, lying inert on the bed. "I don't know. I think . . . I think I saw something. . . ." A deep sense of dread filled her.

"Are you all right?" Athena asked.

"I'm fine. I had a nightmare. Please just leave me alone."

Athena looked like she wanted to say something, but then she shook her head and turned from the bed.

When she left the room, Sloane grabbed her phone and with trembling hands googled "new treatment for neuropsychiatric lupus," hoping to find some new miraculous drug or protocol for stopping the invasion of the disease into her brain, but the articles were the same ones she'd seen for the last two years. No experimental treatments. Nothing new. Nothing to give her any hope. Maybe she was looking for hope in the wrong places.

54

ROSEMARY

Now that Rosemary was feeling better, she wanted to arrange a visit to see Sloane. She punched in the number and waited. It rang once, then went to voicemail. She frowned. This was the third time she'd tried to reach her. "Sloane, darling. It's Rosemary returning your call. Please call me. I'd love to come and see you." Rosemary sighed in frustration. She'd left three messages for Sloane and still hadn't heard back from her. She called Camille.

"Hi, Mom."

"Have you spoken to Sloane?"

"Not since I visited her last week. I've left her a few messages, but she hasn't called me back. I did speak to Whit yesterday, and he said she's been sleeping a lot. I asked about stopping by again, but he said Sloane doesn't want to see anyone. Said she's not exactly herself lately. He said they're waiting for the results of her MRI," Camille said.

This was alarming news. "What? Why did she need an MRI?"

"I didn't want to concern you, but apparently Sloane's condition has declined dramatically over the past few weeks. She's been hallucinating. He's afraid that the lupus is affecting her brain."

Rosemary blew out a breath. This was terrible news. "Poor Sloane. That's the one thing she's always been so terrified about. Does Emmy know?"

"I don't think so. He said that Sloane has insisted he not worry her but promised me that if the MRI results are not good he'd call her."

Rosemary didn't agree with keeping Emmy out of the loop, but she supposed that was not her decision to make.

She was still furious with Faye for making her sound like she was imagining things about Whit, but powerless to do anything about it. Camille had connected with Mac's admin, but she didn't know anything about his report. So Rosemary still had no proof. She thought about Mac, and grief seized her again. She knew there was no way he'd overdosed. Someone had killed him. The same person who had tried to kill her. Why couldn't she remember?

A chill ran through her. Camille had moved back to her own house a few days ago at Rosemary's insistence—she couldn't spend the rest of her life being coddled by her daughter. But Rosemary hired a security firm as soon as Camille had gone. They were expensive, but she could not afford to make herself a target again. Her musings were interrupted by the ringing of her house phone. She looked at the caller ID: Michelle Sommers. Finally! She picked up the phone.

"Michelle. Thank you for calling me back."

"Hi, Rosemary. I'm so sorry it took me so long. We were in Ireland visiting our son, so I only got your message last night."

"How nice. I didn't realize he lived there."

"Just for the next year. He's on assignment for his work. So, what can I do for you?"

"I know you and Peg were good friends, and I'm still trying to come to terms with what happened that terrible day. You mentioned to me that Peg was seeking advice from your husband."

"Yes. Not officially, but as a friend. She believed Whit was having an affair. At first, I wasn't sure I believed her, to be honest." Michelle cleared her throat. "You know, she tended to overreact. But then she showed me receipts she'd found, cellphone records. I'm pretty certain she was right."

"Anything else?"

"Oh yes. She was convinced he was hiding money. Found some receipts for expensive jewelry that he never gave to her. Stuff he couldn't have afforded on his salary."

Rosemary was floored. "That definitely sounds like proof he was cheating."

"Yes. Walter suggested she hire a forensic accountant to go through everything, but then, of course, Whit would be aware. And she was adamant that she didn't want a divorce."

Rosemary sighed. How pathetic that poor Peg still wanted to be with Whit after finding out about all of that.

"Okay. Thanks, Michelle. If you think of anything else, please call me."

"I will. Take care, Rosemary."

She knew in her gut that Whit was on the take, and definitely involved in illegal activities. The problem was that there were obviously some high-placed and powerful people in on it, people who could make anyone too curious disappear.

55

ATHENA

When Athena walked downstairs, Whit was on the phone. He held up a finger, indicating she should wait. When he ended the call, he motioned her over.

"Let's go outside. That was Dr. Porter. He's still away but has the results of the MRI and also the other tests he ordered before he left. The news is *very* bad. Sloane's MRI showed brain damage, not just inflammation."

"Is there anything they can do?"

"No. The neurologist suggested antipsychotics, but with the damage she has, Porter doesn't believe they would help. It's only going to get worse from here. I need some time to process it before telling her. Unfortunately, I have a dinner meeting, but I'll be home around eight. Let's talk then."

She went back inside and watched as he drove away. Things were coming to a head. Athena knew it all had to play out with precision if she was to get what she wanted. Whit's firing Doris would make things that much easier for Athena without the woman constantly observing her. Once Whit was gone, she went to the bedroom he'd been using since Sloane's surgery. The key to his office had to be here somewhere, unless he kept it with him at all times. She stood in the doorway and surveyed the guest room, one not quite as large as the room he once shared with Sloane, but exquisitely decorated nonetheless. Where to start? Going first to the low dresser against the far wall, she went through each drawer, careful to replace every item in the same way she'd found it. Next, she searched the closet, going through the pockets of every pair of pants and every jacket. With Whit's sizable wardrobe, this was time-consuming. No key.

The night tables produced nothing either. Then she had a thought. It was a long shot, but the only place she hadn't looked was the bathroom. Naturally, the room was three times the size of the average bathroom, Athena thought wryly as she took in the large vanity boasting nine drawers and a center cabinet in addition to a linen closet on the far wall. She let out a whoosh of air and sat on the commode before attacking all those drawers and shelves, when suddenly an idea occurred to her. Could it be? She swiveled around, lifting the lid of the antique toilet tank. Bingo!

Clutching the key in her hand, she hurried downstairs to Whit's office and, taking a deep breath, smoothly inserted it. The sound of the lock turning was gratifying. Finally, she was in. Closing and locking the door behind her, she leaned her back against it and took another deep breath. There was no time to waste.

A brief glance around the room made clear the reason Whit spent so much time locked away here. Beautiful leather volumes filled built-in bookcases made of mahogany so dark it almost looked black. The hunter green walls and jewel-toned rug gave the space a rich, warm feel. In one corner sat two leather wing chairs with a small round table between them. She took a seat behind Whit's uncluttered desk and pulled the handle of the top drawer on the left, the one that looked most like a file drawer, but it didn't budge. She quickly determined that it was the only locked drawer. Pulling two bobby pins from her pocket, she inserted them into the lock, keeping the one on the bottom still and wiggling the top one until the lock turned.

She quickly thumbed through the hanging folders until a thick one labeled "Estate Planning" caught her eye. She placed it on the desk and opened it. Inside were copies of Whit's and Sloane's wills. She took the phone from her pocket and methodically scanned each page, which she'd read later. Casting an eye over the other files, she saw little of interest—health insurance information, credit card statements, and other household matters—until she noticed an unlabeled folder with a red star on it. Bank statements in the name of an LLC, which she scanned into her phone before returning the file and closing the drawer. She'd have to hope Whit would assume he'd forgotten to lock the drawer. Athena looked at her watch. She'd been in the office a little over eight minutes.

Standing, she went to one of the bookcases and knelt down to open the cabinet doors. She blinked in confusion; her brow furrowed as she took a closer look. She couldn't believe what she was seeing. She snapped pictures of the items, one by one, then put everything back as it was. Rocking on her heels, she closed the doors and stood.

Sloane was asleep when Athena walked into the bedroom, and the sound of the door sensor beeping did nothing to rouse her. She would have to let her know later that the laptop hadn't been in his office. Sloane looked like death warmed over, but no wonder, Athena thought. Anyone would look like that with the combination of potent drugs she'd been given. Drugs that were actually making her sicker, not better.

After returning Whit's key to its hiding place, she sat on her bed, opened the PDF she'd scanned, and began to read. Finally— the answer she'd been seeking. If Sloane died, Whit stood to inherit everything. He'd already been placed on all the house trusts, and so the residential real estate holdings would be his. And now that he was cotrustee with Sloane of the foundation trust and in control of all its assets, all that money would be at his disposal alone once Sloane was gone. Sloane Montgomery had to die. And soon. She would talk to Whit when he came home tonight and make him see that the only merciful thing to do was to relieve Sloane of her misery.

56

WHIT

Whit was wiped out when he got home a little past nine. The house was quiet, and when he stopped by Sloane's room, he sat on the bed.

"How are you feeling?"

"Some pain, but I'll survive."

"Athena said you haven't been sleeping well and you refuse to take a sedative. I called the doctor, and he said sleep is integral to your recovery. You need to take one." He picked up the bottle on the nightstand and opened it, putting a pill in his hand, then passed it to her with a cup of water. "I insist."

Sloane took the pill from him, and he watched as she put it in her mouth and drank from the cup. "Good girl. I'll be back to check on you in a little while."

He continued to Athena's room and knocked on the door.

"How are you doing?" she asked. "Have you decided what to tell Sloane about the test results?"

"Let's take a drive. I don't want her to overhear."

"But with Doris gone and Yvette's shift over, there's no one here. Do you think it's a good idea to leave her?"

"I just gave her a sedative. She'll be out for hours. And we won't be gone that long."

They made small talk as Whit drove, until they reached Montrose Park and he put the car in park. He turned to face Athena.

"I've thought about this a lot, and I don't think I'm going to say anything to Sloane. What's the point of being cruel? It's pretty clear that she's not going to get better. I don't want to make her final days any worse."

"I have to agree. I don't think she's ever going to improve."

"It's so hard. I'm only coping at all because of you. The only thing I look forward to anymore is seeing you every night." He paused a moment, then went on. "I don't think I could make it through this if you weren't here. The outlook is so bleak. If only the doctor had given me more hope, but no amount of medication can reverse the damage to her brain."

Athena spoke calmly. "I haven't wanted to say anything, but I've seen this before. Once things progress to this level, there's no going back. The possible neurological disorders are horrendous. Physical things like peripheral and sensory neuropathies, paralysis, and seizures. And even worse, the psychological possibilities—confusion, personality changes, paranoia, mania, schizophrenia. The memory loss and confusion are already manifesting. There's nothing we can do except watch her suffer until she dies . . . unless . . ."

Whit's hand reached out to grasp hers. "Unless what?"

Athena squeezed his hand. "She could have a stroke at any time, descend into a vegetative state, hover between life and death. It would be cruel to let that happen. You know Sloane would want us to do something. Imagine this elegant, refined woman of such intelligence and charm being reduced to an incoherent and paralyzed shell of her former self."

Whit sighed. "I don't want to see her suffer either, but . . ."

Athena leaned in closer to him. "You know better than anyone what she's been through with her illness. How hard it's been. She's not a wife any longer. Sloane knows that. You know that she doesn't want to live this way. She's said the same thing to me over the past few weeks. We owe it to her to help her end her pain." She paused. "I know you can't bring yourself to do it. But I can. I'll be her angel of mercy."

"Her angel of mercy?"

Athena nodded. "Sloane isn't really living anymore. We have to end her suffering. You've been so good to her. The best gift you can give to her is to help her escape her pain. You know there's no hope for her now. We're only prolonging her misery." She gave him an earnest look. "You've told me yourself that she never wanted to end up like Harold's wife."

"She doesn't, and who would? I did promise her that I'd never let her end like that. I just didn't think I'd ever be faced with that choice. But I can't stand watching what this is doing to her. Are you really sure you can do this?" Whit asked.

"It's the only way."

He closed his eyes for a long moment. "I guess it really is the only merciful thing. If the doctor had given me any hope——" He sighed. "I just can't believe it's come to this. But I did promise her."

Athena gave him an encouraging look. "It really is the best thing. But you can't be here; it will look suspicious. You need to go out of town, be gone when it happens. Didn't you tell me the final inspection for the foundation's Richmond project is this week? Why don't you go there tomorrow?"

"Okay. You'll do it while I'm gone?"

"Yes."

"How?"

"I'll give her five extra oxy pills. It will be painless. She'll just go to sleep. Respiratory failure."

"And you're sure she won't suffer?"

"Positive. She's suffering now. This will end her suffering. This time tomorrow night, she'll be out of pain."

"I'll leave in the morning. Thank you for everything, Athena. You're the only bright light in this terrible situation."

She leaned in, and her lips met his, but she quickly pulled away. "I'm sorry. I shouldn't have done that," Athena said, looking down at her hands.

"Don't apologize. It's like we were brought together for a reason. You're my soul mate."

She gave him a long look. "I look forward to our story continuing," she said. "For now, I'm going to check on Sloane. Try and make her comfortable on her last night."

57

ROSEMARY

Rosemary smiled when she saw Emmy's number on her caller ID. "Sweetheart! How are you?"

"Hi, Gram. I'm fine, but I'm worried about Mom."

Rosemary wondered if Whit had finally told her what was going on with Sloane and the MRI. "Has something happened?" she asked.

"I haven't talked to her in over a week. Every time I call, it goes to voicemail. I get texts from her every day saying she's okay, just really tired, sleeping a lot, but it isn't like her not to want to talk. I called Whit, and he told me she's on some new medicine that makes her sleep a lot."

"She hasn't returned any of my calls either," Rosemary told her, beginning to feel an edge of uneasiness.

"Something's wrong, Gram." She sighed. "Did you know that they fired Doris?"

"What? Why?"

"Doris called me this morning to tell me. Whit accused her of stealing a piece of Athena's jewelry."

"That's outrageous! Doris would never do that! She's been with Sloane forever. She must be devastated."

"She is. That's not all. She said that Whit and Athena have dinner together every night and are always whispering conspiratorially. I think he's having an affair with her, and Athena set Doris up to get her out of the house. I'm scared, Gram. I feel helpless being so far away. Please, can you go to the house and see what's going on?"

Everything Mac had found came flooding back to Rosemary.

She was ready to blurt it all out to Emmy but stopped herself. Emmy was three time zones and twenty-three hundred miles away. There was no point in panicking her granddaughter until Rosemary went to the house and saw Sloane for herself.

Keeping her voice even, she said, "Aunt Camille and I will go over first thing in the morning, and I'll call you as soon as I've seen your mother. You can talk to her then."

She heard Emmy exhale. "Thank you, Gram. Please call me right away, okay?"

"Of course, I will. Everything will be fine. You'll see." Rosemary hung up, looking out the window at the darkening sky. There would be rain tonight and more tomorrow; the forecast was calling for severe thunderstorms over the next several days.

Next, she rang Camille, speaking before her daughter even finished saying hello. "I just heard from Emmy. She's not spoken to Sloane in days. Whit has fired Doris. Something is very wrong. We need to go over in the morning and see what the hell is going on."

"They fired Doris?"

Rosemary recounted what Emmy had told her. "Is it a problem for you to take off and come with me in the morning?"

"No, of course not."

"Good. I'll have Anthony drive me. We'll pick you up at nine."

Rosemary clicked off and sat back in her chair, feeling a growing apprehension. She'd assured Emmy that everything would be fine, but she knew her words were hollow.

58

SLOANE

Sloane spit out the sleeping pill Whit had given her and slid out from underneath the covers, her legs wobbly as she stood. She'd known for sure something was going on between Athena and Whit when, the other night, she'd crept to her window to overhear their conversation on the patio as they sipped wine together like they were the married couple in the house. The words Whit spoke, his voice warm and mellow, had been carried up to her with the night air. Words like "soul mates" and "life together." She hadn't been able to clearly hear their entire conversation, but there was no mistaking that Whit was romancing Athena. The young woman's face in the moonlight was filled with adoration as she looked up at Whit. Sloane had felt her stomach drop as she'd watched Whit touch Athena's hand.

She glanced at the clock on her nightstand: 9 P.M. A flash of headlights caught her attention, and she moved to the window. She watched as Athena got into the passenger seat of the Porsche, with Whit at the wheel. Where were they going at this hour? She disarmed the alarm and with great difficulty crept from the bedroom and walked to the hallway. The effort caused beads of sweat to roll down her neck. Athena's bedroom door was open, and the room was empty. She hobbled to the stairs and looked up. Maybe her computer was in the guest room where Whit was staying. She got up, not bothering to disarm the room chime since she was alone in the house.

She wasn't sure she had the strength to climb the stairs to the third floor, but she had to try. Inhaling deeply, she steeled herself and clutched the banister. Taking each step slowly, she paused to breathe between them, terrified of falling and hurting her hip. When she reached the top of the stairs, she sat on the landing and drew her knees up to her chest, willing her furiously beating heart to slow down. As her breathing became easier, she inched along the corridor, pain slicing through her body, until she reached Whit's bedroom. His door was closed, but a faint light shone from beneath it. She pushed it open and went in. The bed was made, and Whit's colognes and sundry items neatly arranged on the dresser. She walked over to it and opened each drawer, but no computer, only Whit's clothes. Moving to the closet, she opened it and saw pants, jackets, and suits—most were still in the closet in the bedroom they normally shared. Like the rest of the room, everything was arranged neatly. A few pairs of shoes on the floor, some shoeboxes on the top shelf.

Sloane blew out a breath. A small leather briefcase caught her attention. She'd bought Whit a Peter Millar for his birthday a few months ago, so what was this? Reaching up, she pulled it down, took it over to the bed, and opened it. Inside was a manilla folder. She pulled it out and began to read. As she did, a paralyzing chill went through her. It was a report. From Rosemary's friend Mac.

Her heart began to thud. How had Whit gotten this report—the one that Rosemary wasn't able to find? If the report went missing the night Rosemary was attacked, that would mean Whit was involved. Had he been the one to attack her? But why? A wave of dizziness came over her, and she put her head between her legs. In a few minutes it passed, and she sat up again to read over the report. When she reached the part about the HUD ribbon cuttings, she thought of Whit's idea to combine government housing with her new initiative at the foundation. What in the hell had he gotten involved in?

Clutching the folder, she returned the briefcase to the closet and sat back down on the bed to catch her breath. She had to call Camille! Suddenly, she felt something drip onto her hand and saw that her nose was bleeding. She jumped up, looking at the bed to make sure no blood had landed there. Whit couldn't know she'd been in here. She went to his bathroom to grab a handful of tissues and held one against her nose. She needed to get back downstairs before Whit and Athena returned to the house. She was about to leave the bathroom when she decided to look through the drawers in the vanity. Pulling them open one at a time, she saw each was neatly arranged with toiletries. When she opened the bottom drawer, she noticed a small red box nestled in the back corner. She reached in to grab it. Flipping it open, she gasped out loud. It was a Patek Philippe World Time watch. The same watch Peg's father had always worn and had been claimed for insurance money. Just like the one that burned in the fire that had killed him! She'd never seen a watch like this on Whit's wrist.

Sloane picked it up and, hoping against hope that it was just a coincidence, turned it over. Engraved on the back were the initials JMB—James Mitchell Barkley—Peg's father. How had Whit gotten the watch that supposedly burned in the fire? A terrifying thought occurred to her. Could Whit have set the fire?

Sloane put it back and fled from the room.

She began to tremble, her whole body cold and shaking. Only because adrenaline was coursing through her was she able to scramble back to the stairs and thud painfully on her butt back down to her bedroom. Slamming the door and pushing a chair up against it, she collapsed, panting. They were planning to kill her. She had to do something. But what? She was at their mercy. They could do whatever they wanted, and there was no one here to stop them. It struck her like a thunderbolt now, the reason she could never get through to anyone or receive calls from Emmy or Rosemary or Camille. Whit had to have blocked their numbers on her phone, but she could unblock them! Had he intercepted her email from Carlson Labs too?

Think, she ordered herself. First, she'd call 911. Tell them to check Whit's bedroom for the evidence. Then she'd call Emmy and the others. Tell them to come. Her breathing was growing more regular now. Sloane hobbled to the nightstand and swept her hand across its top, feeling for her phone. The phone, she realized with horror, that wasn't there.

59

ROSEMARY

The car pulled up to the tall building on Connecticut Avenue, and Rosemary peered out the window as Camille exited the glass lobby doors. Anthony knew better than to get out and open the car door for her. From the time she was a child, Camille had insisted that she could open her own door, thank you very much. A blast of cold air shot in with her as she slid next to Rosemary and gave her a quick hug.

"Good morning. I hope you slept better than I did. I couldn't stop thinking about Sloane all night, and that driving rain was so loud I could barely sleep," she said to her mother.

"I'm afraid I didn't sleep much either. Thank heavens it's stopped." Rosemary's back was rigid, her hands clasped on her lap, and the two women remained silent as Anthony maneuvered through the busy Washington streets. The drive took just twenty minutes, but every minute seemed like an hour. As the car pulled into the driveway and up to the front entrance, Rosemary felt a tightness in the pit of her stomach and closed her eyes, seeing in her mind's eye all the times her son had stood there to greet her when she arrived at this house.

Camille put a hand on her leg. "Are you all right, Mom?"

Rosemary opened her eyes. "I'm fine. Let's go."

Anthony had the wheelchair waiting before opening Rosemary's door, helping her into it. "Shall I push it for you?" he asked Camille.

"I'll take her. It might be better if Mom and I go to the door alone," Camille said, and guided Rosemary's chair to the front door, avoiding the puddles on the walkway. She rang the bell and they waited. And waited. Camille rang again. This time the door opened, and Whit stood before them, making a great show of looking at his watch and frowning.

"What are you doing here?" His tone was unwelcoming.

Rosemary wished she could jump up from her chair and knock his jaw off with her fist. "We've come to see Sloane," she said, glaring at him.

"I'm sorry, but she's sleeping. You'll have to come back another time. And please call before you come. I feel bad that you wasted a trip, but the doctor has asked me to keep visitors away. It's cold and flu season. We can't risk her catching something. And she can't have visitors tiring her out." He gave them a small smile. "I'll let her know you were here, and that you send your best."

"We have no intention of tiring her out. We just want to see her for a few minutes," Camille said.

Rosemary inched her chair closer to the open door. "No one has spoken to her. Her own daughter hasn't been able to talk to her. If Sloane is too sick to even speak to any of us, then she shouldn't be lying in a bed upstairs. She should be in a hospital being seen to."

Whit stepped outside, closing the door behind him. "I appreciate your concern, but I assure you she's receiving the best possible care. She doesn't need to be in a hospital full of germs. As soon as she's up to having visitors, you'll be the first to know. Now, if you don't mind, I need to get back inside." Turning away from them, he went back into the house, shutting the door in their faces.

Rosemary's heart was beating so fast she thought she might have a heart attack. "That son of a bitch," she said through clenched teeth. "He's going to hurt her, I know it."

"Come on. He's never going to let us in. We've got to get Emmy back here. He can't refuse to let *her* in," Camille said, gripping the handles of Rosemary's chair and wheeling her to the car.

"Just stay in the driveway for a few minutes while I make a call," Rosemary directed Anthony. She tried Sloane's number, although she knew it would go to voicemail the same way it had all the other times. It rang once. Voicemail. Just like Emmy's and Camille's calls. Had Whit taken her phone away?

"Mom, we have to call Emmy."

Rosemary had already tapped her contact. "I'm calling her right . . . Emmy," she said when she heard her granddaughter's voice. "We're at your mother's. Whit won't let us in to see her. I know she's in trouble, Emmy. You've got to get here as soon as you can."

"I knew it. I knew something was wrong. Can you try calling her doctor, Dr. Porter? Maybe he can tell us something. I'll book a flight and call you right back with the details." The line went dead.

"She's getting a flight. Suggested we call Porter. What do you think?" Rosemary said to Camille.

"You could try, but HIPAA laws are going to prevent him from telling you anything. I thought about calling the police, but what would I say? That a respected senator was refusing to let us in his house? They'd laugh at us," Camille said.

Rosemary's phone rang. "Emmy?"

"I have a one o'clock flight out of LAX that gets into Dulles a little before nine tonight. I'll text you the flight number."

"We'll pick you up and go straight to your mom's," Rosemary told her, and hung up. "She'll be in at nine tonight."

"Okay. I'll come to your house after work, and we can leave together from there," Camille said.

Rosemary nodded. "Good. We can go in a minute, Anthony. I want to wait a few minutes to see if Whit leaves. We can pretend to leave and then circle back. Just ten minutes or so."

A loud clap of thunder made the two women jump. Then the rain started. "Here it comes again," Camille said. "The torrential rain and thunderstorms that were forecast."

How fitting, thought Rosemary.

60

SLOANE

Sloane's head was pounding and every nerve on fire when she woke up. She discovered that she was lying on the floor. She must have passed out. Momentarily disoriented, she tried to remember how she got there when the events of last night all came rushing back to her. Whit and Athena. Plotting to kill her. The last thing she remembered was pushing the wing chair against the door. The exertion must have been what caused her to lose consciousness. She sat up and rubbed her legs, trying to massage the pins and needles away. She moved on all fours to the nightstand and braced herself against it as she stood on shaky legs. Everything she'd discovered came flooding back. That's right: She was going to call 911, but then she couldn't find her phone. It must be in the drawer, she realized, pulling it open. Pushing aside books and papers, she leaned in closer, but it wasn't there. Frantic, she scanned the room, trying to remember the last time she'd used it. *Think. Think!* The chair started to move, and she jumped.

"What do you have against this door?"

Whit.

She heard him groan as he pushed further until the door opened. "Sloane, what the hell?"

She feigned innocence. "I don't know. I must have had another hallucination."

She was light-headed, her pulse racing. She couldn't let him know what she'd found. She had to pretend everything was okay until she got her phone back. *Breathe,* she told herself. The door opened and he entered.

Whit stared at her, his face stony. It took every ounce of self-control to keep her expression impassive. His brow creased.

"You don't look so good," he said. "Let me help you to bed."

She resisted the urge to shrink away from him. "Just tired," she murmured.

He put his arm around her waist and half carried her to the bed.

"Do you know where my phone is? I want to call Emmy," she said, sliding her legs under the covers. "I haven't talked to her in a few days, and I just want to hear her voice. Can you please give me back my phone?"

He gave her a puzzled look. "What are you talking about? I don't have your phone."

She ran her fingers through her short hair, frustrated. "I always keep it on my nightstand. It's not there, or in any of the drawers." She might be forgetful lately, but the phone had not disappeared on its own. Either he or Athena had taken it. They were trying to keep her isolated so they could kill her.

"I'll ask Athena to come help you find it. I have to be on my way soon. I'm driving to Richmond today, remember? To make sure the final inspections go okay on the new shelter?"

She wanted to yell at him every profanity she knew. He'd never mentioned any trip to Richmond. He was trying to confuse her. But she wouldn't give him the satisfaction of thinking he was upsetting her. At least he'd be gone, and then she could call the police without him stopping her. "Have a safe trip."

He leaned over to kiss her. She wanted to pull away with every fiber of her being, but she kissed him back. "I'll call you later. Love you," he said.

Go to hell, she said to herself.

"I'm going to lock the door until Athena comes up, just to be safe." Whit had had the lock reversed the same time that the chime was installed.

"What? That's ridiculous. I'm not going to do anything! You

can't lock me up like a prisoner. Besides, you'd hear the door chime if I opened the door. I thought that was the whole point of it."

"Sloane, you just admitted you had another hallucination last night and pushed the chair against the door! And you almost leapt to your death the other day. If you have another hallucination, you could hurt yourself before we got up here. It's just until Athena comes up."

He hadn't seemed to worry about that last night when the two of them had left her alone. But then again, he had probably hoped she *would* jump to her death. Seeing it was useless to argue, she simply nodded. Once Athena came up, she'd get her phone back, and then she'd call for help. If he was going away, that meant she had time before they tried anything.

After he left, she got out of bed to keep searching. Fighting waves of dizziness, she bent down to look under the bed and the dresser, thinking maybe she'd dropped her phone. After thoroughly searching, she still hadn't found it. Despondent, she sat on the bed and rang for Yvette on the intercom.

Athena's voice came through instead.

"Where's Yvette?" Sloane asked.

"Whit gave her the day off. Is there anything I can do for you?"

They had thought of everything. There was no one here to help her. Sloane wrapped her arms around herself and rocked back and forth, a terrifying sense of helplessness filling her. "I need my cellphone. I have a call to make."

"I'll be right up."

Sloane squeezed her eyes shut, holding her breath to keep herself from sobbing. She had to appear calm. She couldn't let Athena see that she knew what they were planning. She heard a loud thunderclap and walked to the window. Rosemary's car! Thank God!

Why were they just sitting there? *Look up, look up!* she wanted to yell. She'd go downstairs. She turned from the window and went to the door, but when she turned the knob, it didn't open. Of course he'd locked it. Shit! Running back to the window, she banged on it with her fists, but a loud clap of thunder muffled the sound. And then it began to pour.

Whit hadn't let them in the house. Tears of frustration rolled down her cheeks as she pounded on the window in vain. She watched, desolate, as the car drove away until it disappeared from sight along with her hope of being rescued.

A few minutes later, the door opened, and Athena walked in, smiling at Sloane.

"I brought you a protein shake."

As Athena sat on the bed with the drink in her hand, a hot stab of pain radiated across Sloane's chest, constricting it so tightly that she thought she would suffocate.

She stared at the drink, wondering if Athena had poisoned it. She stalled. "Thanks, I'll have it in a little bit. Have you seen my phone?"

Athena shook her head. "Sorry, no."

"May I borrow yours, then? I'd like to call my daughter."

Athena hesitated. "Um, sure, I'll get it in a few minutes."

Tears of frustration spilled onto her cheeks and her voice rose. "I want to call my daughter."

The look on Athena's face told her everything she needed to know. She was never going to talk to her daughter again. Sloane felt as though all the air had left her body as she tried to take a deep breath. She was going to die in this room. She'd never see Emmy again; never see her get married or have children.

"Please, Athena. You don't have to do this. I need to call my daughter."

Icy fingers of fear crept up Sloane's spine when Athena stood up and shut the door.

She turned around to face Sloane and said flatly, "I can't let you do that."

61

ROSEMARY

Rosemary was still shaken from this morning's encounter with Whit, and although he'd been studiously polite, she'd caught the glint of steely coldness in his eyes. She tried to stay on an even keel until Emmy arrived tonight but was unable to concentrate on anything for long. Reading didn't help, and TV was a waste of time too. She checked and rechecked emails, and scanned news articles on the internet, but it was no use. All she could think about was Sloane.

Outside the weather raged, the slanted rain pelting furiously against the windows. This would be one of those storms that knocked out power and flooded streets. She decided the best way to stop thinking would be to take a short nap, and then her phone rang. "Hello?"

"Gram. My flight's been delayed because of weather. It looks like a bad one there."

Damn. Could anything else go wrong? "What are they saying? Do they have any idea when they can depart?"

"No, not right now. I'll just have to stay here and wait. I'll call you the minute I'm on the plane and ready for takeoff. Any news on your end?"

"Nothing. But no news is good news, right? Hang in there. You'll be here soon. I'll wait for your call. I love you," Rosemary said, and slid from her chair to the sofa for that nap.

"Mom."

She felt a hand shaking her shoulder and opened her eyes, surprised to see Camille. "Oh, you're here. I was worried you might have problems because of the weather."

"I left a little early, so it wasn't too bad. We can have a quick dinner and then head to the airport in about forty-five minutes. That should give us plenty of time."

"Emmy's flight was delayed. She called earlier to let me know. I'm waiting for a call from her. What time is it?"

"Seven thirty. Why don't you call her and get an update?"

Rosemary took her phone from the coffee table. There was a missed call and a text message from Emmy. She must not have heard Emmy's call while she slept. "I have a text from her," Rosemary said, swiping it open. "She's booked on a midnight flight. One stop with a layover. She won't arrive until early tomorrow morning." Rosemary looked at Camille in dismay.

"I'll stay the night, and we'll leave first thing in the morning," Camille said.

As soon as her driver stopped the car in front of Arrival Door 4 at Dulles Airport, Rosemary spotted Emmy waiting outside. "There she is," Rosemary exclaimed.

Camille and Anthony opened their doors at the same time. Rosemary watched as her daughter sprang out and ran to Emmy, wrapping her arms around her. As Anthony took Emmy's luggage to the trunk, the two women got into the car.

Emmy slid into the back seat and hugged Rosemary to her without letting go. "Gram, I can't believe this. If something happens to Mom . . ." She shook her head, crying softly.

The drive from the airport to Sloane's house in the morning rush hour was agonizingly slow, and Rosemary found herself drumming her fingers on the leather seat. When the car finally turned in to the driveway, they saw a black sedan parked in front of the house.

"Whose car is that?" Rosemary asked.

"I have no idea," Emmy said as Anthony came to a stop.

Before he turned the engine off, Camille opened her door and leapt out of the car. Leaning in, she said, "Come on, Emmy. Mom, you stay here for a minute till we see who that is."

"No way. I'm coming with you. Have Anthony get my chair," Rosemary commanded. Once it was brought around and Rosemary maneuvered herself into it, Camille got behind the chair and pushed as they went to the entrance.

Emmy punched in the key code, and as she pushed the door open, they heard voices coming from the living room. The three of them crossed the hallway and found two men in suits, one sitting and one standing with his arm perched on the fireplace mantel. They were talking to Athena.

"What's going on here? Where's my mother?" Emmy yelled angrily.

Athena and the two men stopped talking and turned to look at them.

"Emmy, I'm so sorry," Athena said, rushing to her and extending her open arms to the girl.

Emmy pushed her away. "What are you talking about? Sorry for what?"

Camille put her arm around her niece's shoulders. "Who are these men, and where is my sister-in-law?" She straightened to her full height and looked down at Athena.

One of the men stepped forward. "I'm Detective Monroe, and this is Detective Zelinski. We'd like to talk to you." He steered the three women to the sofa, and when they were seated, his gaze rested on Emmy. "I'm very sorry to tell you that your mother is dead. I'm so sorry for your loss."

"No," Emmy cried. "No!" she repeated, shrieking.

"How did she die? When?" Camille stood, her voice cold as ice.

Detective Monroe flipped back a page on the pad he held and, looking down at what was written there, began speaking. "Athena Karras, Mrs. Montgomery's healthcare worker, discovered her body at approximately 5 A.M. this morning when she went to check on her. She was unable to wake her. It appeared to her then that Mrs. Montgomery was not breathing, and when she touched her body, it was cold. She attempted to administer CPR, to no avail. Upon further examination, Ms. Karras determined that she had expired and called 911 at 5:22. A bottle of pills next to her bed will be taken for analysis." He looked up from his notes. "Your mother's body will be released to the family after the medical examiner's evaluation is completed—most likely no more than twenty-four to forty-eight hours from now," he said, closing the notepad.

The three of them sat without speaking. Rosemary was still trying to take it all in when Athena came over and knelt in front of Emmy. "It happened sometime in the night. When I went into her room this morning, I couldn't wake her. She wasn't breathing, Emmy. I tried CPR, but it didn't help. That's when I called 911."

"I don't understand. How did she die?" Emmy's eyes were red and puffy, and her tearstained face mottled.

"They're not sure yet exactly what happened. But I found a bottle of pain pills . . . oxycodone . . . by her bedside. I don't know if she got confused and took too many, or what happened," Athena explained patiently.

Emmy sprang up from the sofa and glared at Athena. "That makes no sense. Why didn't *you* give her the pain medicine? Why was it just left there by the side of her bed? And why would she be so confused that she'd take an overdose of pain pills? It's ludicrous. You're lying!"

"She had an early dinner, and then told me she wanted to sleep and not to disturb her until the morning. Emmy, please, listen," Athena said, rising to face her. "You've not been here to see the steep decline in your mother's condition. She was losing her memory, having hallucinations. She was terrified of what might come next. She wasn't herself."

"Where is she?" Emmy said, choking the words out. "I want to see her."

"Her body has been taken to the medical examiner's office for a forensic evaluation," the detective said.

Rosemary stared at him in incredulity. Her body? Forensic evaluation? Could his words to Emmy be any colder or more brutal? The poor girl's face turned white, and she looked like she was going to be sick. Rosemary hated herself for not having insisted upon bringing to light all she'd discovered earlier. If she had, Sloane would probably still be alive.

"Does Whit know?" Emmy asked.

"Yes. He's on his way back from Richmond, but I haven't had any updates. I can call his office and find out if you'd like," Athena said.

"I want to see my mother. Now," Emmy said, ignoring her.

Rosemary saw the two men exchange a look, and finally Detective Monroe nodded. "Fine. You can follow us to the ME's office. Ms. Karras identified the body, but as a family member, we'd like your identification as well."

62

WHIT

When Athena called Whit to let him know that Sloane was dead, he had immediately checked out of the hotel and begun the drive back to DC. He was glad that he hadn't been there to see Sloane's dead body lying in their bed or seen them carrying her from the house. Emmy was probably on her way to the morgue right about now to see her mother's body.

Life was going to be different without her. So much had changed. He thought back to his initial election to Congress and when he'd first met Robert. The senator had become first a mentor and eventually a valued friend to the new House member, coaching and educating him on all things political. Robert had gone over his speeches with him, even giving Whit access to his own speechwriters when Whit ran for Virginia's newly vacant Senate seat.

Robert had done a lot for him, he admitted, but he'd gone too far when he'd taken Peg's side. That had infuriated Whit. Who did Robert think he was, anyway, this rich senator who had generation after generation of wealth and patrician lineage behind him? What did he know about growing up on the edge, always feeling like you didn't quite fit in, wondering every year if your parents would be able to afford your private school tuition, taking charity from friends' families when they invited you to stay in their summer vacation homes or winter ski chalets? No one who hadn't lived it could understand what it was like to know you were less than, to feel like you were pretending to be something you were not and waiting to be discovered for the fraud you were.

"Shit," he said aloud as he pulled up to the house. The damn reporters were milling around outside. Whit stopped the car and got out as the reporters swarmed around him.

"Please," he said, "we'll have a statement for you later, but I would be grateful if you would give us some time for privacy while we deal with this tragedy."

"So sorry for your loss, Senator," a young female reporter said. "But could I ask you one question?"

Whit hid his fury and his expression remained bland from years of practice hiding his true feelings from the public. "Perhaps later. Thank you," he said, getting back into the car. "Ignorant bitch," he said to himself.

He pulled up the driveway and, getting out, he stood for a moment looking up at the house he loved so much. Now all he had to do was get through the next few days with equanimity, and all would be well.

It had been a hellacious week. Between the police investigation into Sloane's death and the constant barrage of the press, the family had been through the wringer. Throngs of reporters blocked the driveway entrance for hours in hopes of getting a statement from him. Emmy was an emotional wreck.

The medical examiner had released Sloane's body after he had completed the autopsy and found oxycodone, Bactrim, and belladonna, along with all the other medicines she'd been taking for her lupus. Clearly, the oxy overdose was the cause of death. The police had questioned all of them, but they were focusing their questions especially on Athena, as she'd been both the last person to see Sloane alive and the one who found her body.

Whit and Emmy had finished making the arrangements at the funeral home. The funeral would be in a week. Sloane's body was still with the coroner, as the cause of death was not yet determined to be accidental or the result of foul play. When the toxicology report came out, it would become apparent that someone had been making her sick. That was where Athena would come in.

They stood outside together, next to Emmy's rental car. "Before you go back to your grandmother's house, why don't you stay and have dinner with me," Whit said. "I could use the company. And besides, this is your home. You should be staying here."

She cast a derisive look at the driveway and Athena's Prius. "Why is Athena still here? Mom's gone, and I think she killed her. I can't believe you're letting her stay."

Whit sighed. He couldn't very well tell Emmy the truth—that he had to handle Athena with kid gloves so as not to be implicated in Sloane's death. "I know, honey. She'll be moving out in a few days. The detectives asked me to encourage her to stay until they clear her. She has dual citizenship, so we don't want her disappearing. I can't stand it either, but I have to pretend that we're on good terms."

"Well, they'd better figure it out soon. I need to go," she said, getting into the car.

Athena wasn't downstairs when Whit walked into the house. He went upstairs and knocked on her bedroom door.

He heard shuffling behind the closed door before it opened, and she stood there in a belted robe. "Whit." Athena smiled at him.

"May I come in?" he asked.

"Of course." She swung the door wider. "Please, sit," Athena said, pointing at the only chair as she settled herself on the edge of her bed.

"You've been so wonderful, Athena. So understanding. You're the one who's kept me going through all of this. I want to do something to show you how very grateful I am to you and how much I care for you." He pressed his lips together. "There are some things I want you to have."

Athena's gaze flickered, and she said nothing.

Whit got up from the chair and held out his hand to her. "Come with me," he said, leading her to his bedroom, the same room in which Sloane had died.

"What are we doing here?" she asked, her eyes darting around the room.

Whit strode to the bed, where he'd placed a small box. He removed the lid and turned to Athena. "These are some things I want to give you as a token of my appreciation for all you did. And for freeing Sloane from her pain."

Athena stood still, hesitating.

"Please. Come and see," Whit said.

She crossed to the bed, peering into the box, and gave Whit a puzzled look. "What is this?"

He took out a black silk kimono embroidered in silver and gold thread and covered in brilliantly colored floral designs, laying it out on the bed. Next, he lifted a blue velvet box, opening it to reveal a magnificent pair of pink conch pearl earrings.

"These are beautiful, Whit."

"I've chosen these because they have meaning. That is a Japanese wedding kimono. And the earrings . . . the pearl earrings are from Greece." He took Athena's hands in his and searched her face, hoping she would accept them.

Finally, she lowered her gaze and ran her hand across the silky fabric of the kimono. "Thank you," she said in a quiet voice.

He handed her the box with the earrings. "Get some rest now. We've been through a lot. Let's get through the next few days, and then we can make our plans."

They said good night and parted. Whit undressed, showered, and settled onto the cool, crisp sheets, relieved to bring this stressful day to a close. He had fooled them all. He fell asleep with a smile on his face.

63

WHIT

Whit had moved back into the main bedroom. He'd had it professionally cleaned and aired out, and all of Sloane's belongings boxed up for Emmy to go through later. He was surprised by how emotional the day had turned out to be and had gone to bed after he'd given Athena the gifts. It felt strange being in the large bed by himself, and when he first awakened this morning, he half expected to see Sloane's slim shape underneath the blankets. He was eager to get back to work and put this all behind him. Being in this big house alone save for the staff was giving him way too much time to think. In a few more days, they would meet with their estate attorney, and Sloane's will would be read. He already knew its contents, since they'd done their estate planning together, but it would mean that everything was officially over.

He thought back to the past two weeks and smiled. He'd orchestrated everything beautifully. He was finally going to be his own man, with unlimited wealth and power at his fingertips, and he wouldn't have to answer to anyone. All of Sloane's money now belonged to him, and it would make him an even more powerful force to be reckoned with in DC. The White House had always been a dream of his—now it was a distinct possibility. It was a shame that he had to cast Athena aside. He would have enjoyed consummating their relationship, but there would be plenty of women for that. He needed someone to take the fall, and she was getting what she deserved, after all. What kind of a healthcare worker kills her own patient? She'd probably done it before, so actually Whit was doing the world a favor.

He had fooled everyone. Especially Sloane. After Peg had accidentally shot Robert, Whit had seized the opportunity and grabbed her hand. Turning the gun toward her head, he'd slipped his finger over hers and pulled the trigger. Robert was dead and, in that instant, Whit knew he would take his place by Sloane's side. All he had to do was get rid of Peg. He had never planned for his marriage to Sloane to be forever. He didn't know how in the beginning, but eventually an accident would befall her. But then a better plan revealed itself. It had crystallized when they met with her doctor before her hip surgery, and Porter explained how certain antibiotics could cause a lupus flare. It wasn't hard for Whit to get his hands on Bactrim and change out her pills. Then all he had to do was look up things that mimicked brain involvement to make her believe she was losing her mind. Belladonna did the trick. It would cause hallucinations, and his research revealed where he could get it. He'd swiped the bottle of dilating eye drops from his eye doctor's office at a recent visit. Those were easy enough to add to her tea, or whatever she happened to be drinking.

But to really make her believe all hope was lost, he had to do more. It really was brilliant. He thought back to the things he'd done that made even Athena realize that the most merciful thing was to put Sloane out of her misery.

Like the time he went to her room when she was asleep. He moved around to the side of the bed and nudged her softly. She didn't awaken. He glanced at the nightstand next to her and saw the nail scissors. Athena must have forgotten to put the manicure kit away. He hated seeing things out of place. As he picked up the small scissors, an idea occurred to him. He began cutting Sloane's hair in uneven swipes. She'd always been so vain about her hair. She'd wake up in the morning and think she'd given herself a haircut in her confused state. He pulled a long piece in the front and cut it to the scalp. He stood back and admired his handiwork. It would push her over the edge and serve to further convince her that she had lost control of her faculties. Putting the scissors on the pillow next to her, he smiled at his inventiveness and retreated from the room.

And when he'd taken her from the house and merely driven around, telling Athena they were going to the doctor, it was all a ruse. There had never been any MRI or follow-up visits. It had been a piece of cake to fool everyone. He'd worried about Emmy, of course, and then he did some research and came up with the idea to spoof a California number and text Sloane with it, claiming it was Emmy's new phone number. He'd known that simply blocking Emmy as he'd done with Rosemary's and Camille's numbers wouldn't be enough. So he sent fake messages from Emmy to Sloane's phone. He'd also texted Emmy's real number from Sloane's phone while she slept, temporarily unblocking it, then blocking it again so Emmy's responding texts would never come through. He made sure to call Emmy with regular updates to let her know that Sloane was sleeping most of the time.

He did feel a little bit bad that Sloane had had to suffer, but with her illness, all he'd really done was hasten her demise. Wasn't it better that she had died in her prime, forever remembered as young and beautiful?

And now he could finally be free of Madelyn. Of course, he'd never stopped screwing her, and she was a good lay. But she'd gotten way too possessive. He couldn't wait to tell her it was really over this time. He didn't need her, Fred, or their money anymore. He was finally a truly rich man.

And what could he say about Athena? She had come into his life like a miracle. In the beginning, he'd only planned to frame her. To make it look like she was the one making Sloane sicker and sicker, until Sloane died when she accidentally took an overdose of painkillers. He'd made sure that the staff saw them dining together every night, taking evening strolls. When Athena had actually offered to help him kill Sloane, it had taken everything in his power not to whoop with glee. So far, no charges had been brought, but he had a feeling tomorrow would be a bad day for Athena Karras.

He picked up his cellphone and dialed Detective Monroe.

"Monroe."

"This is Senator Montgomery. I'm afraid some items of my wife's have gone missing. A pair of pearl earrings from Greece, and a one-of-a-kind wedding kimono from Japan."

Whit had waited for this day his entire life, he realized as he drove to the meeting. He hadn't been more than ten years old when he came to understand that those who had more looked down on those who had less, and Whit had always been one of those with less. His parents had always done well enough, but it was nothing compared to the over-the-top wealth of most of his friends. And then he'd married Peg and her money, but it turned out the joke was on him, because there *was* no money. And the envy that burned in him grew greater and greater when he looked at Robert and all the riches he'd grown up with. But finally, Whit would get everything he'd worked for, everything he deserved after all these years. The kickbacks he'd been getting from Dominic Peterson were peanuts compared to what the contractors were paying him.

It was easy money. They had made connections with a handful of General Services Administration officers who tipped them off to the bidding on the new HUD multifamily apartment complex construction. Then the contractors that Whit and his band of raiders worked with would come in just under the low bid and be awarded the project. Cut a corner here and there, padding with numerous "change orders," and there was money to be made for everyone. It had started when Bishop was governor and Whit did him a favor by backing a bill that increased funding to HUD for housing in his state. They became friends, and soon Whit was making more money than he ever could have dreamed.

There had been no hitches for a couple of years, until that idiot contractor made a stupid mistake and caused the Chicago fire that would have certainly ended all their careers if they'd been connected to it. The architectural drawings called for copper wiring, but to be a low bidder, he needed to save money somewhere. The

contractor substituted aluminum wiring, thus giving him a substantial savings, since copper was four times the cost. That would
have been okay if he hadn't used copper terminals with the aluminum wiring, which caused a chemical reaction that started the fire
six months later. The fire destroyed the building and killed thirty-
five people in a matter of hours.

There had been some tense moments when they all worried the
contractor would try to make a deal and roll over on them, but on
their behalf, Peterson had sufficiently impressed upon him the fact
that it was in his best interest not to do so. That is, if he wanted to
keep breathing. They arranged for his family to be taken care of
while he served twelve years in prison. To make sure they covered
all their bases, they had dissolved the LLC associated with him,
and were forming a new one today.

Smiling to himself, Whit turned onto an unpaved road that led
to the rustic cabin belonging to Vice President Bishop. Meeting
here guaranteed privacy. There would be no press or curious by-
standers, merely an off-the-record transport of the vice president
to his private residence by the Secret Service—no formal motor-
cade, no lights, no limos. A "flow of traffic" event with four un-
marked black Suburbans; one for the VP, two for the Secret Service,
and one for the White House Military Office. No stopping traffic,
no going through red lights, no noise.

As he parked the Bentley, he saw that he was the last to arrive.
He walked up the steps to the porch and nodded at the two suited
men with earpieces, who waved him into the large room that took
up the entire first floor. They were seated at a rustic farm table—
Vice President Bishop, Congressman Horner, Fred Sawyer, and
Faye Chambers.

"Come on in, Whit. Let's get to work," the vice president said,
beckoning with his hand.

Whit sat at the empty chair and gave the documents in front of
him a cursory scan.

"I think the first order of business is to review the list of proposed new projects and decide which ones we want to have our new guy win bids for. What do you think?" Bishop looked around the table.

"Agree," Whit said. "We've been to the dance before, so we have a good idea which ones are the most profitable. And it's time to start building in Chicago again, since our vice president's auspicious memorial address last week." There was laughter around the table.

"Okay, then," Bishop said. "Let's go down the list and prepare the required paperwork. We need to get this all signed and sealed today."

The work was tedious, and after two hours, Fred pushed his chair back. "I need to pee."

"Why don't we all take a short break," Bishop said. "There's coffee and snacks on the kitchen counter. Help yourselves."

Faye stood up and put a hand on Whit's shoulder. "Can I talk to you outside for a minute?"

"Sure." Whit followed her out the back door, where they stood on the grass together.

"You left me in a bad spot with Rosemary, you know. I thought you were going to have her taken care of in the hospital. I did my part to make sure we weren't implicated. Do you think I enjoyed letting that clown smack me on the head? I'm lucky I didn't have a concussion."

"I tried, Faye. The guy we hired was supposedly the best. If Lawrence hadn't come back to the house, he would have finished the job at her house. After that, the family was on high alert. It's not my fault she came through. At least he got the job done with Mac. And besides, there's nothing that ties either you or me to anything. Stop worrying. She's got nothing. Let's go back in now; I could use a coffee."

Back at the table, Whit passed out the papers for the new nonprofit they'd established. "Let's get these signed, and I'll file them with the state agency."

"Hold on," Horner said, looking it over. "I'm not sure I want my name on this. What if someone discovers I'm part of this LLC?"

"I've told you. We registered the LLC in Delaware because the state doesn't require disclosure of the principals. You don't have anything to worry about."

"But these things have a way of coming out. You know that the opposition is always digging around to find dirt. How can I be sure I'll be anonymous?"

Whit fumed inside and tried to keep his voice even. How many times did he have to explain things to this dolt? He'd never understood why the vice president had brought Horner in.

"For the hundredth time, Horner, we've set up four separate LLCs, each one owning the next, just to be safe. The resident agent is a dead guy with an address of an abandoned lot."

"But don't you have to give a contact number or email, or something?" he said.

Was this jerk for real? "Look, the Gmail address I created in the dead man's name is the primary mode of communication, and the state is none the wiser. There is no way anyone can connect any of us to the new company. We dissolved the old LLCs to stay one step ahead."

Everyone was looking at Horner. "Okay, fine," he finally said. "I guess I'll sign."

"All right, everyone." The vice president rose and nodded at each of them. "Job well done. Now we sit back and wait for the windfall."

There were slaps on the back and laughter as they gathered everything up and went to their cars. Whit couldn't stop smiling as he drove away, picturing the extraordinary new life he was about to embark upon.

They were back in business, all their problems solved. Sloane's death had eliminated the last one—how to hide the money. The succession of bank transfers until the money landed in an offshore account was becoming too cumbersome for the large amounts he was now making. But like a miracle, the Emerson-Chase Foundation had come to his rescue. Triad III was just the first shell company he'd moved money through. With sole control of the giant entity, he could now move money around with ease. It was just a matter of ironing out the final details. And then, no answering to anyone or anything. He felt like the king of the world.

64

WHIT

The next morning, Whit woke up early and in a good mood. Sloane's funeral would take place in two days—a private affair for family only—and then he could get on with his life. This entire ordeal had been hard—her illness had taken a toll on him. He was ready to go back to a normal life: one with no sick spouses, no clinging women looking to him to solve all their problems. After showering and dressing, he sat down and dug in, savoring the taste of the sausage—an indulgence he rarely allowed himself. Taking a final swallow of coffee, he grabbed his briefcase and headed to the foundation, where he would take charge.

When he arrived, the receptionist greeted him.

"Good morning, Senator. I'm so sorry for your loss. Mrs. Montgomery was a wonderful woman. Is there anything I can get you?"

"Thank you, Rebecca. Just some coffee. Black."

"Yes, sir. Shall I take it to Mrs. Montgomery's office?"

"Please."

He continued to Sloane's office, which would now belong to him. He'd already contacted a decorator to redo the office—he'd keep the de Kooning, of course—and combine his with Brianna's next to it. He needed more space.

He turned the knob on the office door, but it was locked. What the hell? He was about to go find Rebecca when she appeared in front of him with his coffee. He bit back his irritation and spoke in even tones. "The door's locked. Do you have a key?"

"Oh no, I don't. Let me see if Brianna's in yet." She scurried past him and was back in moments. "I'm afraid she's not in yet, but she should be here any minute. Would you like to have a seat in the waiting area until she arrives?"

"Fine."

He followed her back and took a seat, fuming. Firing Brianna was going to be his first order of business. He needed his own finance person anyway. One who would cooperate and be paid handsomely to turn a blind eye to all the money that would be flowing through the charity. He checked his emails and read through some news updates while he waited. At 9:05, she finally arrived.

"I'm so sorry, Senator. I didn't know you were coming in today. I'll get the key right away."

"I emailed you last night to let you know that I needed to take care of a few things this morning. I guess you don't check your email after you leave here."

Brianna didn't answer. He followed behind her as she wheeled down the hall. She went into her office and came out with the key. "Here you go. Apologies for not seeing the email. But I've been so upset with Mrs. Montgomery . . . I can't think straight. She was a wonderful woman. I'm so sorry for your loss."

"Thank you," he said coldly, and turned on his heel.

He inserted the key in the lock and opened the door. He could still smell Sloane's perfume in the air. Oh well, all traces of her would be gone soon enough. The high-backed chair was turned facing the window. Suddenly, it swiveled around to face him.

Whit's mug crashed to the floor and his mouth dropped open. He clutched his chest as sudden pain telegraphed across it. He must be seeing things. Impossible—Sloane, alive! Smiling at him.

He felt his knees threaten to buckle and grabbed the back of a chair for support. "B-but . . . how c-can . . . you're dead," he stammered, his voice growing hoarse.

She laughed. "That's funny. I feel very much alive." She looked past him and spoke again. "Don't I look alive, Emmy? What do you think, Athena?"

He spun around, almost losing his balance. Athena and Emmy stood in the doorway.

"I've never seen you look better, Sloane," Athena said.

Whit staggered backward and turned around to face Sloane once more. "I don't . . . I . . . I don't understand. We planned your funeral. How can you be . . ."

Sloane rose from the chair with an air of serene authority. "I'm very much alive, Whit. The only thing that's dead is your future."

His heart was pounding as he struggled to grasp what had happened. He turned to Athena, glaring. "What did you do? How . . . what . . . who *are* you?"

"I'm your worst nightmare, Senator Montgomery. The woman who's going to put your ass in prison." She reached into her pocket and pulled out a badge. "FBI Special Agent Athena Pamfilis, at your service."

65

ATHENA

It hadn't been easy for Athena to pretend to be falling in love with a man she despised, but her training as an undercover agent had served her well. Now she relished the shocked look on Whit's face. She had been inserted into the Whit Montgomery case by her bosses at the FBI soon after Whit began making arrangements to hire a home healthcare worker for Sloane. The investigation had started long before, but when the opportunity presented itself for Athena to get inside the house, it was too good to pass up. By that point, the FBI was also looking into the possibility that Whit was involved in the shooting death of his wife and Senator Chase. Despite the incident being ruled manslaughter and suicide, Athena's initial task was simple: determine the extent of Whit's scheme to defraud HUD and find out whether Sloane was Whit's partner in the scheme. If she stumbled upon anything related to the shooting, that would be a bonus. From the start, Athena knew it would be easy to grab Whit's attention and make him believe she was infatuated with him. Blinded by their arrogance, powerful men always underestimated her.

It had been a delicate balance, luring Whit to confide in her and at the same time making sure that Sloane wasn't suspicious or jealous. She'd had to make Whit believe that Sloane was starting to be jealous of all the women surrounding him so he couldn't be persuaded to let Athena go. She'd felt terrible about framing Doris, who was now back with Sloane, but Doris's suspicion of Athena had become an obstacle to the investigation. Her cover had almost been blown when Rosemary's friend Mac had found that Facebook page from her last assignment. Athena had been working undercover at a pharmaceutical company and hadn't realized a colleague had posted the picture of their softball team online. Athena's own Facebook page with her cover name had since been deleted, but unfortunately the tag still showed the name she'd been using on that assignment. When Athena read the text from Rosemary, Clint scrubbed the page, but it had been a close call.

At its core, this case was one of simple public corruption and fraud. Conspiracy to commit murder was icing on the cake. What Athena had never expected was Whit's scheme to kill Sloane. In the beginning, she'd suspected that Sloane and Whit could have conspired to kill their respective spouses in order to be together, but it soon became obvious that Sloane had deeply loved Robert. Athena quickly realized that Sloane had nothing to do with her husband's death. From day one, Athena recorded all of her conversations with both Whit and Sloane.

When Athena finally gained access to Whit's office, she discovered the Bactrim, belladonna, and strong sedatives in his bookcase. Her training as a naturopathic doctor made it easy for her to put the pieces together. She realized that it wasn't the lupus, but Whit who had been making Sloane sick.

Once she found everything, she knew they had to get Sloane out right away. She'd called Clint.

"Things have gone sideways in a hurry."

"Shit, what happened?" he asked.

"He's been poisoning her. It was never the lupus. It's been Whit all along."

"Whoa, slow down. What are you talking about?"

She told him what she'd found in Whit's office and what it meant.

He whistled. "Good thing you have a medical background. What the hell? So that's why he made her sign him as a trustee on the foundation. We've got to stop the operation . . . right now. And we need to get her into a hospital ASAP and determine how bad off she is."

"I know! I bought us a little time, though. Maybe there's a way to still get the evidence on the VP."

"No. There's no time. What if he plans on finishing her off tomorrow? We can't take that chance."

"Well, I know he isn't going to kill her by tomorrow."

"How can you be so sure?"

"Because I convinced him to leave the house for a few days."

"How did you do that?"

"I may have told him that I would . . . kill her . . . and that maybe it would be better if he wasn't around when I did it."

"What? Have you lost your mind?"

"I'll keep watch over her room tonight. He'll be gone in the morning, then I'll tell Sloane everything and we can plan our next move."

The next morning, she'd gone to Sloane as soon as Whit left for Virginia.

Sloane looked terrified when Athena walked into the bedroom. "I need to call Emmy."

"I can't let you do that," she'd told her.

Sloane had shrunk back. "I know what you're doing. You're going to kill me!"

"It's okay. I'm here to help you." Athena pulled a chair up next to the bed and took Sloane's hand in hers. "I'm not who you think I am."

Sloane sat in shocked disbelief as Athena disclosed everything to her.

"I don't understand," Sloane said. "If you're FBI, then you have no medical training? You've been lying all this time, taking care of me with no idea what you're doing? How did you even get the job?"

Athena put a hand up. "I'm a naturopath by training, and for the last two years I've worked as an undercover agent for the FBI. The care agency has no knowledge of my real identity, but, well, the FBI can arrange things without seeming to. We've been monitoring all your phones, and when Whit called to make the request for a home healthcare worker, we moved in. It isn't the lupus that's been making you sick; it's Whit. He's been giving you Bactrim, as well as belladonna. I found it in his office yesterday. That's why you've been having hallucinations, fever, mental confusion. Belladonna is poisonous. Bactrim exacerbates lupus flares. And you're sleeping so much because he's been dosing you with sedatives. We need to get you to a hospital. Have you checked out and see what needs to be done to try and reverse the damage he caused."

"Belladonna? Isn't that a plant?"

Athena nodded. "It's used in homeopathy, but it can be poisonous. You might have heard of nightshade. People have mistakenly eaten the berries and died. He was adding it to your tea and other drinks. Easy enough to do with eyedrops used by ophthalmologists, which aren't harmful as eyedrops, but when consumed, very poisonous. He somehow got his hands on a bottle."

"So all those times he said he took me to the doctor, when I couldn't remember—he was lying?"

Athena nodded. "At the time, I thought you really were sick, so I didn't suspect anything like that. My handler, Clint Winston, said the surveillance team that was following him saw him drive you to a medical building and go in, but of course they didn't follow him inside. Clint tried to determine whether you'd been seen, but they wouldn't tell him due to privacy concerns. My guess is that he never took you in to actually see the doctor, but you can call the office yourself and confirm."

Sloane shook her head, her mouth open but saying nothing. Finally, she burst into tears. "He made me believe I was losing my mind! I bet there was never any MRI either. Why would he do it? I'm no threat to his career."

Athena waited for the shock of Whit's machinations to sink in before she delivered the next bombshell. "We've also been investigating him for Robert's and Peg's deaths. We have even turned up evidence that he was involved in the death of her parents. We believe he's planned to kill you from the very beginning. Your foundation is the perfect vehicle for him to launder money."

"He did kill them! I found Peg's father's watch. The one supposedly destroyed in the fire. And a report he stole from Rosemary!"

Athena listened rapt as Sloane filled her in on what she'd found in the guest room last night.

Sloane's lips were pressed in fury. "He is absolute filth. And if he is responsible for Robert's death too . . ." She began to cry again, shaking her head back and forth in disbelief. "I married this monster. I moved him into our house!" She rocked forward, wrapping her arms around her knees. "What have I done? How could I be so stupid! He should be put away somewhere forever." Sloane's breath was coming too fast, getting ragged.

Athena put a hand on her arm. "Try to calm down. I'm here to help you. The FBI has been watching everything he does. We have the proof to put him away on everything but Robert's and Peg's murders. We have information from Congressman Horner that Vice President Bishop is involved, and Horner's helping to get us proof. But I can't risk leaving you here any longer."

Sloane's face looked even more gaunt than usual. Her eyes met Athena's. "What are you going to do?"

"I need to get you out of this house. You're very sick." She took a breath, giving Sloane time to absorb what she was telling her. "I've been playing him, making him think I'm falling for him. I told him I would give you a fatal dose of sleeping pills tonight while he's away."

"What? Why don't you arrest him now?"

"We're planning to. We had hoped to wait until after Whit's meeting with the VP, Congressman Horner, and a few others in four days. Horner is working with us and was going to be wired for the meeting." Athena gave Sloane a brief summary of how the conspirators were stealing money from HUD housing projects. "We needed Whit to get the vice president on record, proving that he's a part of the scheme. We think they were involved with the contractor who was arrested in connection with the Chicago fire. But we can't risk your life. We have to get you out now. Once that happens, Whit will know we're onto him."

"What? All those innocent people who died . . . The children! They profited off of that as well. They have to pay," Sloane said.

Athena was all too aware of the tragic consequences of Whit's greed and what it had cost her. Her own husband had died in the fire that was caused by the contractor Whit and his fellow criminals had helped scam into being awarded the building contract. She wanted them all to pay—it was the reason she'd been so dedicated to this case—but no matter how much she wanted justice for her husband, she couldn't allow Sloane to become collateral damage. "Whit will pay. We can arrest him. But I'm afraid the vice president will get away with it."

"No! He has to be exposed. I don't understand. Why do you have to abandon it if you arrest Whit?"

"Once we take you out of the house and the FBI takes him into custody, the investigation falls apart, because the meeting with the VP will never happen. The reason we've been waiting was to get to Bishop. But we have to get you out now, get you to a hospital."

"No, you can't let Bishop get away. You can't let him go on stealing from people, ruining lives. Whit already thinks you're going to kill me. What if you do?"

That was when they'd come up with the plan. They had to make it look real. Athena's 5:22 A.M. call brought the arrival of an FBI agent, posing as a medical examiner, to take the body away. The police were brought in on the operation to convince the remaining household staff that Sloane was really dead. But it still had been surreal for Athena to watch Sloane wheeled out on a gurney with a sheet covering her from head to foot.

Sloane was moved to a safe location in the hospital, where she waited—until Athena brought Emmy to her. The three of them huddled in the room, outlining the plans for the coming days—the planning of the funeral, their confrontation with Whit, the police follow-up.

"What about Gram? And Aunt Camille?" Emmy had asked. "Can I tell them the truth?"

"We can't take the chance of their knowing your mother is alive. Something might slip. It's too risky," Athena had told her. "It will only be for a few more days."

66

WHIT

Whit was still struggling to grasp what had happened over the past twenty-four hours. How the hell could he have been so duped? Athena, an FBI agent? Making him believe Sloane was dead. Horner being wired for their meeting. Now it made sense to him why that traitor was asking all those ridiculous questions. Whit wanted to wrap his hands around Athena's neck and squeeze the life out of her. His face burned with fury as he played her interrogation over in his head. After he was arrested, they'd taken him to the federal courthouse in DC and stuck him in a windowless room while he waited for his lawyer. The smug look on her face infuriated him.

"You treacherous bitch," he'd spat at her. "All those dinners and long conversations. It was all bullshit."

Unruffled, she took a seat across from him. "Do you kiss your mother with that mouth?"

He glared at her. "How dare you come and live in my house and pretend to take care of my wife. Is that even legal?"

Ignoring his question, she folded her hands in front of her and leaned forward. "We've been watching you for a long time now. But we didn't know for sure that you were a cold-blooded killer. We know all about kickbacks from the contractors, rigging the bid process, stealing from the American people. How can you look yourself in the mirror, knowing all the pain you've caused to so many people?"

"I'm not saying anything to you until my lawyer gets here." Whit didn't understand why he hadn't yet arrived. He'd placed the call as soon as he'd been arrested.

"See you at the bail hearing," she said. "There's someone else who wants to see you."

The door opened, and Sloane walked in as Athena left. Despite still appearing frail, she looked better than she had in weeks. She took a seat across from him, her eyes cold.

"I just want to know one thing. Did you kill Robert?"

"Of course not. Peg did, you know——"

She put a hand up. "I don't even know why I bothered asking. Like I can believe a word that comes out of your mouth. You are loathsome, Whit Montgomery. A sociopath. That's the only explanation I can come up with to explain how you could do all the unconscionable things you've done." She narrowed her eyes. "Making me believe I was losing my mind. Dosing me with things to make me hallucinate and make my lupus worse. What kind of an evil person does that?"

"Sloane, you don't understand."

She stood. "You're right. I could never understand what drives someone as depraved as you. I hope you rot in prison for the rest of your life. Do you even feel guilty about those poor people who lost their lives in that fire because your inferior contractor cut corners? It's your fault that all of those people are dead."

"You can't blame me for that. I had no idea that he would screw up the electrical."

"You don't take the blame for anything, do you? I'm not going to waste another breath on you. I'm just glad they'll put you away where you can't hurt anyone else." She stood and walked to the door, opening it. Stopping, she turned around and looked at him. "Athena tells me it's worse for good-looking men in prison. I have a feeling you're going to learn the meaning of regret."

Before he could respond, his lawyer, Adrian Hodges, came into the room. "The judge is ready for you now." The marshal escorted them down the hallway and into a courtroom. After the charges were read, Whit pled not guilty, and his lawyer asked for bail.

The assistant U.S. attorney, an uptight bitch with slick black hair and a short skirt, gave him a disgusted look, then turned to the judge.

"Your Honor, we ask that the defendant be held without bail. Not only does he pose a serious threat to any witnesses related to the fraud and public corruption charges, he is a substantial flight risk."

Adrian countered with his argument. "My client is a respected senator, a pillar of the community with no prior offenses. He poses no threat to anyone, and to deny him bail is a gross miscarriage of justice. He can surrender his passport and post his houses as collateral. They have a combined value of over thirty million dollars."

The judge made a decision. "Bail is set at twenty-five million dollars, with the houses as collateral. The defendant will surrender his passport and will not leave the state."

Short Skirt gave Whit a nasty smile. "Your Honor, none of the houses are owned by Senator Montgomery. They are in trusts, and his name has been removed from them. And considering that he tried to kill his wife, I sincerely doubt she'd be willing to put any of them up as collateral. Additionally, all assets in his name have been frozen, pending the outcome of the public corruption and fraud charges."

"In that case, bail is denied." The gavel came down sharply.

Whit turned to his attorney. "Do something!"

"I'm sorry, Whit. We'll have to regroup. Nothing I can do right now."

As he was leaving the courthouse, Athena stopped for a final dig.

"Just for the record, I was never attracted to you. In fact, being around you made my skin crawl, you malignant narcissist." She pulled something from her pocket. "Here." She handed him a large blue stone with a painted evil eye on it. "My turn to give you a present. Where you're going, you're going to need it."

67

ROSEMARY

Rosemary had one stop to make before picking up Camille. As Anthony made the familiar turn, she opened her purse and took out her compact and refreshed her lipstick. When the car came to a stop, he opened her door and helped her out.

"Would you like me to walk you up, ma'am?" he asked.

"No, thank you. Just hand me my cane."

She took a deep breath after she rang the bell and waited for the door to open. A uniformed woman ushered her in and showed her to a room off the hallway.

Faye was waiting for her, and despite everything, Rosemary's first impulse was to embrace her old friend. But common sense prevailed, and she simply nodded instead.

"Thank you for coming," Faye said, her voice shaking. She looked as though she'd aged ten years since Rosemary last saw her.

Her eyes rested on the electronic ankle bracelet around Faye's leg.

"I didn't do it for you. I came because I'm hoping to understand. Why?"

Faye sighed. "I lost my way. I don't know. Maybe it was after Reggie died. You know, he was the straight arrow, the one who kept me constant. Afterward——" She stopped, lost in thought, then her hand flew to her mouth. "Where are my manners? Would you like some tea, coffee?"

Rosemary shook her head. "This isn't a social visit, Faye. I'm not staying long. I just want to hear from your mouth how it is that you almost had me killed."

"Never one to beat about the bush," Faye joked weakly. "I never wanted to hurt you. It started off innocently enough; go along on the vote and be included in the boys' club. I wasn't born with a silver spoon like you and Reggie, and despite his family money, his inheritance had to be split with five siblings."

"So what are you saying? That you were poor? You had to do it? You've lived a privileged life yourself, Faye. If you were anyone else, you'd be sitting in jail right now awaiting trial. But you get house arrest because of your connections. I'm so disappointed that you let your greed turn you into this." She was beginning to think that coming here had been an exercise in futility.

Faye shrugged. "Everyone in this town is greedy. It's easy to pretend you're not, when you have all the money you could ever want. But it's not just the money. I liked being included. Finally being on the inside after all the years only looking in. Politics isn't exactly kind to women. And I got used to the money. When you started looking into things, I panicked."

"Well, I hope it was worth it. All those people died in that fire. How can you sleep at night?"

"I had nothing to do with that."

"What about Mac? He was my friend. How could you?"

Faye's expression remained neutral. "I have no idea what you're talking about. From what I understand, Mac fell off the wagon. So sad."

Rosemary shook her head. "I don't even know who you are anymore. I'm so disappointed in you."

Faye narrowed her eyes. "You're disappointed in me? Who cares? Why couldn't you just mind your own business?"

Rosemary shook her head in disgust and stood. "Goodbye, Faye. God help you."

She turned and, not bothering to wait for any response, walked out of the house. "I'm finished here, Anthony," she said as he shut the car door.

"Ms. Camille's now?" he said as they drove away.

"Yes."

She leaned back in her seat and closed her eyes, thinking of all that had been lost in the past few years. First, Peg's parents—her dear brother and his wife. Despite there being no proof, she still believed that Whit was responsible for their deaths. Then her darling Robert and Peg. Rosemary supposed she would never know the truth of what actually happened that day. One thing was for sure; they had coddled Peg way too much. It was the one area of disagreement between Sloane and Robert, and Rosemary used to think Sloane was being unreasonable. But now she saw that Sloane had been right. Maybe if they'd made Peg take more responsibility for herself, Robert would still be alive. It was a source of guilt the two women shared.

She wished she had known that Athena was an FBI agent. Then Rosemary wouldn't have played amateur detective, and Mac too would still be alive. *Stop*, she told herself. *You were only doing what you thought was right.* If she'd learned one thing in her eighty-two years, it was that most things are out of our control. The best we can do is live with integrity and purpose and try our utmost to do our best. She'd devoted her life to her family, loved them with her whole heart, but in the end had been powerless to keep them safe. It wasn't her job, after all. Her job was to love, to help, and to pray for them—and that, she knew, she had done well.

68

ATHENA

Athena closed the door of the whitewashed bungalow behind her and strolled along the pebble path to the beach, where she sat on the low stone wall, burrowing her toes in the cool sand. It was early, the sun still low in the sky, but the day promised to be a hot one. She scanned the blue-green water of the Aegean Sea and breathed in the heady mixture of salt air and fragrant wild oregano. She was home. Crete—the Greek island where her parents had been born, and the place Athena had always felt so connected to. Although she'd been born in America, this was the place that held her history and the soul of every one of her ancestors.

After Whit's arrest, Athena took some long overdue leave from the bureau. The case had taken a greater toll than she'd expected, and at the end, the tension and stress had been almost unbearable. It was as if she'd been holding her breath for all those weeks, and only now could finally exhale.

The case ended successfully. The vice president received double the usual sentence for a public corruption charge due to the loss of lives from the faulty wiring. Even though the contractor had been charged with manslaughter, not Bishop, the judge was disgusted by his involvement and gave him the maximum of five years. After his arrest, Whit agreed to a deal in which he pled guilty to the attempted murder of Sloane and the public corruption charges in order to avoid a trial and charges regarding Mac's murder and Rosemary's assault. Instead of a potential life sentence, he got fifteen years. Sloane had immediately initiated divorce proceedings. His assets were gone, and his life, for all intents and purposes, was over.

He had been clever enough, Athena thought. Despite analysis indicating that the fire had been arson, no concrete evidence tied Whit to it. His claim that the watch in his possession had been given to him by Peg's mother before the fire was impossible to disprove. The insurance company could pursue charges against him for fraud, but they'd have a hard time collecting the money, as his assets were all gone. There was also insufficient evidence to prove that he'd murdered Peg. The other politicians, as well as the GSA insiders who awarded the contractor bids in states that had been complicit in the scam, all went down. The only one who escaped unscathed was Madelyn, who was now free to enjoy her husband's money without the encumbrance of his presence.

Naturally, Athena had moved back to her own apartment, but she'd continued to see Sloane over the next ten months, and a strong bond was forged between them. It was wonderful to watch Sloane become healthier each week. A house that had been so dark just a short time before was nowadays filled with an incredible lightness. Athena loved observing Emmy and Sloane's interactions, remembering her own mother and all that they'd shared.

Athena's FBI cover story had for the most part been a fabrication. The daughter of Greek immigrants, she was indeed a widow, but that was the end of any similarity to her real past. Born Athena Pamfilis, she'd grown up as an only child in Chicago. Her mother had been a great believer in natural health remedies, and Athena remembered neighborhood women coming to the door at all hours for her mother's advice and therapies. She never turned anyone away. At times she was irritated that her mother's afternoon or evening was taken up when Athena wanted her attention, but as she matured, she recognized how selflessly and indelibly her mother had touched so many lives. It was the reason Athena had chosen to pursue medicine at Southwest College of Naturopathic Medicine in Arizona.

Athena stood and crossed the sand until her feet were touching the clear water. How she loved this glorious island, with its dazzling white buildings and miles of perfect beaches. The first time she'd brought her husband here, he'd fallen in love with it too, and that had made her love him even more.

Leaning over, she plunged her hands into the water and splashed her bare shoulders with the refreshing coolness. She'd never planned to have a career in the FBI. She was going to build her practice, and her husband, Dimitri, a social worker, would continue his work with families in need. The day of the fire, he'd been on a case visit and had gone back into the building to try to rescue a toddler who'd wandered off. He never made it out alive. He wasn't even supposed to be working that day. The two of them had planned a long weekend, but the doctor on call at her practice came down with the flu and asked Athena to fill in for him that morning. So Dimitri went to work too. If we only knew how those seemingly mundane decisions can have monumental consequences.

Afterward, only the twin devils of hatred and vengeance kept Athena going. She couldn't punish the contractor, but she could make retribution to other criminals her life's work. And so she'd left medicine and found her way to the FBI. The universe had delivered poetic justice when she'd been assigned to the case that would ultimately bring down the conspirators whose greed was inadvertently responsible for the fire that killed her husband.

The Montgomery case had turned out to be different in many ways. As layer after layer of Whit's vileness had been peeled away, Athena realized that bringing a man like him to justice could finally fulfill and end her need for revenge. And then there was Sloane, who reminded her so much of her own mother, with an iron will and a passionate need to help those who couldn't help themselves. Sloane understood loss. The losses Sloane had suffered made her softer, and that softness had begun to thaw the icy hatred that had encased Athena's heart for so many years.

Athena had finally allowed herself to grieve. She had cried more in the last few months than she had since the tragedy. It was as if a thick curtain had been opened, and she could see outside of herself. She'd been given an incredible freedom to break down the walls she'd built up around herself; to open herself and say to the world, *I'm ready to embrace life again.*

She raised her eyes to the sky, shielding them with her hand to see a dazzling golden aurora pulse around the sun. When she looked away, the dancing sunspots shimmered on the water, electrifying her vision. It felt like a message from the heavens.

Athena strolled back up the beach to the cottage. Wiping the sand from her feet, she slipped on the sandals she'd left on the porch. She wound through the twisting alleyways and side streets of the old town, enjoying the aroma of jasmine and bougainvillea. She caught sight of her reflection in shop windows. Her white sundress contrasted with her tanned arms and legs, and her wide-brimmed hat made her appear young and carefree.

Finally approaching the beautiful Venetian harbor of Chania, she sat at one of the waterfront restaurants and ordered a frappé. The sounds of Greek being spoken all around her made her heart glad, and she inhaled deeply, savoring the moment. Even after being here for just two weeks, she felt more relaxed than she had in years. Her mother had always said the Greek islands were a balm to the soul, and she was right.

SLOANE

Sloane breathed in deeply, feeling stronger than she had in months. She had slowly regained her health after Whit's arrest and imprisonment. She wasn't sure she'd ever be able to forgive herself for being blinded to Whit's true character or to the abuse Peg had suffered. The healing had been a long and gradual process, and as she became stronger, one of the first things she'd done was to visit the cemetery. It was a warm day in April when she stood next to Peg's grave, the sun shining on the white headstone. She placed the vase of daffodils in front of it. "I'm sorry, Peg. Sorry that I didn't believe you, and sorry you suffered. I pray you're finally happy and at peace. Forgive me." She'd uttered the words out loud and swept her hand across the top of the marker before turning away. Next, she'd walked the short distance to Robert's grave and knelt. "My darling Robert, I will hold you in my heart forever. I love you. Until we meet again," she said, and recited a verse from William Butler Yeats: " 'For I would ride with you upon the wind and dance upon the mountains like a flame!' "

The visit had been a catharsis, and over the following months, Athena became her own Florence Nightingale, ministering to Sloane, encouraging her, challenging her to continue fighting her way back to wholeness. And Doris, wonderful Doris who was like a mother to Sloane, devoted herself to caring for her. When Sloane gazed in the mirror these days, the woman she saw reflected there looked healthy and radiant.

Now Sloane sat on the ferry's hard bench as sunlight splashed across the blue water in iridescent dots. She leaned back against the wood and closed her eyes, the bracing smell of salt air filling her nostrils. The gentle rocking of the boat was hypnotizing, bringing forth memories of long ago. The last thing she'd put in her suitcase was the light turquoise shawl that she'd brought on her honeymoon with Robert all those years ago. She remembered that sometimes the nights were cool in June.

She heard the grinding of gears as the large ferry slowed and circled to turn. She rose and went to the railing, watching as the vessel inched closer to the dock, and then Emmy appeared next to her, taking her hand. Excitement bubbled up inside her, and she turned to Camille and Rosemary. "Come see how beautiful it is," she said, pointing toward land. The four of them stood together as the boat docked at the harbor and the wide gangplank was lowered, meeting the ground with a deafening clang. Soon they were in the midst of droves of people disembarking, suitcases and bags bumping into one another.

Sloane took in the sheer beauty as she walked along Chania's waterfront. Emmy and Camille were on either side of her. Rosemary walked with one hand holding her daughter's, and the other clutching her cane. A wide smile broke out on Sloane's face when she saw Athena.

In an instant Athena was running to them, embracing each woman, her eyes filled with tears. "Welcome, welcome! I'm so happy you're here!"

"This is going to be the best girls' trip yet," Sloane said, hugging Athena to her. "Thank you for inviting us." When Athena had asked them to come, she had insisted the four of them stay with her in the simple cottage she'd inherited from her parents.

"Come, I have a table for us," Athena said, leading them to one overlooking the water. A bottle of champagne sat in an ice-filled bucket. "Sit, my dear friends. I'm so thrilled to see you."

"Petros," she called to the waiter. "Will you bring glasses for my friends? And a dish of mezedes?"

"You look wonderful, Sloane. Positively radiant." Athena smiled at her. "And so do you, Rosemary. All of you."

Rosemary's blue eyes crinkled. "Mind over matter!" She pointed her cane at Athena. "By the end of the summer, I'll be walking without this contraption."

Athena nodded. "I believe it. You're one amazing woman."

The waiter arrived bearing a large tray and placed tall-stemmed glasses in front of them one by one, followed by a platter of aromatic appetizers. "You must have ouzo with mezedes. It is custom," he said in a jovial voice, placing five shot glasses of the clear liquid on the table. "On the house."

"How perfect," Sloane said, lifting her face to the sun and then raising her glass. "Let's each make a toast," she announced.

"To friendship," she said.

"Justice," Athena said.

"Loyalty," Camille spoke.

"Women," Emmy said.

"And to forgiveness, of ourselves and others," Rosemary said in closing.

As they drank, Sloane looked at each of them, these strong and courageous women who had helped bring healing to her body and to her soul. She was glad to be alive. It was a start. Forgiveness would take longer, but she would give herself time. For now, at least, she could start by forgiving herself for surviving, when the man she loved hadn't. Maybe this golden place, this country where she and Robert had loved each other so well, would once more fill her heart with joy.

Sloane raised her glass again. "To hope."

ACKNOWLEDGMENTS

It takes many hands to bring a book to publication, but it is the readers who bring it to life. And so, first and foremost, we thank you, our readers, for your loyalty and enthusiasm. Huge thanks as well to librarians, booksellers, and book bloggers for helping to bring our work to new readers.

To our dream agent, Jenny Bent, you are everything and more an author could ever hope for in an agent. Boundless gratitude for your faith in us and your dedication to finding us the perfect publishing home. We are thrilled to be in your capable hands, and what a bonus that we get one another so well. A special thanks to Nissa Cullen and Victoria Cappello at the Bent Agency. To our fantastic editor, Jenny Chen, we knew from the moment we first spoke that you were the editor for us, and your brilliant insights and careful eye made this a far better book. To Mae Martinez, thank you for your keen observations and input—we loved your aha moment! Huge thanks to Jennifer Hershey for welcoming us into the Bantam family, and our deepest thanks to the entire Bantam team: Sarah Breivogel, Mark Maguire, Allison Schuster, Emma Thomasch, Steve Messina, Pam Alders, Fritz Metsch, Paul Gilbert, and Scott Biel.

To Dana Spector at CAA, thank you for your creative vision, energy, and help in bringing our stories to life on film, and to Oliver Sanderson for your adept handling of all those critical things that happen behind the scenes.

To Leslie Wells, who worked with us as the story evolved and helped to smooth out all the rough edges, your advice and notes were invaluable and took the story to the next level. Thank you!

Appreciation to our beta readers—Christopher Ackers, Dee Campbell, Honey Constantine, Lynn Constantine, Tricia Farnsworth, Kim Howe, Rick Openshaw, Jeff Schwartz, and Wendy Walker—not only for taking the time to read the book but for your invaluable comments and feedback as well.

There are always experts in their fields who so willingly share their time and knowledge. To them we owe a debt of gratitude. To Heather Constantine, CRNA, and Lori Jensen Cretella, MD, for sharing your expertise regarding our medical questions. To Special Agent Christopher Munger for your help with all things FBI. And to our friend in the Secret Service for authenticating plot points. Thanks to Stanley Constantine, JD, for always answering our legal questions. And to Michael Constantine for technical advice on building and construction.

After reading draft after draft for what seems like a thousand times, we are always astounded at the eagle-eyed proofreading of Jeff Schwartz, who catches even the smallest typo. How did we miss all of that? Thank you for finding it.

As always, thank you to our families for their love and support. You make it all worthwhile.

One final note. We never take for granted the generous and supportive community of writers to which we belong. Thank you for always being there to listen, encourage, cheer, and console. We are fortunate indeed to be among you.

ABOUT THE AUTHOR

LIV CONSTANTINE is the pen name of sisters Lynne Constantine and Valerie Constantine. Lynne and Valerie are national and international bestselling authors with over one million copies sold worldwide. Their books have been translated into twenty-eight languages, published in thirty-three countries, optioned for development in both television and film, and praised by *USA Today*, *The Sunday Times*, *People*, and *Good Morning America*, among many others. Their debut novel, *The Last Mrs. Parrish*, was a Reese's Book Club selection.

livconstantine.com
Instagram: @livconstantine2
Twitter: @livconstantine2

ABOUT THE TYPE

This book was set in Walbaum, a typeface designed in 1810 by German punch cutter J. E. (Justus Erich) Walbaum (1768–1839). Walbaum's type is more French than German in appearance. Like Bodoni, it is a classical typeface, yet its openness and slight irregularities give it a human, romantic quality.